Wilson has mastered the art of creating a romance that manages to be both sexy and sweet, and her novel's skillfully drawn characters, deliciously snarky sense of humor, and vividly evoked music-business settings add up to a supremely satisfying love story that will be music to romance readers' ears.

—*Booklist*, starred review, *#Moonstruck*

Making excellent use of sassy banter, hilarious texts, and a breezy style, Wilson's energetic story brims with sexual tension and takes readers on a musical road trip that will leave them smiling. Perfect as well for YA and new adult collections.

—*Library Journal*, *#Moonstruck*

#Moonstruck is delightfully entertaining with banter and sizzle. Sariah Wilson definitely dials up the heat and tension with this fake relationship. Ms. Wilson developed a great cast of characters in Maisy's siblings and friends with a cameo of Zoe and Chase from *#Starstruck*. *#Moonstruck* can be read as a standalone in the *#Lovestruck* series. Fans of Lauren Layne, Erika Kelly, and LuAnn McLane will enjoy *#Moonstruck*.

—*Harlequin Junkie*, *#Moonstruck*

#Moonstruck is a deeply romantic and dazzling love story. This heroine has to undergo some personal growth and work through her emotional baggage in order to get the man she wants and accept love. This is a great character-driven story for romance fans to devour.

—*Fresh Fiction*, *#Moonstruck*

#AWESTRUCK

#AWESTRUCK

SARIAH WILSON

Montlake
Romance

Text copyright © 2019 by Sariah Wilson
All rights reserved.

Published by Montlake Romance, Seattle

www.apub.com

Amazon, the Amazon logo, and Montlake Romance are trademarks of Amazon.com, Inc., or its affiliates.

ISBN-13: 9781542040006
ISBN-10: 1542040000

Cover design by Erin Dameron Hill

Cover photography by Wander Aguiar

Printed in the United States of America

For Kameron,
Even though I know you'll never read this story

CHAPTER ONE

"Someone in this room is going to prove that Evan Dawson is not a virgin."

Even though my boss sounded completely serious, I couldn't stop my snicker from escaping. This was why she had called an emergency meeting? Who cared? Evan Dawson had done so much worse than possibly lie about whether or not he'd done it.

"Ashton?" Brenda raised one eyebrow at me from behind her black-rimmed glasses. "You have something you wanted to say?"

The gaze of every intern currently working for the Portland, Oregon, branch of ISEN (International Sports and Entertainment Network) landed on me, and I coughed to hide my discomfort at being called out.

I fought the urge to pull down my ponytail and cover my face in a curtain of red hair. "No, I didn't. Sorry."

Brenda nodded briefly, satisfied that she'd shut me up so quickly. She was not a woman anyone crossed, for any reason. There was the minor fact that her grandfather owned ISEN, her dad was the current CEO, and she was his only child. Someday the entire national company would all be hers, and she never let us forget it. Her dad had required her to "work her way up," and among other responsibilities, she was in charge of the intern program for this branch. It was common knowledge that if we played ball and made her happy, we would have the job of our choosing in whatever department we wanted.

Ever since I was a little girl, I'd wanted nothing more than to be the official announcer for the Portland Lumberjacks.

Brenda had the power to make that happen for me.

As long as I played along.

And apparently what she wanted was to discredit Evan "Awesome" Dawson, the quarterback for my beloved Jacks and one of the best players in the entire NFL.

Brenda went on. "For years Evan's been playing up his aw-shucks, boy-next-door, wholesome white-bread routine to sell sports drinks, cars, and anything else that might appeal to flyover states. And I don't believe him. I think he's lying, and we're going to prove it. And our ratings will go through the roof."

Ah, the ratings. One night after work, Brenda had gone out with us lowly interns and gotten tipsier than she'd probably intended. She'd confided that she was determined to make our ratings skyrocket, forcing her casually sexist grandpa and dad to pay attention to her and what she was capable of. That she was sure if she could break one great story or scandal, they'd finally get over the fact that she was a woman, and she'd get promoted to a vice president position.

It looked like she intended to use Evan to get there.

An image of Evan flashed up on the screen behind Brenda, and I knew why she didn't believe him. To say he was gorgeous would have been seriously underselling it. Tall, athletic body that looked like it had been carved from a boulder, chiseled jaw, bright-blue eyes, and dark-brown hair. A bank account that bred zeroes. And that all-American smile that still, after all these years, made me a little weak in the ovaries.

The world should have been his own personal sex-musement park to which he had a season pass. It was definitely hard to buy that one of the most perfect male specimens to ever walk the earth was an actual virgin.

But I knew what a jerk he was underneath that pretty, polished exterior, and I was down for whatever evil plans Brenda had. Especially if they meant my getting the chance someday to work with Scooter Buxton, voice of the Jacks.

"Isn't that his story to tell or not tell?" Talia, the only other female intern, spoke up. "I mean, if he were a woman, this isn't even a conversation we'd be having. We'd be applauding his commitment to his personal choices, not trying to prove that he must be a liar."

Much as I was up for destroying Evan Dawson's life the way he had once ruined mine, Talia might have had a tiny point.

Given that scary look currently brewing on Brenda's face, she did not agree. "This is the story. Feel free to excuse yourself from pitching if you have such an issue with it." I wondered whether Talia would be fired at the end of the day or if Brenda would be generous and wait until Friday. Our boss did not enjoy being challenged. "Pitches will start in twenty minutes. I'll assign the person who can best show me how you'll get this story. And you know I take care of people who deliver. Get to work!"

It was actually a little unfair how I was about to get assigned to this story and beat out every other intern. There was no conversation as everyone rushed back to their cubicles and started typing on their computers and phones. I did some cursory research on Evan's stats for the season so far, but there was little else I had to do.

Because I'd gone to high school with Evan Dawson. I knew him. Not biblically, obviously. Because then I could have marched into Brenda's office and won her approval.

But I'd known him. I'd been head over heels in love with him.

And he'd broken my heart in the most public, most humiliating way imaginable.

I'd hated him ever since.

No one in this room knew him the way that I had.

And no one else had the same kind of connections that I did.

I considered my options in exposing him as a liar. There was the obvious—seduction. Getting him into bed would be proof he wasn't a virgin. And mildly tempting as that icky idea might have been, if gossip was to be believed, many had tried, but none had been chosen.

It shocked me a little that my mind went there first—considering doing something gross and unethical. But I'd played by the rules once before. I'd lost out on multiple internships while I was still in college to boys who were willing to do whatever it took to succeed. Who would lie, cheat, steal, and basically sell their own mothers if it meant getting the job. I'd tried succeeding on my own merits. It hadn't worked. Ruthlessness and naked ambition superseded everything else, as one recruiter had told me, saying I wasn't cut out for sports reporting.

But I had to succeed. It was all my grandma had talked about since I was a kid—how I would reach the highest echelons of success in this industry, something she'd never been able to accomplish. Which couldn't happen if I didn't find somewhere willing to take me on.

With ISEN I'd traded on my family name and the charitable organization my grandmother had started. I would have done a lot worse just for a chance. Multiple, constant rejections did that to a girl. Women already had a hard time getting a foot in the door in this industry; now that I had finally made it inside, I wasn't about to let this opportunity slip away from me. I would be ruthless. I would be ambitious and driven and do what I had to do to succeed.

But sleeping with Evan was a step too far, even for me. I considered trying to get one of his teammates to rat him out, but the guys on the team would be a dead end. The players would protect their beloved QB at all costs. He had led them to four Super Bowl wins in the last few years, and no one wanted that particular train to be derailed. Although I was willing to take the chance if it meant getting him out of Portland permanently. Our backup QB would be just fine.

Which left the wives and girlfriends (WAGs) of the Jacks. They would know the gossip. They would have heard things they didn't let get out to the general public. I didn't know any of the WAGs personally, but I knew someone who did.

I picked up my phone and called my older sister on her cell. It rang once before she answered.

"Aubrey Bailey-Price." Why did she answer that way? Like, she could obviously see it was me calling. Why was she all lawyer all the time?

"Hey, Aubrey. It's Ashton."

"I know." Aha! See? Totally called it. "What do you need?"

"Why do you assume I need something? Can't I just be calling to say hi?"

She let out a long sigh, and I could just see her pinching the bridge of her nose, as she so often did in conversations with me. "I'm in the middle of something important, so if you could quickly get to why you're calling me, that would be great."

"Last year you did some work for Malik Owens. Something you said he and his wife, Nia, owed you for."

I held my breath, waiting for her response. Aubrey took her attorney-client confidentiality very seriously, and the only reason I knew even that little bit about the Jacks' defensive end was because she had been a tad bit drunk, and I had pressed her for information.

"How did you . . ." she sputtered, obviously not remembering what she'd told me. "I never would have . . ."

"I don't know the specifics, and you don't have to give them to me. But I need your help. I have to find an in with the Jacks. I've got to get some intel on one of the players, and the women are my best way in. If they owe you, I need you to call in that favor with Nia and set up a meeting."

"Which player are you trying to get intel on?"

I hesitated, not knowing which way this would go. Aubrey had been friends with Evan in high school, which was how I had known him. He, along with half the football team and cheerleading squad, had hung out at our house all the time. It was how I had developed such a serious crush on him.

"Evan Dawson."

"Really?" She sounded both surprised and, worryingly enough, delighted. My whole family knew the saga of Ashton and Evan—how he had shattered my teenage heart and single-handedly destroyed my entire high school experience. Aubrey, for some reason, had always thought that I had overreacted to the whole situation because I'd been, in her words, "so unbelievably young" and that I should have let Evan apologize to me when he'd tried to.

"Yes, really. Are you going to do it or not?"

There was a long pause, and I wondered if she had hung up on me. "What am I supposed to tell Nia?"

Yes! I threw my free hand in the air. Getting Aubrey to even consider it felt like a total win. "Just tell her you have a younger sister who recently graduated with a degree in broadcasting and communications who loves football and wants to get an insider's peek into the lives of NFL players and their significant others."

All true. So it technically wasn't lying.

Another long, quiet pause. "And what's in it for me?"

"Uh, undying love, adoration, and worship from your younger sister?"

"Rory already adores and worships me."

"Debatable, since both activities would probably entail holding still for longer than ten seconds." Our younger sister had the attention span of a gnat on coke. She was like what would happen if a fidget spinner could procreate. "And did you just make a joke?" It was very un-Aubrey-like.

"Possibly." She sounded pleased with herself, which was good because it meant this was going well.

Until it didn't.

"Tell you what," she said. "I have this huge case I'm working on, and I'm in the middle of depositions right now, and it's taking up all my time. Problem is, I'm also on the planning committee for the upcoming ten-year reunion. If you promise to help me out with the reunion however and whenever I want, I will set something up with Nia Owens."

It was difficult to know how to respond. I wanted to thank her, get off the phone before more damage was done, and just pay her steep price in order to make this happen.

The other part of me knew how dangerous it was to give Aubrey a blank check like this.

But beggars couldn't be choosers. "I promise. Whatever you ask me to do to help out with your high school reunion, I will do it."

"Without question."

I rolled my eyes. "Yes, without question, oh mighty master."

"Excellent. You'll be hearing from me soon." We hung up, and I had a serious moment of dread as I tried to imagine what sort of demented Aubrey-dictated nightscape I'd just agreed to.

I began typing up a generic outline and waited at my cubicle for my chance to pitch Brenda.

A head popped up above my shared wall, surprising me. It was my work husband, Rand. Which I'd thought was a stupid name until I found out his actual name was Randolph, and at that point, I no longer blamed him for shortening it.

"What are you going to say?" he asked. Rand was cute, in a metro-lumberjack kind of way. Thick beard, light-brown hair, brown eyes, lots of ironic flannel.

"As if I'd tell you," I scoffed. We'd been flirting for a few months, but I knew nothing would ever come of it. Because I suspected that he would have slit my throat and walked over my bleeding-out corpse to get ahead at this network. So would every other intern on the floor, so I couldn't blame him for that, either. "But I am going to win the assignment, just so you know not to waste your time."

His eyes narrowed at me in wry amusement. "What? You think because you're young and hot you'll get chosen? Brenda doesn't swing that way."

Thanks to my ridiculously fair skin, I could feel the blush starting at my throat and working its way up to my cheeks. I didn't really think of myself as hot. I wasn't a troll or anything—I was tall and had red hair, hazel eyes, and a decent figure, given how often I worked out or played sports. I'd even had a couple of semiserious boyfriends in college. But thanks to Evan and his buddies, in the deepest, most private part of me, I couldn't see myself as anything other than some ugly, pathetic wannabe.

"It's because I'm better at my job than you," I finally managed when the blush died down. Sometimes it felt like Rand flirted with me just because he enjoyed making me flush fifty different shades of red.

"We'll see," he said with a wink, going off to pitch his take on Evan's story.

I waited about half an hour longer, drumming my fingers on my desk. The line outside of Brenda's office had cleared, and I made my way over to her door.

Which was open, so it wasn't my fault for eavesdropping. Although it wasn't really eavesdropping; it was just standing somewhere that the two women inside couldn't see me and holding really still while listening intently.

"Maybe we can take a different tactic with this story. Honestly, it isn't that big of a deal if Dawson is a virgin. Lots of people hold off. I mean, there are so many famous celebrities who are waiting or did wait until marriage. Like Lolo Jones, Adriana Lima, Maisy Harrison of Yesterday, or Zoe Covington, Chase's wife. All that aside, just in the NFL alone you have Tim Tebow, Russell Wilson, Philip Rivers, Manti Te'o, Prince Amukamara—"

Brenda held up her hand, cutting Talia off. She'd done the opposite of what Brenda had asked for. Brenda hadn't come to praise Evan Dawson but to bury him.

"That isn't quite what I wanted, but I suppose I can consider it." My boss's tone indicated that no consideration whatsoever would be taking place. "Next!"

I avoided making eye contact with Talia as she left the office, not wanting her to see how sorry I felt for her. I went in and sat down in the chair next to Brenda's desk. She was typing something on her computer and staring at her screen.

Brenda was intimidating not only because of her attitude, her confidence, and the power she held over all of our lives but also because I'd never seen her as anything less than immaculate. Like today—her pale-blonde hair was done up in a tight French twist, her business suit looked custom, and she wore high heels that made me think of stilts. I was always impressed with her ability to balance on her impossibly high shoes. I wondered if she did yoga.

"Wow me, Ashton."

Her command stopped my bizarre brain tangent. "While I don't know for sure one way or the other if Evan Dawson is still a virgin, what I can tell you is that he used to be quite the rebel back in high school."

That made her look away from the computer. "How do you know that?"

"Because I went to high school with him. I know him." Knew him, to be more accurate. I hadn't spoken to him in ten years. "He got busted for drinking, partying, shoplifting. If I remember right, he was even part of a group of kids who stole a police car and went for a joyride."

I had her complete and total attention. "How come I've never heard any of this?"

Because my father was an entertainment and sports attorney who the head football coach had retained to keep Evan out of trouble and to keep his records sealed. "Juvenile offenses. But I remember it. So I know that he's not what he seems. That there's more going on with this story than what he tells the world."

She leaned back in her chair. "Very interesting. Almost impressive."

I had managed to almost impress her! Part of me wanted to keep the streak going and tell her I was the one who had given him the nickname "Awesome" during my freshman year of high school, but people never believed me. They always assumed it was something that had started when he went off to college. I decided to leave that fact out, as it might have made me seem a little desperate.

Which I totally was. "And because I grew up with him, I can get access to him now." Whether or not that was true didn't matter, only that I was promising Brenda something no one else would even consider.

Because Evan was notorious for being tight-lipped with the press. He did his NFL-mandated interviews but gave away very little, keeping to one- or two-word answers. He didn't go on sports shows and generally stayed quiet at press conferences. "I can talk to the people around him, too. Find out the real scoop. Maybe even find some women who will come on the show and say they've hooked up with him. And I'm helping my older sister with her ten-year reunion, which is also Evan Dawson's ten-year reunion. Lots of potential people to interview there, too."

She nodded, considering my pitch. I needed to seal the deal. "He broke my heart. Publicly humiliated me at school. I've been waiting ten years to pay him back. If anyone wants to see Evan Dawson brought down a peg or two, it's me."

Brenda smiled at me like I was her new best friend, and it was honestly a little unsettling. Like the way a great white shark might smile at a sea lion she was about to devour whole. "Excellent pitch, Ashton. I'll let you know."

It wasn't quite the response I'd been anticipating. I'd thought for sure she'd tell me right then and there that I had the story. I stood up and walked out of the room, hoping she'd call me back.

She didn't.

If I didn't get this assignment, I was going to be super pissed. Mostly because I had promised to become Aubrey's reunion beck-and-call girl, and that would not be fun.

And because no one else was as personally invested as I was. No one else wanted to see Evan Dawson pushed off his pedestal as much as I did.

"Didn't go as well as you thought?" Rand asked as I flopped down into my office chair.

"It went just fine," I told him through clenched teeth. Now was not the time to poke the bear. There might be teeth, claws, and blood in response.

He didn't get the message. "Too bad. The Winnowing is coming, and I bet this would have helped you get hired on to an actual paying position."

As Rand kept talking about how he was sure his own job was secure, I realized I'd been so focused on what I could do to ruin Evan that I hadn't even thought about the Winnowing. Brenda talked about the Winnowing often—she hired a lot of interns and a year later gave only about a quarter of them a job. It was an effective scare tactic to keep us all in line and doing whatever she asked.

Our year was nearly up. We'd been hired in January, and it was November.

I had to stay here. I had to become an announcer for ISEN. It had been my dream my entire life.

"May I have your attention?" Brenda stood on a low coffee table just outside her office. "I wanted to thank everyone for their pitches, but I've selected the intern who will break this story wide open for us."

The interns from the outer cubicles came forward, all eager to hear her announcement. I'd been so cocky about getting the assignment, it just occurred to me that despite my history with Evan, I realistically had a one-in-thirty chance.

My heart leaped up in my throat, making it impossible to breathe.

Rand waggled his eyebrows at me, as if to say the story was his, and I couldn't even give him a good sarcastic retort since my nerves and displaced heart were threatening to suffocate me.

"The intern I've selected is . . . Ashton Bailey!"

Relief washed over me, and there were some mumblings and half-hearted claps in response to Brenda's announcement.

I'd done it. I'd won.

It was the first step to making all my dreams come true.

"Ashton, can I see you in my office?"

I nodded and hurried forward. I sat back down in the seat I'd recently vacated.

"I want this to be your first priority. Spend your days getting this story. You don't need to physically be here every day while you're working on this. Come into the office once a week to check in with me, and send me an email every time you get new information. All of your other responsibilities are suspended. I'll have the other interns pick up your slack." Oh, they would love that. "You probably won't be keeping normal business hours while you investigate, but anything you need to do in order to uncover the truth about Evan Dawson, I want you to do it. Got it?" Brenda's voice was strong and determined. And strangely invested in getting the result she wanted.

"Got it," I said. She was offering me a lot of freedom. Which I planned on taking full advantage of.

When I got to my cubicle, I should have been a good sport about winning, but I couldn't keep the grin off my face.

"Huh. Maybe I was wrong about Brenda's preferences," Rand remarked.

"Stereotypical man. A woman turns you down, she must be gay. I already told you, I'm better at this than you. When are you going to learn that I'm always right?"

He smiled at me, showing that despite our teasing, he didn't hold a grudge. He'd still take every advantage, but that was just how things worked on this floor.

Despite my bragging to Rand that I was always right, there was something I'd been wrong about.

Apparently Brenda wanted Evan Dawson off that pedestal every bit as much as I did.

It made me wonder why.

CHAPTER TWO

Aubrey had arranged a lunch date for me with Nia Owens on Monday. I spent the entire weekend either freaking out that this wouldn't work or worrying that Nia would be as protective of Evan as her husband would be.

I got to the restaurant early and told the hostess I was expecting a guest. She seated me next to one of the windows facing the street. Another rainstorm started, raindrops lightly drumming against the panes as they fell. I tapped my fork against the table while I waited, my leg restlessly bouncing in time to my tapping.

"Hey, are you Ashton?"

I looked up to see a petite, well-put-together woman smiling at me. She had dark-brown eyes and black hair that hung to her shoulders. I stood. "I am. You must be Nia."

We shook hands, and she sat down across from me, taking off her coat and placing her umbrella on the floor. "Did you watch the game?" she asked.

"We're a Jacks family. I always watch the game." I'd missed the first twenty minutes of it but watched the rest. The Jacks had defeated the Cleveland Browns last night, which had put everyone in Portland in a good mood. I mean, not that it was that great of a victory. My two sisters and I could have played against the Browns and won, too.

We looked over the menu quietly and placed our order when the waitress returned. After she left, Nia folded her hands together and gave me a level look. "So what did Aubrey tell you? About Malik and me?"

"My sister is serious about confidentiality. She said in passing that you owed her a favor, and she was nice enough to let me cash it in."

Nia twisted her mouth to one side. "Good to know. I am planning on helping you, even if I don't buy that you want to do some 'day in the life' thing. I know how ISEN operates. But I want you to appreciate what this favor means, so I'm going to tell you why I owe your sister."

She paused when the waitress returned with our drinks: a water with lemon for me, an iced tea for Nia.

Nia added some Splenda to her drink before stirring it. "Last year, during Malik's contract negotiations, a woman came forward claiming that she had given birth to Malik's daughter. She was trying to extort half a million dollars from us to buy her silence. And you know how Chester Walton is about things like that."

Chester Walton was the very conservative owner of the Portland Jacks. A retired Texan oil tycoon, he took his players' reputations seriously. There had been more than one Jacks player let go because of things like this—committing adultery or fathering a child with a woman who was not his wife.

He was the reason I knew that if I could expose Evan Dawson as a liar and a fraud, he'd be fired. Chester Walton would never tolerate his golden boy's halo being dimmed.

"Your sister managed to keep that gold-digging ho at bay until a paternity test came back, proving Malik wasn't the father. Which I could have told her to begin with, because my man does not cheat on me. Then your sister went above and beyond and got the woman to sign a confession, legally stopping her from trying to come after us again, promising financial damages if she in any way tried to speak out against Malik or me. Anyway, Aubrey saved our future, Malik got his renewal and salary increase, and I promised to owe her a big one. Now tell me what you're really doing."

Some small part of me immediately considered that I could take this story to Brenda if I needed to. It wasn't *Evan Dawson's not a virgin* level good, but it was still something.

Even if it's a betrayal of your sister and the very nice woman who just agreed to help you?

I couldn't be that evil. Nia had trusted me, and I could, at the very least, do the same in return. "I don't think Evan Dawson's a virgin, and I want to prove it. Because it can't be true. Just look at him."

"That man is fine," Nia agreed. "I've never seen him sneak off with any groupies. I don't think I've even heard any gossip about him. I know lots of women have tried, but no one's succeeded. I think it is true, and you're not going to find anything that says otherwise. But that's not my problem. And since it's not going to hurt the team or my husband's career, I'd be happy to introduce you and get things rolling."

"No," I quickly retorted, cursing my quick tongue when I saw her reaction. Although I was willing to share some of my story, she didn't need the whole thing. "I mean, he'd just lie about it, right? I need to get close to the other women like you. The WAGs. Someone there has to know something."

"Before we move forward, I need you to promise me one thing. You won't lie just for ratings."

It wasn't hard to agree. "I promise." It was one thing to scheme my way into a job; it was another to be a reporter or an announcer and deliberately lie to sports fans. I could be cutthroat and truthful. "I would never do that."

"Good." She nodded. "You remind me of Aubrey. She's trustworthy, too."

"Ugh, don't compare me to my ultra-perfect sister who can do no wrong."

Nia laughed.

"Do you have one of those?" I asked.

"Girl, I am one of those. My poor sister is constantly hearing it from our mama: 'Why can't you be more like Nia?'"

The waitress put down a tray of sourdough bread as our laughter faded away. Nia cut herself a piece and chewed slowly, thoughtfully.

When she finished, she said, "You know, initially I thought this was about you wanting to meet one of the players. Which would require setting you up a great Instagram account. A lot of NFL players use that app as a dating tool. I'd make you my friend, which would then have you showing up in their feeds. Easiest way to meet an athlete. But it will also work for getting you in with the women. You need to focus on Tinsley Hale."

"Jamie Hale's wife?" From what I could remember, Tinsley Hale was a former Lumberjill. The Lumberjills were the Jacks' cheerleading squad. She'd broken the team's rules by dating offensive lineman Jamie Hale, but all had been forgiven once they got married. "Isn't she, like, the managing director for the Lumberjills now?" I asked.

"She is. And she knows everything about everyone. There's a party tomorrow night to celebrate the win against Cleveland and to do a kickoff for Tinsley's favorite charity." Tuesdays were days off for NFL players. "I'll get you in as Reggie Franklin's date. The girls don't fight over him, so you'll seem unthreatening."

Reggie Franklin was one of the practice squad players, which basically made him expendable to the team. There was always a chance he could land a starting position, but not a great possibility. Which meant his earning potential was extremely low and made him not quite as desirable a player as the other Jacks.

"The thing with Tinsley is she loves doing work for the Jumping Jacks organization. The one that's for sick kids? Figure out a way to help them, and you'll have your in."

"That's my family's charity. I'm on the board," I told her, excited. This was all working out so well.

"You're one of those Baileys?" she asked.

I nodded.

"Whatever you do, don't tell her that!" Nia shook her head. "Tinsley has to be the star of every situation. You just want to volunteer and help out. She's in charge, and you have to suck up to her. Think you can handle that?"

Oh, I had a black belt in dealing with and sucking up to difficult women. "I think so."

"Good. So I have a homework assignment for you. Today or tomorrow take some pictures of yourself for Instagram. Do some inside, some outdoors. Try lots of different looks. Let me see your cell."

I put in the password and handed it over. Nia fiddled with it for a few minutes before handing it back. "I added my contact information and put Instagram on your phone. Create an account and email me your username, and I'll follow you. Tinsley will probably investigate you, and we want her to see that we're friends. I'll get a bunch of the other girls to follow you, too."

The waitress returned with our food, but for the first time in forever I couldn't eat. I was giddy that this was all going so well. Hopefully within the next forty-eight hours I'd have everything I'd need to ruin Evan Dawson and land my dream job.

Nia wasn't done giving me instructions. "Tomorrow night, be at my house at six o'clock. We'll all go over to the party together. Sound good?"

"Sounds good!" I agreed. This was all happening so fast. It hadn't even been hard.

I should have known that nothing in life was ever that easy.

Once the business part was out of the way, I really enjoyed the rest of my lunch with Nia. She was hilariously snarky and loved chocolate and Jacks football, which made her the perfect potential friend.

Sariah Wilson

When I got home, I did as she asked and took about a bajillion pictures of myself, sending them over to her first for approval. She picked out her favorites, and I posted them to my newly created Instagram account, including the hashtags she told me to use.

At first Nia was my only follower, but within an hour I had multiple follows from WAGs and Lumberjills. I didn't know how she'd accomplished it but figured it was better not to ask.

The next day, as per Nia's instructions, I went and got my hair done, my toenails and fingernails painted, and my eyebrows waxed. It was pretty far away from my usual casual tomboy style, but I did as I was told. I chose a skirt and blouse that I thought said "hanging with the girls!" It was also the girliest outfit I owned.

It took me about half an hour to drive from my condo to Malik and Nia's mansion in Lake Oswego. And their house was practically on top of the lake. I parked my car on the street and ran through the drizzling rain, wishing I could better see the view of the water behind their home.

When I knocked on the door, I half expected a snooty British butler to answer. But it was Nia in an expensive-looking red minidress. Her gaze traveled from my head to my feet, and before I could even tell her how amazing she looked, she said, "Oh, nuh-uh. You are not getting in my car dressed like that. Come inside. I will find you something else to wear."

"You're, like, a foot shorter than me. Nothing you own is going to fit me." I stepped into the foyer, and she took my coat and hung it up on a rack.

"Never doubt my closet game. My bedroom is this way. Malik! We need a few minutes!"

"All good, baby," he responded from another room. "Let me know when you're ready."

I had only a second to take in all the luxurious surroundings before she had hustled me into her custom closet, which was obviously a shrine to the patron saint of designer fashion and accessories. It was probably the same size as my entire condo. She was right. I shouldn't have doubted her closet game.

She started pulling short, sparkly, clubbing-type dresses off her racks, piling them on a bench in the middle.

"Aren't those more male-centric outfits? I thought I was supposed to dress up for the girls."

"We are. Don't you watch *Real Housewives*?"

"Not if I can help it," I joked, but she shot me a brief, withering look in between pulling dresses.

"This is how women like this dress up for each other. You're supposed to blend in. And you'll stand out in that raggedy broken-down-librarian outfit. No offense."

"Total offense." Not really, but I felt like I should probably stand up for my fashion choices.

She then began holding the dresses up against me and discarded them in a pile on either my right or left based on what she saw. When she had finished, she picked up the smaller pile and handed it to me. "I think any of these would work. Pick the one you like best. Join us in the living room when you're ready."

Before I could protest that I was afraid I might get lost trying to retrace my steps, she'd left. I took off my skirt and blouse and started trying on dresses. As I'd feared, most of them became super-micro-dresses on me. So, so short.

My mom always said the right length for a skirt was at least two inches below your cellulite. Finally, I found one that met her criteria. I put on the silver spangly one that actually reached midthigh. My shoes matched well enough, and I even managed to find Malik and Nia in the kitchen. They were grinning at each other, whispering. He had his arms wrapped around her and was nuzzling her nose.

And even though I was always surrounded by overly affectionate couples in my own family, for some reason this hit me funny. Made my heart twinge. Some part of me whispered, *I want that.*

I cleared my throat, hoping it would clear my head at the same time. "I'm ready."

"Let's get going!" Nia gave her husband a quick kiss, and I followed behind them to their four-car garage. We piled into a white SUV, and to my delight, Malik had the local sports station on the radio.

"There's Evan's house," Nia commented as we drove down their street. It was another mansion on the waterfront surrounded by large trees. "Lots of the guys from the team live in this neighborhood."

If things went the way I hoped they would, Evan wouldn't be in that house for much longer.

On our way into the city, we stopped by an apartment complex to pick up Reggie. He said a brief "what's up" to me when he got in the back seat.

He was a handsome guy, but I was on a mission. And it wasn't to date a man who'd probably be kicked off the team in a year due to injury since the coaches would use him as a tackling dummy for the starters.

Apparently the disinterest was mutual, since he spent the entire car ride on his phone. He didn't say anything to me for the rest of the evening.

Sadly enough, still not my worst date ever.

Tinsley was hosting the celebration/Jumping Jacks kickoff party at her penthouse in one of the swankiest buildings in downtown Portland. The doorman let us up after making sure that our names were on a list. Turns out the paparazzi yelling Malik's name and taking his picture didn't work as a valid form of identification, and Malik showed the doorman his driver's license. Now satisfied, the doorman pointed out which elevator we should use. The elevator went right inside the penthouse. No hallways or anything.

Even though I feared for my ability to sit down in this dress, I quickly saw that Nia was right. Every woman at the party was dressed in a similar fashion, and I would have been out of place in my other "Amish girl during Rumspringa" outfit.

Two of the defensive linemen called Malik and Reggie over, leaving me with Nia. She took a compact out of her purse and checked her lipstick. "Let me make the rounds, and I'll come back later to introduce you to Tinsley, okay? Find a quiet corner, and don't talk to anyone yet."

"Okay." Because that wouldn't be awkward. Showing up at a party and avoiding every person there. Totally normal behavior, right?

I went over and grabbed myself a drink just to give my hands something to do. Even though I knew it was only my imagination, it felt like everyone in the room was staring at me. I recognized all of the players and even some of their significant others. I wanted to talk to the team about plays and strategies for their upcoming game that Sunday but didn't want to incur Nia's wrath.

"Did ya know I've got a weakness for redheads?" I turned to see the Scottish kicker, Finn MacNeil, standing just behind me. I could see why Rory had a thing for him—light-brown hair and dark-green eyes, a devilish smile, fantastic athletic build, and a burr on his *R*s that could fluster a girl.

Not that I was flustered. Much. I focused on the drink in his hand, remembering his near-DUI conviction that had been dismissed by a judge. Brenda had run a story about it, questioning favoritism for professional athletes, but it hadn't gotten her the ratings buzz she'd hoped for. Finn was definitely trouble, and not why I was here.

"Yeah, I hear you've got a weakness for whiskey, too. I wouldn't recommend either," I said, quickly excusing myself since I wasn't following Nia's instructions.

My phone buzzed. Hoping it was Nia telling me to find her, I was disappointed to see that it was just a text from Aubrey.

> Need you on Thursday
> evening, Reunion Monkey!

I sighed. She was not going to make this easy.

21

Wanting a distraction, I took myself on an uninvited tour of the penthouse. I smiled at groups of people as I walked by them but didn't slow down to start any conversations. I found a room with a door slightly ajar and decided that meant I could go in.

Given the brown leather couches, the framed jerseys, and the massive TV that could have moonlighted as a movie theater screen, I guessed this was Jamie's man cave. The Cleveland game was paused on the TV. I hadn't had the chance to see the beginning of it yet and figured this would be the perfect way to do what Nia wanted. The remote sat on the coffee table, and I rewound the game to the initial kickoff, settling onto the couch.

I started narrating the game out loud. "The Cleveland Browns won the coin toss and have elected to receive. Number 42, alcoholic and womanizer Finn MacNeil, lines up his kick. And it's a beautiful one, straight and strong to the Browns' ten-yard line. Where it's picked up by"—I didn't know the names of the Browns players off the top of my head—"the return specialist, Number 14."

It was a bad habit I had whenever I watched any type of sporting event. I couldn't help but do the play-by-play. At our family get-togethers, they made me do it in my head. If I ever forgot, I was pelted with couch cushions. But I was alone now, so it didn't matter.

The Jacks defense held the Browns at the line of scrimmage and quickly got the ball back. The Jacks offense came out onto the field. Evan Dawson threw the ball to the team's best wide receiver, Ian Sommers. Sommers had magic hands and a vertical leap that would make a frog jealous. He hardly ever missed a throw. But Dawson had hurled it wide, and no one on the planet could have caught it.

"Bad throw. You're killing me, Dawson!"

"If it makes you feel any better, we win."

Someone had entered the room behind me, and the sound of his voice scared me, causing my heart to slam hard against my chest. I put my hand up, as if I could calm it down.

But my fear turned to dread when I realized I recognized that voice. It had been a long time since I'd heard it, but there was no mistaking it.

I turned slowly, hoping it was all my imagination. Or that someone had spiked my drink. Or that I was lying in a coma somewhere, and this wasn't actually happening.

But it was happening. In reality, and vivid Technicolor.

It was Evan Dawson.

CHAPTER THREE

He stood there in a charcoal-gray suit tailored to fit him perfectly, showing off his broad shoulders and strong arms. He didn't wear a tie and had left his collar open. His blue eyes sparkled, and the light in the room gleamed on both his soft hair and perfect teeth. Although I knew what he looked like, I had forgotten how much more breathtaking he was in person. Like the camera couldn't capture all the pretty.

And I hated the fact that even though he was my mortal enemy, I was still attracted to him. I figured that said something not great about me.

I'd known going into this evening that running into him was a possibility; I'd just hoped that fate would be kind and not force me to talk to him.

Apparently not.

"Sorry if I startled you."

I got to my feet, not liking how his standing gave him a height advantage over me. Even then he still had a good four inches on me. I wondered how badly I'd just embarrassed myself.

"How long have you been lurking?" *Creep,* I mentally added but refrained from saying out loud. It probably wouldn't help my cause if I verbally abused him right off the bat. Even if he deserved it. I needed this group to accept me, not to have its most powerful member ban me from all of its extracurricular events.

He gave me a self-deprecating smile, and I told my knees to hold freaking still. "It wasn't lurking. Just observing. And it was however long doesn't make it weird."

Too late, I mentally retorted. Sometimes I worried that I thought things so hard and so loudly that my thoughts would turn into speech bubbles like in a comic book. I refrained from looking around to see if it had finally happened.

"You look like you're thinking mean things about me."

Maybe the speech-bubble worry was legitimate, and he really could see them. "You're a psychic? A mind reader?"

"What's with all the hostility? You're that upset over one failed pass? One mistake?"

Not just one mistake. A series of them. But he meant the Browns game. It was then that it dawned on me he didn't know who I was. He didn't recognize me.

Which was like him just tossing handfuls of salt and dumping pitchers of lemon juice into my wounds.

He'd practically ruined my teenage life, but I hadn't been significant enough to merit even a single memory.

"You seem familiar," he said, still behaving like he could practically read my mind. He scanned me, tapping his forefinger against his mouth, as if thinking deeply. "I saw you earlier today on Instagram."

What was it Nia had said about Instagram? That athletes used it as a dating app? Why had Evan Dawson been scrolling through his feed looking at chicks if he was still so pure and untouched? And of the thousands of pictures he must have had access to, given all his connections, was I really supposed to believe he saw my recently uploaded pics and actually remembered them? Maybe it was just a line.

Then he added, "You're friends with Nia Owens, right?"

So, the Instagram thing wasn't just a line? He knew Nia followed me there?

Or else he'd seen me arrive with her.

One of his abilities that had rendered him so "Awesome" was his keen observational skills on the field—the way he could take in everything around him and make the right play, taking his time to get everything just right before he passed the ball.

Apparently it applied to his regular life, too.

"Instagram?" I finally managed, keeping some of my anger in check. "Trolling for possible hookups?"

That charming, teasing grin I remembered so well popped up on his stupid, handsome face. "Haven't you heard? I don't do that."

"I have heard it but don't much believe it."

Now he just looked amused. "Really? Why not?"

The man already had an ego so big that the mansion down in Lake Oswego was probably a necessity, just to have enough room for the both of them. I wasn't about to add to it. Instead, I just made an indistinct gesture with my hand as my answer. "I think you know."

Another grin, this time at my expense. "So . . . do you always narrate games while you watch them?"

"Yes." It wasn't weird. It was what I wanted to do as a career, and I wasn't going to let him make me feel dumb about it. "The announcers are who make the games entertaining."

"Oh. Not the football players? The men out on the field doing the actual work?"

I did not want to banter with this guy. He seemed to think we were having some kind of adorable rom-com moment, and I was considering how far I could get after I hit him upside the head with that autographed Mickey Mantle baseball bat in the corner before the police showed up to arrest me.

"I stand by my statement."

"If Bob Costas came in this room . . ." Evan walked around the couch, keeping his left hand out of sight behind his back. What was that about? "You'd what?"

Jump up and down and scream like a total fangirl? Start crying hysterically? Lose my ability to speak? They were all distinct possibilities. "I would . . . be excited. And there might even be some fainting involved."

"And I'm not faint-worthy?"

Once upon a time, maybe. Now? Not even a little. I didn't say anything, but my expression must have conveyed my thoughts as he began to laugh.

I heard the sound of ice hitting a glass, and I saw a glimpse of something pink near his hand. Possibly an umbrella. My curiosity usually got the better of me, and I couldn't help but ask, "What are you drinking?" I knew that after he got out of high school Evan had stopped drinking. Another thing he was famous for in the media. Which made some sense, given that his parents had been killed by a drunk driver when he was fourteen.

If he'd started up again, that would definitely be newsworthy.

And given the embarrassed look on Evan's face, my suspicion might not have been too far off. "Nothing."

It was not nothing. "Let me see it."

"No."

Like I was a kid again and back home with my two sisters while we played Keep Away, I made a grab for the drink behind his back, but he easily kept it out of my reach. Frustrated, I made another lunge, but he switched hands and moved the drink around to his front, holding me at bay.

"You do realize the Jacks pay me a lot of money to keep things in my hands. Big hulking men have to tackle me in order to get things away from me."

His words were hot against my neck, and I realized then just how close I'd gotten to him. How good he smelled, how broad and strong he was. I looked up at him, and those piercing blue eyes that danced with amusement were the only things that snapped me out of the spell he'd put me under.

What was wrong with me? Seriously? I hated Evan Dawson. I was working to ruin his reputation and get him publicly humiliated and then fired. Why hadn't my body gotten the memo that we were not allowed to be attracted to him?

I stepped back, letting out a deep breath that I hadn't realized I'd been holding in. "Fine. I don't really care."

And even though it was unintentional, my reverse psychology worked. He showed me his drink, which was, in fact, pink and had an umbrella. "It's nonalcoholic, if you'd like to try it." He held the drink out to me, and it gave me weird, traitorous little shivers to think about putting my lips on something his lips had been on. "I haven't tasted it yet. I'd never live it down if the guys saw me with this."

"Then why carry it around?"

He shrugged. "The bartender called it an Awesome Dawson. What was I supposed to do?"

"Try 'no thanks.' Like what you supposedly say to all women."

"There's no 'supposedly' about it." He placed the drink down on the table. Then he undid the buttons on his suit jacket and sat on the couch, lounging on it like he owned the place. "I do say no a lot."

So, so cocky and arrogant. I added it to the mental list of reasons I couldn't stand Evan Dawson.

"Why so interested in that part of my life?" he asked, and I momentarily panicked. I was making all kinds of digs about his supposed virginity. *Way to tip your hand, moron.*

"No reason." Yeah, that was real smooth and definitely threw him off the scent. I wanted to slap myself in the forehead.

"Is your boyfriend not measuring up?"

Why did that make me so indignant? "I don't have a boyfriend." And if I did, our private life would have been just fine, thanks. I couldn't say that, though. I needed to get the spotlight off me and back on him. Maybe I could get him to admit to something. "What about you?" What if he had a secret girlfriend who would spill all his secrets?

The jerk actually winked at me. "I don't have a boyfriend, either."

"Usually or just now?" I asked.

"I'm into women. And before you ask the question I know you're dying to ask, no girlfriend, either," he added, popping my hopeful balloon. "But the night is still young."

The boyfriend thing could have taken this story in a whole new direction. Too bad.

Nonexistent relationships aside, it dawned on me that Evan Dawson was flirting with me. I wanted to go outside and key his car, and he was *hitting* on me. Like I was some football groupie excited just to be in the same room with him.

The thirteen-year-old former fan inside of me was giddy.

But my logical adult side told her to shut up. I was in control of our hormones now. We would not be responding to his teasing.

Before I could tell him he was barking up the wrong tree, he said, "Now that we know we're both single, I should probably ask if you're here with anyone." Like there was some unbreakable team code? I didn't belong to anybody. If I wanted to ditch my "date" and hook up with someone else, it was none of Evan's business.

"I came with Reggie." Sort of. But he didn't need to know that.

Was it my imagination, or did his face fall a little?

And why wasn't I taking advantage of this? It was the perfect way to shut down this conversation. *I'm dating your teammate, sorry. Have a good night, and keep your masculine wiles to yourself. Oh, and I'm going to get total revenge on you. 'K, thanks, bye.*

Instead, I added, "He did it as a favor to Nia. I've heard about the Jacks' parties, and I wanted to see one for myself."

"That's good, given that Reggie's longest and most serious relationship has been with his cell phone."

Why did I want to laugh?

Evan Dawson is not charming. He's not. Not charming.

"Do you want to get out of here?" he asked, shocking me out of my internal mantra.

"And do what?" Because if he was telling the truth, he didn't mean that the way other men usually did.

He shrugged one shoulder. "Whatever you want. What do you say?"

Why was I tempted by his offer? What was going on with me? Why was some small part of me ready to throw away the past and see where this would lead?

If I didn't snap out of this, it was going to lead me straight to unemployment.

But I still didn't want to deliberately offend him.

"I say it would be really rude of me to ditch my friends. Have a good night."

I moved to walk past him, and he reached out, gently grabbing my wrist. Fireworks exploded up and down my arms. That reaction stunned me. It had to be a fluke. Static electricity. Jupiter moving through my seventh house. My body's trigger warning that something awful was about to happen.

"You know, you haven't told me your name."

It reminded me that despite being this all-consuming figure in my teen years, he didn't remember me at all. And then I realized that he hadn't bothered to introduce himself. That I was just supposed to already know who he was because he was oh-so-important to all us little people and our pathetic lives.

That I totally knew who he was before I ever even saw his face was beside the point.

It was enough to restoke my anger, which had been slowly dying out. I jerked my arm away. "It's Ashton."

"That's not usually a woman's name, is it? Although I used to know a girl named . . ." His voice trailed off, and I finally saw recognition dawning in his eyes. "Ashton? Ashton Bailey? Is that you?"

To be fair, I looked nothing like I had when he knew me. I'd had frizzy carrot-orange hair that had deepened over the years to a much darker shade of red. I'd grown at least six inches and now had curves where I was supposed to have them. LASIK eye surgery instead of glasses. No more braces.

He stood up quickly, like he wanted to hug me or something, and I flew backward, hitting the backs of my knees on the coffee table and falling butt-first onto its surface. Where I knocked over his Awesome Dawson drink on Nia's dress. "Just great," I muttered.

Evan offered me his hand, intending to help me up. I didn't need his assistance. "I'm fine," I told him through my clenched teeth, trying to brush off some of the pink drink. It didn't seem like it was going to stain, but now I'd have to get the dress dry-cleaned. I scooted over and got up, putting the couch between us.

As if he sensed my concern, he stayed put, his hands in his pockets. "I can't believe you're here. I tried for a long time to get in touch with you. To apologize."

It was true. About a year after he'd graduated from high school, he reached out to me on Facebook, and I blocked him. Not only because I didn't want to hear his excuses, but also because I was worried that I might be tempted to cyberstalk him.

Then there was the email he'd sent me. "So Sorry" had been the subject line. I deleted and then undeleted that email multiple times over the course of several months before emptying out my inbox's trash once and for all. Then I changed my email address.

Admittedly, he probably could have tried harder if he'd really wanted to get in contact with me, but he didn't. And I'd done everything I could to keep him away.

"Now the hostility makes a little more sense. Come to dinner with me on Thursday. Let me explain and make this right between us. Please."

I should have agreed. It would have been the perfect opportunity to grill him without him realizing it. But I'd been holding on to my anger against Evan for so long that I didn't know how to let go of it.

His calling me hostile did not help.

"On Thursday I have to help my sister plan your ten-year high school reunion."

"Aubrey, right?" When I nodded, he continued. "What about tomorrow?"

"Isn't Wednesday your hardest day?" Many an NFL player had complained about it.

"It'll be easy to get through if I know you'll let me take you out and talk to you."

He was so cheesy, but sadly enough, some part of it was sickeningly charming. At the very least God could have made him boring and stupid. So that there'd be an easy way to resist him. Oh no, Evan Dawson had to be the ultimate winner of the human race's genetic lottery.

I wouldn't fall for it again. "I have an intramural basketball game tomorrow night."

"Really?" His eyebrows lifted in surprise. "That's what you're going with?"

It did sound like a bad excuse, but it was the truth, and I didn't owe him an explanation. "That's what I'm going with."

He considered me, the right side of his mouth lifted in a half smile. "I'm guessing if I ask you out for Friday night, you'll be busy then, too. I don't know that this has ever happened to me before. Like we've already established, usually I'm the one who spends my time saying no."

I couldn't help myself. I rolled my eyes so massively hard it could have been seen from outer space, which made him laugh. Even his stupid laughter was rich and velvety and melted another micro fraction of my defenses.

"Come on, Ashton. Have dinner with me."

"Do you hear that?" I asked him, cocking my head to one side. He went still, listening. "That's the sound of this, never happening."

I strode out of the room, head held high. It was the perfect note to leave on. Or it would have been, if he hadn't been laughing.

I couldn't believe I'd just had a conversation with Evan Dawson. Where I'd said and done stupid things that amused him. On the plus side, pink drink spillage aside, I looked amazing. So at least I'd always have that.

I nearly ran right into Nia and the very blonde woman I assumed was Tinsley. Nia made the introductions, and I shook Tinsley's hand. "Those are such cute shoes!" I told her.

I had no idea whether they were fashionable or not, but I'd learned at an early age you could never go wrong with other women by complimenting their style choices. Especially footwear.

"Thank you!" she said, grinning. Tinsley looked like a stereotypical ex-professional cheerleader. Tan, in great shape, perfect waves of long hair cascading down her back, blinding white smile. "Nia tells me you'd like to become involved with our Jumping Jacks program."

"I can honestly say it's my favorite charity."

"Perfect. I'm having tea here this Saturday with some of the other committee members to give out assignments, if you're interested."

"Yes!" I needed to rein in my enthusiasm, given their startled expressions. "Definitely. That sounds great. What time?"

She told me to be at the penthouse at two o'clock. In the middle of saying our goodbyes, Evan walked out behind me, brushing past me as he did so.

"Excuse me, ladies. Nia, Tinsley, always a pleasure to see you."

The two women said their hellos and goodbyes as Evan shot me a look that made it pretty obvious we knew each other. After he walked away, it took less than a half second for Tinsley to ask, "You and Evan?"

"No. Nope. No. There is no me and Evan. I just ran into him. In there." I waved my hand over my shoulder. I was supposed to be here to impress her, not to give the image that I was looking for a player to nab. I also needed to keep my I HATE EVAN DAWSON metaphorical T-shirt to myself. "He's not my type." That was a total lie, as he was the type for every breathing woman on the planet. "I am not interested in dating him. At all."

I was protesting so much it was like I was a freshman at a liberal arts college.

"You'd be one of the very few women here who could say that," Tinsley said with an enthusiastic smile. "Evan is the Jacks' white whale. Nobody ever lands him. And given the size of his, er, contract, many women have tried and failed."

I doubted that but knew enough not to say so. I just smiled back. I hoped it looked real.

Maybe every other woman had tried and failed to get what they wanted from him.

I planned on being the one who succeeded and exposed him as a lying fraud.

CHAPTER FOUR

Early in the morning I sent off an email to Brenda, letting her know that I'd started my quest to expose Evan and giving her what little information I had gathered.

It wasn't much, and her terse, curt reply let me know it.

I got Nia's dress dry-cleaned at a place with a two-hour turnaround and texted to ask if I could bring it by. She said sure, and I made the long drive out to her home. It was weird not having to show up to work. I liked being able to do what I wanted when I wanted.

Don't get too used to it, I told myself. It wouldn't be long before I'd be making my way up to the big show, getting to announce for the Jacks.

Before I could even knock on Nia's door, she threw it open. "Come in! We have so much to talk about. Such as how Evan liked your photo. Because he's into you."

What? What photo? Oh, right. Instagram. My whole body scoffed at the idea that Evan Dawson could ever be attracted to me. "That's a little far-fetched. Just because he likes the picture doesn't mean he likes me."

"Maybe not. But it's still a click in the right direction. Or maybe I jumped to my far-fetched conclusion because of this." She held out her phone to show me one of my Instagram photos. With a comment from Evan Dawson.

ashtonbailey610
Portland, Oregon

5 likes

ashtonbailey610 Um, yeah. So...this is me. Any thoughts?
awesomedawson_4 Gorgeous redhead with a fiery personality to match!
1 DAY AGO

Add a comment...

He called me gorgeous? Why did that both thrill and infuriate me at the same time? What kind of game was he playing?

Did he really feel that bad over what had happened in high school? He should. But it wasn't my job to absolve his guilt. He could live with it, as far as I was concerned.

I'd certainly had to.

"I'm guessing you hadn't seen that yet. Which means he's not trying to slide into your DMs."

I nodded. "He kept insisting he wasn't trying to slide into anything."

That made her smile. "Come inside. Would you like some tea?"

"Sure."

She took my winter coat and her dress and hung them both in the same place as she had last night. I followed her into the kitchen, where she had a darling pink-and-green-porcelain tea set on the table.

I had barely sat down when she pounced on me.

"Gorgeous? Fiery personality? Okay, you need to tell me what really happened," she said as she poured some herbal tea into my cup. "I know what you said last night, and I don't believe a word of it. What is going on? Because there were some serious vibes happening between you two."

"There were no vibes," I told her.

"Please. I am a professor of vibeology and know it when I see it. I want the whole story."

I hadn't told anyone the Evan Dawson story in a really long time. I blew on my drink and took a small sip.

"Come on, I'm dying of curiosity. Spill!"

I put the cup down. "I skipped first grade."

She shot me a "what does that have to do with anything?" kind of look.

"Apparently I used to finish worksheets before the teacher even finished passing them all out and constantly begged her for more to do. The school worried about me becoming bored and wanted to keep fostering my love of learning. They met with my parents and recommended that I be skipped into second grade. Because I was so tall, smart, and mature for my age, everybody agreed. And it was fine. Until I got to high school."

Nia's brown eyes were wide, her chin resting on her hand. "And what happened in high school?"

I included the age/grade-skipping thing only because my entire family thought it was relevant to the story. "When I was a freshman, I was thirteen years old. Which made me five years younger than my older sister and her friends, who were all seniors. Including Evan Dawson. My home was the place to hang out for the cheerleaders and football team, and one day while I was in the basement playing *Madden*,

Evan asked if he could join me. I gave him the extra controller, and we played for hours."

I remembered how we had laughed and joked, the way he'd ruffled my hair when I said something he thought was funny.

While I had thought it wildly romantic at the time, I later realized it was how you'd treat an adorable pet.

"We played video games almost every day. We spent a lot of time together. I thought we were into the same kind of stuff, but he probably thought of me as some kid sister. Then the school year started, and I auditioned to be one of the announcers for the varsity football games. I got the position. When everybody came back to the house to celebrate the wins, I was the one Evan sought out and talked to about the games. He made me feel special. Important." When he'd talked to me, he'd made me feel like I was the most interesting person in the entire world. That nothing else mattered to him but that moment and being there with me.

And I had convinced myself I was in love with him. Now I recognized it was just a really gigantic crush, but I had deluded myself into thinking we were Romeo and Juliet, only with less dying in the end.

"You fell hard, didn't you?" Nia asked, and I noticed her expression had shifted from interested to sympathetic.

"The hardest." I nodded. Back then I had done nothing but think about Evan. My grades slipped, and I didn't care. I just knew he and I were meant to be and someday would run away together. Preferably after I got boobs.

I took another sip of my considerably cooled-down tea. Nia stayed quiet, just letting me ramble.

"Did you know I'm the one who gave him his nickname? He came running out onto the field, and I said, 'He's so awesome,' in this ridiculously dreamy voice, and it stuck. Everybody started calling him 'Awesome' Dawson after that," I told her. "I was so proud of being the person who'd started it." I had doodled "awestruck" on the covers of all my school folders. A way to admire him without anyone else knowing.

"I didn't know that."

Nobody seemed to know where his nickname had originated. Except for me. "More than anything else I wanted him to take me to a dance. To have that teen romance moment, you know? Walking down the stairs with the handsome guy at the bottom waiting for you, only able to say, 'Wow,' because you look so amazing. Homecoming came and went. A couple of others, like an autumn-themed one and the Halloween dance. Still nothing. I even got so delusional that I thought maybe he was waiting for a really special dance to ask me. Like the prom. Then Sadie Hawkins was coming up. If Evan wasn't going to ask me, I decided to ask him. To finally tell him how I really felt. I thought maybe he was just shy or didn't know I liked him, too, so if I said it first, it would make it easier for him."

"Oh no," she groaned, covering her face with her hands, peering at me from between her fingers. "What did you do?"

"I wrote him a letter. A handwritten letter that was, like, six pages front and back, all about how in love with him I was and how I knew we'd end up together and then inviting him to the Sadie Hawkins dance." I had poured my little teen heart into those pages. Exposed my soul in a way that had made me beyond vulnerable.

"What happened with the letter?"

"I left it in his locker. I remember how sick to my stomach I felt the entire day, waiting for him to say something, do something. I looked for him in the halls and couldn't find him. When school ended, I knew he had to have seen it by then. I waited by the locker room, knowing he'd be there for practice."

Nia let out a frustrated sigh for me.

"He finally showed up and stopped smiling as soon as he saw me. He told his friends to go ahead, friends who were all snickering as they passed me. Which I didn't really pay attention to because all I cared about was Evan. My voice shook so hard when I asked him if he'd gotten my letter. He wouldn't make eye contact but said he had. I asked if he wanted to go to the Sadie Hawkins dance with me. And then he finally looked at me with so much pity in his eyes and said, 'You're just a kid, Ashton. It's not going to happen.' That was the last time we spoke." Until last night.

Nia stirred her tea absentmindedly. "I mean, that sucks to get your hopes dashed, but it doesn't seem that bad. All of us have had our fair share of rejection."

"Oh, that's not the bad part. And I wish it was only about rejection. I spent that entire weekend crying my eyes out. The following Monday when I got to school, it felt like everybody was laughing and pointing at me, but Aubrey told me it was all in my head. Turns out it wasn't. Evan had taken pictures of my letter and forwarded them to the entire school. People kept quoting lines to me and calling me 'Stalker.' At first it was funny to them, then it turned mean. Like I became the school's official punching bag."

"That is so sad." Nia put one of her hands on top of mine. She must have heard how my voice turned thick as I fought back tears.

"Yeah. He was the shining star. The prom king. The kid who walked on water, who would take them to state. A god among men at that school, and I was some nobody freshman who didn't know her place. Everybody wanted to make sure I remembered I wasn't good enough for him. I tried to talk to Evan about it, to ask why he'd done this to me, but he avoided me. Didn't come over to my house anymore. Until one day out of the blue, he sent me a text. He asked me to meet him on the football field at the fifty-yard line after the game, at midnight. Said he had something he wanted to say to me."

I paused, remembering how excited I'd been. How I'd had to sneak out of my house because, given the constant harassment at school, my parents never would have let me go off to meet him. I had convinced myself he was going to apologize, beg my forgiveness, and we'd finally be together.

And that he'd make everyone stop being so horrible to me.

"I showed up a little early and waited. Just after midnight the sprinklers came on. Only somebody had added dyed soapsuds to the tops of the sprinklers, and they covered me and the grass in a bright-blue coating that took a long time to wash off. As I ran off the field, I was being videotaped by Evan's friends, who yelled awful things as they threw eggs at me. Told me how pathetic and ugly I was, how desperate and sad. A total loser. Everyone I knew saw that video."

My voice had started to shake. Even though it had been ten years ago, talking about it made it feel like it was happening all over again.

"Things only got worse. People wrote cruel things on my locker. They egged our house almost every weekend. I couldn't walk down the hallways without being bullied. My sister even got kicked off the cheerleading squad for beating up the captain after she said something awful to me." It had surprised me that Aubrey's popularity couldn't shield me. It wasn't only Evan who stopped coming to our house to hang out. Everyone stopped coming.

"And if it was bad at school, it was worse online—where there were no adults to step in if things got too out of control. Friends I'd had since elementary school ditched me. As far as they were concerned, I was toxic, and nobody wanted to be tainted by being seen with me. I started having panic attacks and went into a pretty dark depression. It was miserable. My parents had to pull me out of school, and I was homeschooled for the next couple of years."

I was trying to tell the story matter-of-factly, and I was definitely downplaying how serious it had been, how much my family had worried about me, and how it had taken me a long time to feel like myself again.

"I did go back my senior year, mostly because I wanted to play basketball and get scouted. By then most of my tormentors had graduated, and I'd changed and grown up enough that it wasn't an issue any longer."

My plan had worked—I'd received a full ride to the University of Oregon to play basketball for them.

"Did he ever apologize?" Nia asked.

"No. Not while we were in school together. He did try to reach out after he graduated. Sent an email, which I never read. He also tried to message me on Facebook, but I wasn't interested in his excuses." And I'd never understood why he'd been so mean. If he hadn't liked me, fine. If he'd thought I was too young for him, okay. I had thought that, at the very least, we were friends. Who treated their friends like that? Why humiliate me in front of the entire school?

And why stand by and say and do nothing while everyone tormented me?

Nia stood up, took off her long dangly earrings, and laid them on the table. She was muttering under her breath. "Mess with my girl like that? I don't think so."

"What are you doing?" I asked and got up to follow her as she left the kitchen. She picked up her purse. "Where are you going?"

"I'm driving out to the stadium, and I'm going to find Evan Dawson, and then I'm going to beat the living sh—"

"Whoa!" I held up both my hands. "While I very much appreciate the support, I don't need you to fight my battles. I can handle Evan. And if you did something like that, it would get Malik in trouble."

That seemed to cool her off slightly. "He can afford the fine. So can Evan."

"True, but I can't afford to scare off Evan entirely and lose my chance to get the inside scoop from the other women." Like it or not, Evan was the team captain. He did hold a lot of sway with the other players and, by extension, their wives and girlfriends.

She let her purse drop back on the table. "Okay. Fine. But now I hope you do find somebody he's slept with."

"I'm pretty sure I will. But I have to stay calm and keep my wits about me. Because I don't intend to just get mad. I intend to get Evan."

CHAPTER FIVE

After spending the afternoon hanging out/strategizing with Nia, I headed home to my condo to have dinner. I reheated some poached salmon and wild rice and ate while I watched ISEN for a little while. Then I changed into my uniform for the game. My intramural team, the Portland Storm, was playing against our number-one rivals in the league, the Portland Pioneers. It wasn't a playoff game, but the outcome would be a pretty good indication of who would win the league championship in the end.

The Pioneers proved to be worthy opponents, and the game was intense. The score was close, and we were up by only four points. I played center, being the tallest person on our team.

Verity had just passed me the ball, and I was about to pass it off to Eliza on my left when a commotion by the gym doors caught my attention.

Evan Dawson stood by the doorway, surrounded by a small crowd of people.

And I immediately tripped over my own feet and landed facedown on the court.

Pain seared through my skull as the ball rolled out of bounds, giving it to the Pioneers.

"You all right, Ashton?" Verity asked, coming over to help me get back on my feet. I took her outstretched hand.

"Yeah. I'm fine." I was not fine. My head was spinning not only because of my injury but also because of Evan's unexpected appearance. What was he doing here?

"Come on, we're still playing," she said as she ran down the court to set up for defense. I did the same, trying to get my head back in the game. Of course the first thing that would happen when I saw Evan again was that I would fall face-first onto the hardwood floor. Sort of ruining my moment from last night where I'd been snarky and awesome and walked away like a boss. No, the universe couldn't let me have that. Things had to be balanced by me totally humiliating myself.

And it wasn't done screwing with me yet. Our coach called a time-out, asking me if I was okay because "you hit your head pretty hard. Everybody heard it." I told her I was okay, and I was, right up until the moment one of the women seated on the bench directly in front of me sprayed her water bottle the wrong way. All over my shorts so it looked like I had peed myself.

"Sorry!" she said, offering me a towel.

Fan-freaking-tastic. I dabbed at my shorts, but it didn't do me much good. It was like there was some universal conspiracy to make sure I suffered nothing but complete and total embarrassment whenever he was around.

Although I was supposed to be listening to my coach, instead I was watching Evan make his way from the door to the bleachers. It was a slow progression as he smiled and took selfies and signed autographs for everyone in the crowd who asked.

"Bailey?" my coach said, and I realized she'd called my name more than once.

"Yes?"

"Do you want to sit out the next quarter?"

Part of me was tempted to accept. To take the easy out, to turn my back on him and ignore him completely.

But now I had something to prove. That he wouldn't unsettle me, and that I was a good player. Better than good. Senior year of college, my team had gone to the NCAA championship game and placed second.

I wanted to show him I didn't suck.

Despite all current evidence to the contrary.

"Put me in. Let's win this," I told the coach. She nodded, and we all piled our hands into the middle of a circle and yelled, "Storm!" before heading back onto the court.

For the next half hour, I pretended Evan Dawson didn't exist. Since I'd spent the last ten years doing just that, I had plenty of experience.

That score went back and forth; sometimes we were in the lead, sometimes the Pioneers were. It was the closest game I'd played in a very long time.

We were down by two points, and the audience had started to count down the time with the clock. Eliza passed me the ball, and I went up to shoot, but one of the Pioneers immediately fouled me. The shot still made it, and the points were counted.

The ref told me what I already knew—that I'd get one free throw. I glanced up at the clock. Two seconds left in the game.

If I missed, we'd go into overtime. It would delay the inevitable confrontation with Evan Dawson I was about to have.

If I made the shot, we'd win.

And I did so enjoy winning.

Everybody moved into position while I stood at the free throw line. The ref bounce-passed me the ball, and I lined up my shoulders and feet. I bounced the ball a few times, clearing my head until the only thing I could hear was the sound of my own breathing.

I squatted down slightly, lifted back up, and released the ball . . .

Nothing but net.

My teammates ran to hug me, jumping up and down as the audience cheered for our victory.

I couldn't help myself. I looked for Evan. Had he been impressed? He was on his feet, clapping and grinning. He even did that guy whistle thing with his fingers.

"Way to go, Ashton!" His voice rang out clear and strong, above all the other happy commotion. He waved, and I quickly averted my gaze.

I stayed in the center of the crowd as my teammates were congratulated by friends and family. Evan remained in the bleachers, as if he was waiting for me to come to him.

When the crowd shifted over to our bench, I grabbed my jacket and my duffel bag, hoping to sneak out quietly. I glanced up and saw that Evan had started walking toward me. Crap.

"Hey, Ashton, you coming out with us to celebrate?" Verity asked me. "We're thinking karaoke." It was what we usually did after winning a game—the single ladies would head out together and do something fun.

"I can't tonight. I have to deal with . . ." My voice trailed off as I pointed at Evan.

"Evan Dawson is here for you? Lucky girl. Tell me all about it at our next practice," she responded, waggling her eyebrows at me as she walked away.

Lucky? Not so much.

Annoyed and feeling a bit stabby? More on target.

Even if he did look sort of yummy in his dark jacket, a slate-gray T-shirt, and his blue jeans.

"Great game! Really intense. You played so well. And I usually hate women's basketball," he said when he reached me.

How did he ratchet my annoyance from an eight all the way up to, like, ten million? "I don't remember inviting you."

"You didn't."

Was that all he was going to say about it? "How did you find me?"

"I called your dad's law firm, and he gave me Aubrey's extension, and she was happy to tell me where you'd be."

Oh, a conversation was going to be had between me and my sister. Maybe a conversation of the physical variety. Because I was going to kill her. And given his role in this fiasco, I'd force my dad to represent me for free after I took her out.

We were starting to attract an audience. I saw a group of giggling teenage girls hanging around by the bleachers, waiting for him. I wanted to be like, "Run! I'm the ghost of Evan Dawson's past! This won't turn out well for you!"

Instead, I said, "Okay. I'm going now."

He fell into step alongside me and then even opened the gym door, letting me go first. I was about to tell him I was perfectly capable of opening my own doors when I noticed the teenage horde was closing in on us. I'd seen videos of what they did to celebrities, and I did not want to get caught in the cross fire. We went around a corner, out of sight of the throng. I grabbed Evan by the shirtfront and pulled him into the empty gym. I held still in the dark, listening to the sound of too much lip gloss and low self-esteem passing us by.

"You know, if you wanted to get me alone, Ashton, all you had to do was ask." His voice was low and almost purring, like a giant predatory cat.

I needed to remember that's what he was. A predator who only looked out for his own self-interests and couldn't care less about other people.

And yet I stood there, still holding on to his shirt, breathing in his scent of soap and some kind of masculine cologne that had my toes curling in.

I forced my hand to release him and backed up, feeling along the wall for the light switch. I found it and turned the lights on, flooding the gym with brightness.

"Thanks for the save," he said, hands in his pockets as he leaned against the wall.

"I didn't do it for you." I couldn't explain why I'd done it at all. "I think they're gone. We can go now."

Instead of pushing on the door and leaving, he walked over to a cart and grabbed the basketball on top. He bounced it on the shiny floor, the sound echoing loudly off the walls. "It's been a long time since I've played."

Nobody cared, least of all me. Before I could say as much, he spoke again.

"I am sorry for just showing up, but I need to sit down and talk to you. I gave up too easy the last time I tried to apologize to you, and I'm not doing that again. Have dinner with me?"

How many times was he going to ask the same question and expect a different answer? "This is your plan? To hound me until I give in?"

"Not hound. Ask nicely. Repeatedly." He took off his jacket, and my traitorous eyes followed the outline of his biceps and shoulders in his shirt.

"Why do you even care? Why is it so important for you to explain?" The words burst out of me; I hadn't intended to speak them aloud.

"Because of all the things I regret in my life, what happened with you is one of the things I regret most. I'd do anything to go back and change it."

Why did that make my eyes fill up with burning tears? "Yeah, so would I. But time travel is still not a thing."

He held the basketball against his stomach, resting his forearms around it. "Right. So the only thing left is for me to beg for your forgiveness after I explain everything to you."

"Not going to happen."

There was a pause as he considered my instant response. "I never figured you for the kind of girl who'd hold a grudge like this."

"It's not holding a grudge. It's just keeping certain memories fresh in my mind so I'm better prepared for having to talk to you." And to keep my hormones in check, because they liked Evan Dawson and everything about him very, very much.

He laughed. "I'd forgotten how funny you are."

Today, it was not on purpose. I let out a long sigh as my response.

"Ashton, please go to dinner with me."

My resolve started to crumble ever so slightly. "Why do I get the feeling you're going to keep asking until I say yes?"

"Because you're getting to know me?"

I'd just about had my fill of Evan Dawson. Especially when he was trying to be cute. I started for the door, but he blocked my path. "Ashton, wait. How about this—we play a game of one-on-one. If I win, you let me take you to dinner and apologize. And if you win, I promise to never bother you about it again."

This shouldn't have been a difficult decision, but it was. Because I was torn between making another grand exit and playing his game to see what would happen. Maybe it was because I'd spent the afternoon reliving my teenage trauma with Nia that now some perverse part of me wanted to hear what he had to say.

And after all these years, I did want an explanation. Just to get closure so I could stop obsessing about it.

Not that I intended to forgive him or anything like it, but it wouldn't hurt to have him believe he was in my corner as I tried to find out the truth about him.

Who knows? Maybe he'd reveal something else at the dinner that I could use for my story. At the very least it might be progress to report to Brenda.

"Fine." I set down my duffel bag and took off my jacket.

And nearly squawked out loud when I saw him taking off his shirt. "What are you doing?"

He tossed the shirt on top of his jacket. "I don't want to get my shirt all sweaty. Not to mention I told you it's been a long time for me, and I just saw how good you are. I need every advantage I can get."

Yes, because being a professional athlete wasn't going to help him at all. "And you think this is an advantage?"

"I don't know. Ask your eyes. They've been glued to my chest for the last minute or so."

He wasn't wrong. His chest was a thing of beauty. Rippling, sculpted muscles and sinews and fading bruises in every color of the rainbow, all of which my fingers itched to touch.

I'd obviously hit my head harder during the game than I'd originally thought. "Are you always this full of yourself?"

"Only when someone gives me a reason to be." He dribbled the ball, walking backward. "Play to ten?"

I tightened my ponytail. "Let's go."

He bounced the ball to me, and I immediately sank my first shot. "Two points, me."

Evan turned out to be a stronger opponent than I'd thought. He had four inches on me, which helped him to block. As did his whole standing super close without a shirt on. It was a distraction and a definite advantage for him. I lost control of the ball more than once due to my idiotic physical reaction to him. Like he was scrambling my senses by being so close and smelling so good and giving off this intoxicating heat that made me want to cling to him like a baby monkey.

"Eight to eight," he reminded me, his words burning against my earlobe, my back pressed to his front as I dribbled.

I could easily pivot out of this and make the shot. Game over.

Instead, I just kept dribbling, like the ball represented what was going on in my mind. Did I want things to be over and never see Evan again?

I turned to shoot, and the ball bounced against the backboard. Evan grabbed the rebound and with an easy layup won the game.

"Yes! Yes!" he said, both arms high above his head. "I win!"

"Okay, okay. Stop dancing in the end zone," I told him. I was all hot and bothered, and I suspected it had nothing to do with the physical exertion and everything to do with the guy celebrating under the hoop.

Had I missed on purpose? I always gave basketball my all, but this time I suspected I'd tried, like, maybe ninety percent. Or eighty-five.

Possibly sixty.

"Dinner, Friday night. Because you have plans tomorrow night, right?" he asked after he'd finished his victory lap around half of the gym. I mopped some residual sweat off my forehead, out of my eyes. So much for worrying about his shirt. This jerk didn't even have the decency to break a sweat.

And how did he remember my schedule like that? "I guess Friday is fine."

"I need your address so I can pick you up. How's seven o'clock?" To my hormones' sadness, he walked over to put his shirt back on.

I did not want Evan Dawson knowing where I lived. "I will meet you at the restaurant. You didn't negotiate picking me up as part of the bet." Ha. At least I still had some dignity left and had won something, even if the victory was tiny.

He blinked slowly, a smile shadowing his lips. "You're right. I didn't. So I'll need your number so I can text you the information."

Why did it feel just as dangerous to give him my number as it did my address? But with no cards left to play, I rattled off my cell number.

And all of my feelings of having won something disappeared when I saw his smirk. He'd outsmarted me in the end.

Evan put his phone back in his pocket and picked up his jacket. I turned off the gym lights as he opened the door.

"Hey, Ashton, do you hear that?"

"What?" I asked, holding still, wondering if we'd set off an alarm somewhere.

He moved closer, again making my senses go nuts. "It's the sound of this, happening." He whistled as he went out into the hallway, leaving me standing in the door with my mouth hanging open.

How did that make me both want to laugh and hate him more at the same time?

CHAPTER SIX

I went into ISEN the next afternoon to tell Brenda about my progress. Rand gave me a hard time about being "the teacher's pet," but I ignored him as I headed into her office. I told her about the dinner date we had planned, along with the charity appointment with Tinsley. Her eyes lit up when I talked about the dinner. She wanted to know when and where, but I told her I didn't know yet.

As if he somehow sensed he was being talked about, my phone dinged with a new message.

> Friday night - Rodrigo's. Meet me there at 7:00. I'll be the one who just crushed you in basketball.

I handed her my phone to let her see his text.

She stared at my screen for a long time. It made me a bit uncomfortable. I wondered if she'd mention the basketball part since I hadn't told her anything about it. I probably should have. It just didn't feel like it was any of her business since it didn't have anything to do with the story. Only the outcome had mattered—that we were going to dinner.

Speaking of, Rodrigo's was a new restaurant that had opened downtown and was basically impossible to get into. Aubrey had been trying for months to get reservations for her and her husband.

Which of course wouldn't be a problem for a guy like Evan Dawson.

"This is really promising, Ashton. Make sure he gets some wine in him, and you have your phone handy so you can record whatever he's saying."

She handed my phone back to me, and I put it in my purse. "For sure." But the idea of getting him drunk in an attempt to make him confess everything felt . . . wrong. When I found out the truth, I didn't want there to be any coercion or trickery involved.

"Even though you don't have any official intel yet, it sounds like you're making progress. Good job, Ashton. Keep it up. And keep me informed."

I promised I would and then pitched in for a few hours to help out with the workload. The other interns all glared and muttered things about me just out of my hearing. It made sense that they'd resent me. I'd resent me, too. I was getting special treatment. But their behavior started giving me nervous flashbacks to high school, and I ended up leaving earlier than I had intended.

After I grabbed some dinner from the bistro where I usually ate lunch, I headed over to Aubrey's house. She and my brother-in-law, Justin, lived in the same upper-middle-class suburb where we'd grown up, just two blocks over from my parents' house.

I knocked on their door, and when Aubrey answered, I got bowled over by my four-year-old niece, Charlotte, and my two-year-old nephew, Joey. "Auntie Ashton!"

"Hey, guys!" I said with a laugh as they clung to my legs. I walked inside slowly, their weight slowing me down.

"Are you here to play with us?" Charlotte asked, her big hazel eyes imploring me to say yes, her red hair in two braids that made her look a little like Pippi Longstocking.

"Charlotte, for the thousandth time, Mommy told you to go upstairs and get dressed. You can't run around in your underwear," Aubrey said, pinching the bridge of her nose.

Now my niece turned her big-eyed puppy gaze on my sister. "No, Mommy, why? I don't wanna wear shirts or dresses or pants."

"Upstairs, right now."

With fake sobs Charlotte heaved herself up the stairs, stopping her crying only when she realized we weren't listening to her. Then she stomped loudly all the way to her room and slammed the door once she got there.

"I am so looking forward to her becoming a teenager. You know, before I became a mom, I had no idea I could ruin someone's day by asking them to wear pants," Aubrey said as she pulled Joey off my leg. "Do you have to go potty?"

"No," he said, scrambling to be put down and then running off to play with his cars.

"I don't have to go potty, either. In case you were wondering."

Aubrey shot me her patented Mom Look to let me know she wasn't amused. Her phone beeped, and she glanced at the screen. "Sh—crap. Izzie's mom just backed out of carpool on Saturday for Charlotte's soccer game."

"Rory could take her. If she remembers. Or maybe I could do it. I do have this thing on that day, though." Hopefully the game would conflict with my Tinsley meeting, and I could back out of my offer. Because I did not want to do carpool for Charlotte and her friends. I'd discovered that transporting a bunch of four-year-olds was like moving multiple serial killers in between prisons.

"You can't take her," she scoffed. "They banned you from all of her games because of how you screamed at that referee. He will personally throw you out again if he sees you there."

"But how would he recognize me, given that he's completely blind?"

Aubrey sighed. "They're four-year-olds. They're not playing for the World Cup. Let me just send out a couple of texts and see if someone else can drive."

So I tended to get a tad bit excited when it came to sports. Especially sports that my family members were participating in.

"Okay, Elia's mom said she would do it. Come into the kitchen. I've got you all set up in there."

By "all set up" she apparently meant she'd raided a stationery store Viking-style and arranged the entire inventory on the table. "What's all this?" I asked.

"It's what we need for the reunion. Here's everything that needs to get done." She handed me a list, and it was seriously longer than the Bible.

"Classmate search, website, mailings, invitations, T-shirts, venue, decorations, theme, awards, slideshows, videographer, photographer, DJ . . ." And there was more. It kept going. "I repeat, what is all this?"

"The stuff I'm taking care of for the reunion." She was in her fridge, taking out juice boxes and putting them in a diaper bag on the counter.

"You said you were *on* the planning committee. Not that you were the *entire* planning committee. Don't you have minions to do your bidding?"

"Yes. I have you."

So not what I had signed up for.

Once she added some fruit snacks and organic animal crackers to the bag, she came over to grab the list from me. "Don't try to eat the elephant all at once. Just take one bite at a time. I want you to start with the classmate search. We need to find mailing addresses for all the members of my class. Everything here on the table is color-coded and organized for the different stages of the reunion. The search pile is in the red folder."

She handed it to me, and it had a list of names and potential phone numbers to try.

"You do realize they medicate people with this level of organization, right?" I asked. "And why mailing addresses? Have you heard of this thing called evites? Or computers?"

"I'm not doing anything as tacky as an electronic invitation. These will be real embossed invitations on a heavy ecru-colored cardstock. Because this is going to be the best ten-year reunion Westlake has ever seen, and it all starts with the invite."

I sat down in the chair, already feeling defeated. There were hundreds of names on this list. "Why do you care what people who haven't seen you in ten years think of you or this reunion?"

She was rearranging the contents of the bag. My guess was she was color-coding and organizing it, too. "I don't care what they think. It's just important to me."

"That's the definition of caring."

"Whatever, Reunion Monkey. Start making phone calls."

It occurred to me that the only reason my sister would be packing a bag was if she was going somewhere. "You're leaving me with all this? Where are you going?"

"Justin and I are going to have dinner in the city tonight. Where we will drink grown-up drinks and eat grown-up food and pretend we're still interesting adults who know how to make actual conversation with each other."

Justin and Aubrey had met in law school, married immediately after graduation, both joined my father's law firm, and gotten pregnant with Charlotte right away. Then they'd bought this home to be near our parents. It was all either a sweet ode to family bonding or a warning for a relationship that was bordering on codependency.

"What about the kids? Who's going to watch them?" I hoped the answer wasn't me. Much as I loved my niece and nephew, they were like mini emotional terrorists ready to take out themselves and everyone around them in order to get their way.

"Mom and Dad are going to take them for the evening. I'm just going to drop them by their house, and then I'll be on my way. And I wouldn't leave you alone with all this. I got a volunteer who wants to help out."

As if on cue, the doorbell rang.

"And there he is now," she said.

"He? You're going to leave me alone in your house with a strange man?"

"Oh," Aubrey said with a wicked gleam in her eye that suddenly made me very, very afraid, "he's no stranger."

She opened the door, and sure enough I heard Evan Dawson's voice for the third time in as many days.

They said their hellos and how are yous, and Joey came over to hold on to his mom's leg while staring up at Evan. His little jaw hung slightly open, and he finally uttered the word *football*.

Evan crouched down to be eye level with my nephew. "I do play football. Do you like football?"

Joey nodded enthusiastically but didn't say anything else.

"I love football, too. But probably not as much as your aunt Ashton does." Evan caught me watching him, and that overgrown idiot winked at me.

It was not charming. It was not. At all.

He stood up, and Aubrey led him into the kitchen, giving him the same introductory spiel she'd just given me. She took out the list of students and split it in half, handing him his part.

"If you'll excuse me for a minute, my daughter has been upstairs and completely quiet for too long. I'll be right back."

The ends of his hair were slightly damp, as if he'd recently showered. He put his jacket over the back of his chair and sat down, the cotton fabric of his dark-green shirt tightening around his muscles.

Why did I notice little details like that about him? What was wrong with me? "You do know that in some states this basically constitutes stalking, right?" I hissed at him. I'd already agreed to hear him out at dinner. What more did he want from me?

"I'm not stalking you. I'm just . . . around you a lot recently. And is this a bad time, or are you just randomly pissed off?"

I clenched my fists. He did not get to make judgments on what my mood should or shouldn't be where he was concerned. "You have ten seconds to get out of . . . Wait, stay right there."

"Indecisive. I like it."

Instead of responding to him, I ran for the stairs, grabbing Joey on the way. I'd been on the verge of forcing Evan to leave when it occurred to me how this had all happened.

Aubrey.

He'd said he'd talked to her.

My sister was not going to interfere like this. I wouldn't let her. I dropped off Joey to play in his room. I found Aubrey in the master bathroom scrubbing lipstick off Charlotte's face and arms. Charlotte again looked at me with her puppy dog eyes, silently begging for assistance.

That kid was on her own. I had something else I needed to deal with first. "Are you serious with this? You're going to leave me here with him?"

"I'm not too worried. It's not like he's going to try to S-L-E-E-P with you."

"You can spell that again," I told her. Definitely not happening. No matter how happy it would make Brenda. Or certain dumb, irrational parts of mine. "You need to toss him out of this house."

She added more cleanser to the washrag she was using on Charlotte's face. "You need to act like an adult. You promised you'd do whatever I asked, without question. He volunteered to help me out, and I'm not in a position right now to turn down that kind of help."

"Yes, I'm sure the superfamous star of the NFL has loads of free time to help plan your reunion. That sounds so in character for him. He is such a devious piece of . . ." I glanced at my niece. "Work."

"I need you to go downstairs and just be nice. Don't swear at him or anything."

"What good would that do me? I can't tell him to go to, er, Hades because I'm pretty sure the devil still has a restraining order out against him." I sighed loudly. "You do know he's forcing me to go to dinner with him at Rodrigo's, right?"

Aubrey stopped scrubbing her daughter's now bright-pink face. "That jerk. Want me to beat him up for you?" The sarcasm was strong in our DNA.

"I would think as an officer of the court you'd be a little more concerned about someone blackmailing me into a date."

"And I think you could have fun with Evan if you'd just let yourself. You don't know. You might actually like him. There could even be sparks."

"Only if I burn down the restaurant in my failed attempt at escape," I muttered.

She rinsed the washrag in the sink. "You could have fun under the right circumstances."

"In these circumstances, am I sedated?"

Aubrey just gave me another Mom Look in the mirror.

My stupid sister. Wanting everybody else paired off. Like she'd been called to be the current incarnation of Noah. "My life is not a one-and-a-half-star movie. Evan and I are not going to fall in love with each other, no matter how much you push us together."

"Like Dad always says, nothing truly great came from a comfort zone."

I folded my arms so I wouldn't be tempted to choke her. "This isn't about comfort zones, Aubrey!"

"Or, a positive attitude will take you far."

"I don't need your sports philosophizing. And I've found that a negative attitude can take me much further." I leaned against the counter, arms still folded. "What is your endgame here? Do you think I'm going to marry Satan? What would our color scheme be? Devil red and brimstone?"

"Who's Satan?" Charlotte piped up, causing us to both turn and look at her.

"The guy downstairs in the kitchen," I told her.

Aubrey rolled her eyes at me. "Are you really telling my daughter that Evan Dawson is the actual devil?"

I shrugged one shoulder. "If the pointy black horns fit. Besides, my job as her godmother is to make sure she's properly instructed on all religious matters."

"Hello? Is anyone home?" someone called from downstairs.

"Why is Rory here?" I asked Aubrey, who suspiciously did not meet my gaze.

"I might have mentioned you two were coming over."

Was this some kind of Bailey family conspiracy? Were they all in on this "let's make Evan and Ashton spend time together" situation? "Promise me this is it. From now on, you'll stay out of my love life."

"Okay, fine, I promise," Aubrey said in an exasperated tone. Like I was another one of her toddlers.

I went downstairs to find Rory before she started hitting on Evan and climbed into his lap. Because I did not need that visual image permanently seared into my brain.

How many meddling family members was I going to have to put up with tonight?

CHAPTER SEVEN

To my surprise I didn't find my younger sister draped across Evan Dawson's lap. Instead, she was standing in the family room, watching him make phone calls to the former students on his list.

Not at all creepy.

She had a big dreamy grin plastered on her face. My little sister was the opposite of Aubrey—flighty, superoptimistic, idealistic, and so full of life.

I had no patience for any of it. Especially right then.

"I just love athletes," she said with a sigh. "They're so . . . athletic."

"Profound observation. What are you doing here?"

"Admiring the view. Man, if being sexy was a crime, he'd get a life sentence."

I shut my eyes and counted slowly to ten. When I opened them, I said, "It's not just about his appearance. Don't you remember the stories I told you about him?"

"Yes, I remember." She shifted her body, almost like she was posing against the wall in case he glanced up at us. "I also remember he tried to apologize to you back then, and according to Aubrey, he's trying to apologize now."

How did Aubrey know that? Just how long had their phone conversation been? I should ask her. She would know. Her job required her to keep track of literally every minute of her day.

Rory kept going. "And I also remember that you hold a grudge longer than anybody not named Hatfield or McCoy should hold one. Like when you thought I broke your talking stuffed animal when you were ten. You were mad about that for years."

"Was not," I scoffed. "And two people saw you do it."

"You can't count Buster as a person. He was our dog." She sighed again. "And I think you're wrong about the kind of man he is now. There's a real he-goes-to-Africa-to-dig-wells kind of thing happening in his aura. Seriously, he's hot enough that I'd date him even if his personality sucked."

Evan was off the phone and smiling as he went over his list, obviously listening in.

"Sound travels," I whispered to her. "He can hear you."

"I know what sound does," she said in her normal tone. "You think I don't want him to know I think he's hot? Hey, cutie, how you doin'?" She said the last part loudly.

Evan's smile widened.

"Don't you have a boyfriend? Ned or Fred something?"

"Ted. Teddy, actually. But Teddy is no Evan Dawson. And he's not my boyfriend." Another happy sigh. "Hey, if you're not going to date him, do you mind if I ask him out? And if you are going to date, can you introduce me to one of his teammates? Like that Scottish kicker is seriously adorable."

It was a well-established fact that Baileys had a weakness for football players. It had started with my grandmother, an heiress who had wanted nothing more than to be a sports reporter for the *Portland Blaze*. She'd ended up with a member of the Jacks as her husband. My dad played college ball, as did Justin before he blew out his knee.

I should be attracted to nice, sweet men. Men who grew beards and kept bees and wrote sonnets about how much they liked my hips. But I was discovering that my body was shallow and easily swayed by muscles and cut jaws and manly forearms.

In the midst of my self-loathing over my poor choices in men, Aubrey breezed back downstairs carrying Joey on one side and Charlotte on the other. She set Charlotte down and went into the kitchen.

"We're off. Evan, please make yourself at home, and you've got my cell number if you have any questions. Thanks so much for helping out."

"My pleasure."

I had one last attempt before they left. "Can't I just take the list home and work on it there? There's no reason we have to be here." Both of us. At the same time.

Aubrey swung the diaper bag over her shoulder. "The master lists do not leave my house. I don't want them to get lost or get stuff spilled on them."

"That won't happen. I'm not Rory."

"Hey!" Rory protested.

"Time for us to go. Come on, Rory, Mom and Dad are expecting you. It's been a long time since you've been home to visit." Aubrey took Rory by the wrist, like she was another one of her children she had to corral.

Rory whined as she dragged her feet. "There's a reason for that!"

"Charlotte, Joey, say goodbye to Aunt Ashton and Evan."

Joey had his head tucked against Aubrey's shoulder and smiled at me. "Bye." Then he gave Evan a little wave. "Bye, football man."

Charlotte hugged me around my legs and then waved widely at Evan. "See you later, Satan!"

There was a stunned silence until Aubrey was back in motion, getting her children and Rory out of the house. The front door closed with the sounds of Aubrey telling her older kid not to call people Satan.

I was alone. With Evan Dawson.

I wanted to follow after them. Seek out refuge in my parents' home. But I wasn't a wuss, and I had already let Evan Dawson control a big part of my life. I wasn't about to give him even more of it.

I'd promised Aubrey, and I was going to do what she'd asked me to do.

Evan stood, walked over to the refrigerator, and pulled out a pitcher of orange juice. He opened a few cabinets, presumably looking for a glass.

"What are you doing?" I couldn't help but ask.

"Your sister said to make myself at home, and I'm thirsty." He located a glass and filled it.

"That's just something people say. They don't actually want you to start snooping around their house."

"I'm not snooping. Just getting some juice. Do you want some?"

I didn't know which annoyed me more—his going into cabinets like he lived here or offering up things that weren't even his. "No, I don't."

Time to stop fixating on Evan. I looked over my list. It wasn't alphabetical, as I'd assumed it would be. In fact . . . I flipped through the pages, reading names. My sister had given me a list of the kids who'd been in theater. The Chess Club. The AV team. The artists. I didn't have a single football player or cheerleader or formerly popular teen on my list.

Evan was at the sink, rinsing out the glass before he put it in the dishwasher. Of course he'd be thoughtful like that.

I glanced at his list and saw that Aubrey had given my former tormentors to Evan to contact. It made me less angry with her that she'd done something so sweet. Even though I didn't need her protection. I wasn't thirteen any longer. I wasn't afraid of them like I had been.

"Your niece and nephew are really cute." Evan sat down, and I scooted my chair back ever so slightly, just so I wouldn't keep accidentally smelling his cologne.

It didn't really work. "Yes, they are. We have excellent genes."

"I would definitely agree with you there." I felt his gaze on me and looked up to see the teasing, sexy smirk on his face.

"Don't do that," I told him.

"Do what?"

"Flirt."

"Why? Is it working?"

A little. "No." I could feel the flush starting and willed it stop.

He leaned in, and I could feel the warmth of him against my exposed skin. "We're all alone now, right?"

"Yes, just the two of us with no witnesses in a room filled with sharp utensils."

He laughed. "Here's to hoping we both make it out of this night alive." I had to refrain from kicking him in the shin. Like I'd stab him. There was no way I was calling my older sister to tell her that I'd stabbed Evan Dawson in her pristine kitchen. She'd probably make me clean it all up.

I decided my best course of action was to ignore him. To do the job Aubrey wanted me to do and then go home. I'd been psyching myself up for the dinner. A dinner that would take place in a neutral area that I'd never been to before. This was different. He was here, in Aubrey's kitchen, at her table. It was like I had these two worlds colliding, and I didn't know how to process it all.

At the top of the list was a speech Aubrey had written out for me. It started off with, "Hi, this is [insert your name here]." I wondered what she would do if I called someone and actually said, "Hi, this is insert your name here." I could tell her that I'd only been following her instructions exactly. It wasn't worth the potential aggravation, even if I would have been amused.

I was supposed to confirm the list members' mailing addresses and ask them if they'd like to order an early-bird ticket. Aubrey said in her notes that she wanted us to sell a hundred early-bird tickets. I wasn't a saleswoman. My sister had recruited the wrong person.

This was apparently not the case with Evan.

"Hi, this is Evan Dawson. I'm calling you about the upcoming ten-year reunion for Westlake." He paused to laugh, and that megawatt smile that had sold a million sports drinks made me feel like I couldn't catch my breath. "Yes, it's really me. Oh, just helping out a friend. Anyway, I wanted to make sure I have your correct mailing address and see if you'd like to buy a couple of early-bird tickets for you and your lovely wife."

Oh, look at me. I'm charming and hot and rich and hot and famous and athletic and hot. Yes, I said *hot* three times in my head. Not even my subconscious was listening to reason about why we were not attracted to Evan.

"Fantastic. I'll put you down for two tickets then. See you there."

He hung up Aubrey's landline. I wondered for a second why he wasn't using his cell, until I realized he probably didn't want a bunch of random people he'd gone to high school with having his private number.

A private number that he'd given to me without hesitation.

I tried not to read anything into that.

"How many early-bird tickets have you sold?" he asked me, and I recommitted to my plan to ignore him.

Which he didn't seem to like. He pushed against the foot of my chair so that I was forced to face him. "What?" I demanded.

He looked slightly confused at my irritation. "Women don't usually ignore me."

"Only because they don't know any better."

"I was only asking how many tickets you've sold."

I scooted my chair back toward the table. "Look, you have your calls to make, and I have mine. We're not here to chat." Why was I hearing my mother's voice in my head telling me to be polite? "And I haven't sold any yet. Although you could just buy all the tickets."

It seemed like a brilliant idea. Evan could easily afford it, and then we'd be done.

"Why would I do that? Then I'd be the only one there."

"Untrue. Your ego is probably your favorite plus-one. I'm sure the two of you would have a fantastic time together."

He grinned and leaned in toward me. "We could go together. You could be my plus-one. Or I could be yours."

My plus-one? He wasn't even in consideration to be my minus-one. I opened my mouth to tell him that, but he kept talking.

"If I bought all the tickets, then I wouldn't get to spend more time with you, enjoying your ever-so-pleasant company. And nobody wants that to happen."

I did! "I want that!"

"Do you really?"

What, he was so amazing and wonderful that I should be grateful just to be in his presence? "Yes. Because if you bought all the early-bird tickets, we could go home."

A wolfish grin lit up his entire stupid handsome face. "Sounds good to me. I'd love to go home with you."

Why did that make my pulse beat so erratically and my breathing go shallow? "Oh please. Mr. Chastity Belt himself wants to go home with me?"

He moved in closer. "I didn't say anything would happen. I may flirt, but that's as far as things would go." I sucked in a deep breath when he reached over to brush a strand of hair from my cheek, delicately tucking it behind my earlobe. His fingertips were calloused and warm and felt way, way too good. "Even if you have me imagining otherwise."

He said the words under his breath, as if he hadn't intended to say them out loud. But I heard them. And my body just reacted with a big *yes, please*, starting a flush I felt in my stomach that traveled all across my skin. Like the kitchen lights had just sunburned me.

And goose bumps broke out everywhere as he took in my flush, letting his fingers drift down from my ear to my jaw, under my chin. "Ashton, there's something I need to say—"

Not yet. Not like this. Not when I wasn't prepared and my defenses were in disarray. "I'm not talking to you about your apology or excuses or whatever."

He leaned back, taking his hand away. "That's not what I wanted to say. Because that's what tomorrow night is for. Tonight is about making sure that Aubrey doesn't murder us in our sleep for not doing what she wanted. I'd forgotten how scary she could be."

That made me smile. Against my will.

And he, of course, noticed. "You smiled! An actual, real smile. I was a little worried you'd forgotten how."

"Maybe that was just a smirk. How do you know I wasn't envisioning your career-ending injury, reducing you to a life of selling used cars?"

Evan leaned back in his chair, his strong forearms crossed against his broad, tight chest. "My finance guy has made sure I'll never have to sell used cars, even if I got cut from the team tomorrow. And that was definitely a smile. That I caused. And I'm going to make it happen again. Maybe even make you laugh."

I couldn't help myself. He was being really charming. Another smile crept up on me.

"Two in a row!" He raised both of his hands above his head, like a ref signaling a touchdown. "This is almost as good as when I won the Super Bowl last season."

I twisted my lips, but it didn't do me any good. I smiled again. "You won the Super Bowl? All by yourself? I'm pretty sure you had some help."

"Yeah, I did. But that got me Smile Number Three."

"Okay, you proved whatever point you wanted to prove. Let's just get back to work."

Evan smiled at me and nodded as I began dialing the first name on my list. His denim-clad knee grazed against mine, and I jerked away, nearly falling out of my chair.

I'd told Aubrey that the only sparks that could happen between Evan and me were of the things-being-set-on-fire variety.

I was wrong.

Because I felt that slight touch zinging around inside me like an electrical current before it exploded into a ball of fireworks in my stomach.

This was bad. Very, very bad.

CHAPTER EIGHT

Despite the fact that my boss had told me I didn't have to come in to work, I chose to go in that Friday morning. Because I'd discovered that idleness didn't really suit me. I liked being busy. And because I didn't want to think too much about my dinner date with Evan later that evening.

Brenda did not help my cause when she pulled me into her office, giving me makeup and hair tips and suggesting that I take the afternoon off to go shopping for a dress. She even gave me her company American Express card. I felt a little guilty taking it, but I couldn't really say no.

I told her about my surprise run-in with him, and the longer I talked, the more withdrawn Brenda became.

She cleared her throat, cutting me off midstory. "Look, I can see that you hate this guy, and I don't blame you, but you need to get him on your side. Win his trust. And that's not going to happen if you keep being openly hostile toward him."

"I can't just pretend like I forgive him." I mean, I could, but then somebody in Hollywood would have to give me an award.

"You'd be surprised what you're capable of when your career's on the line." Her implication was more than clear. "You know the saying: you can't make an omelet without compromising some of your principles."

After more lecturing about how I had to reel in Evan Dawson like he was a prize fish (largemouth bass seemed the best likeness in my wandering mind), she told me to go and get ready. I had, like, seven hours. I didn't need that long, but I texted my younger sister to see if she wanted to go shopping. She immediately replied.

> Meet you at the mall in twenty minutes.

I was about to ask her if she had class or midterms but figured it wouldn't matter even if she did. Rory always did whatever she wanted to do. I headed over to the elevators and pushed the down button.

"Where are you going?"

The sound of Rand's voice startled me, and I put a hand against my fast-beating heart. "Brenda wants me to . . . run some errands for her." Technically it was a dress for me, but I was doing it at Brenda's request. But if I told Rand the whole truth, I'd never live it down.

"Lucky girl. I hope you get your Dawson story. I'd hate to see Brenda's reaction if you don't come through. Especially if it all turns out to be true and there is no story."

I already knew what her reaction would be, and I suspected it would end with my entrails thumbtacked onto the company bulletin board as a warning to all future interns.

"I'll worry about my job, and you worry about yours," I told him with a bravado I wasn't really feeling. I excused myself when my elevator arrived. When I headed inside, I dismissed Rand's trying to screw with my mind and instead thought about my last few encounters with Evan. He might have come across as a charming, arrogant, handsome jerk face, but nothing he'd said ever felt dishonest. I'd never once gotten the impression that he was lying to me.

I pushed the button for the lobby. Tonight would be the true test. I'd figure out what was really going on with him.

And hopefully keep my entrails on the inside of my body, where they belonged.

Rory and I ended up spending a lot more time shopping than we should have, and she offered to drive me home so I could get ready.

And by "drive," I mean she sped through the roads like a crazed maniac who'd seen the Fast and the Furious franchise one too many times.

"You can slow down!" I told her. I liked to be on time as much as the next person, but Evan could wait. Safety first. I was sure he would understand.

"You still have to shower and get dressed and blow-dry your hair and put on some makeup. I don't want you to be late!"

"And I don't want to be a martyr for punctuality!"

She sneaked into a parking spot right in front of my building. She reached into the back seat and handed me my bags. "No more complaining. We're here, and nobody died. Have fun tonight. Relax. Be nice. And give the guy a break, would ya?"

I'd like to give him a break. In three places. And why was every Bailey woman so determined for me to give Evan another chance?

To be honest, I was surprised my mother hadn't weighed in yet. She reminded me of an app on my phone, in that she was always bugging me for updates on my life.

Because somebody had to have told her. Despite her constant assurance that she could keep a secret, Rory only kept secrets in circulation. My mom had to know. Her silence on the subject was disconcerting.

We waved goodbye, and Rory darted back out into traffic. I made my way upstairs to my condo and got ready as quickly as I could. I didn't do a lot of fancy dates at upscale restaurants, so I wasn't quite sure how to do my makeup. And I didn't have time for somebody on YouTube to teach me.

Then I slipped on the little black dress that Rory had helped me pick out. It had been on sale, it fit me perfectly despite my height, and I could wear it both for the restaurant date and to Tinsley's meeting the next afternoon. I put on a pair of black heels that I'd owned for a long time and had hardly ever worn as they made me taller than every guy I'd gone out with. I realized that tonight it wouldn't be a problem.

About twenty minutes later, I was at Rodrigo's, giving the hostess my name. She asked me to follow her and led me into a tiny private room. It had a view of a marina on the Willamette River. Although it was dark outside, the large floor-to-ceiling windows gave me a fantastic view of the city all lit up on the other side of the river. Boats decorated with lights came into the marina to dock for the night. There was an outdoor patio beyond the windows, and I imagined in the spring and summer it would be a wonderful place to have dinner.

There was a small table set for two, with plush armchair-like seats. A single candle burned in the middle of the table, making the room seem soft and romantic.

The hostess set down two menus and promised to send our waiter in. I went over to the windows to better take in the view.

All day long I had wondered: What would he say? What would I say? What would happen on this sort-of date? Some part of me was scared. Anxious. I put my hand over my stomach, willing it to calm down.

It didn't help when Evan suddenly entered the room and said, "Just so you know, technically I got here first. I just stepped out for a minute. But I went ahead and ordered some appetizers, if that's okay."

Was this some sort of competition? Who was the most on time? I turned around to see Evan in a dark-navy suit that fit him just as well as the last suit I'd seen him in. His hands were in his pockets, and he rocked slightly on his feet. Almost like he was . . . nervous.

Evan Dawson, nervous? The man who played a highly intense game every week to sold-out stadiums and millions of viewers all over the country? He was praised for having nerves of steel, for never rushing, no matter how many defensive linemen were closing in on him. How could he be nervous right now?

Had I made him nervous?

"These are for you," he said. He picked up a big bouquet of flowers that had been placed on a side table and handed them to me.

"Oh. Thank you." I'd never had a man bring me flowers before. They were a mixture of pink and purple and white. I recognized the roses but not the other ones. They looked expensive.

I set the bouquet down on the floor next to my feet. One, because I didn't know what else to do with it. It wasn't like I could put it in water. And two, because all morning and afternoon I'd been telling myself that I had to shore up my defenses. Put my armor back on. Not let Evan Dawson in with his charm and smile counting and devastating good looks. I had a job to do, and I couldn't forget it.

And all my good intent nearly went out the window when he said, "You look really beautiful tonight."

I could actually feel my heart soften as it sped up at his words. Sarcasm was my only defense. "Am I supposed to be impressed by all this?" I asked as I sat in my chair quickly, before he could help me. "The expensive flowers, the swanky restaurant?" The compliments?

My snark actually seemed to make him relax. Like he could deal with me better in my natural state. He sat down across from me, draping his linen napkin across his lap. "You don't have to be impressed by anything. But feel free to try and be civil."

This was the problem with eating at a restaurant so fancy. I didn't know which fork to pick up and stab him with.

But even I had to admit I begrudgingly admired the fact that he never cowered when I got snarky and gave as good as he got.

"I don't remember you always being this sarcastic," he added.

My boss wanted me to not aggravate him and get him on my side, but I couldn't help myself. "I didn't used to be a lot of things. I've changed a lot in the last ten years. And I'm not always sarcastic. Sometimes I'm eating. Or sleeping."

He let out a short laugh. "I'd bet all of my Super Bowl rings that you're sarcastic while you sleep. Dinner's on me tonight, so please order whatever you'd like."

I probably should have protested and said I could pay for myself, but I figured he could afford it. I opened my menu, grateful for the chance to block him out, if only for a couple of minutes. Like most of the riverside restaurants in the area, Rodrigo's specialized in steak and seafood. I looked at the ridiculously expensive surf-and-turf option and considered ordering three of them. Just to see what Evan would say.

There were also quite a few French dishes I didn't recognize. A note in the menu said the new head chef had trained at a swanky culinary school in Paris. I decided to stick with food I could pronounce.

Our waitress entered the room and introduced herself as Jeannie. She said our appetizers were on the way and offered to get us a drink. I ordered water, and Evan did the same. I wanted all my wits about me, plus I was driving. Better not to take any chances.

"Are you ready to order?"

I said I was, and Evan nodded. I got a filet mignon, while Evan, to my private amusement, chose the surf and turf.

Jeannie said she'd return shortly with our drinks and appetizers. Evan thanked her, smiling, and she tripped over her own feet as she left the room.

Which I totally got.

Unfortunately.

As I sat in this romantic candlelit room, the moonbeams bouncing off the river outside, the man across from me looking like he'd just stepped out of a man's high-fashion magazine, I again reminded myself to get my armor and defenses back in place. Because he was doing much too good of a job of slowly dismantling both. I was going to hear whatever he had to say, and then it would be done. I was finished letting him lease so much space in my head. If I kept this up, he'd become a joint owner of my brain.

"You graduated from UO, right?" he asked.

How did he know that? Sister interference, or had he looked me up online? "I did."

"And where are you working now?"

What should I say? Should I lie? I hadn't prepared for this question. If I told him where I worked, would he somehow make the connection?

I figured it was better to stick to the truth as much as possible so that I didn't trip myself up later. "At the moment I'm using my degree to fetch coffee from Starbucks and make copies. I'm an intern at ISEN."

"You mentioned you still want to be an announcer. Is that why you're working there?"

Yes, that hadn't changed in the last two days. He might also have remembered that from before. I'd talked about it all the time with him when we were younger. He'd been very supportive, even though back then no woman had ever announced a televised NFL game. "I do still want that. And yes, that's why I'm there."

He picked up a butter knife and twirled it back and forth. "I seem to recall you telling me about how you'd gone to that sports announcer camp in Pennsylvania."

Slightly humiliating that that was what he'd chosen to remember from the time we'd spent together. "It's just something I've always wanted to do." There were plenty of female sideline reporters, but no announcers at a national level for the NFL. Not until Beth Mowins. She was kind of a personal hero of mine. And even then she'd been relentlessly attacked by trolls on the internet for being "too shrill" or "annoying" as she called the game. She'd cracked the glass ceiling hard, and I hoped to follow in her footsteps. "I've spent a lot of time calling whatever I can—college volleyball games, Pop Warner football, the local junior high soccer team's games."

"Do you have a demo? I know some people."

I actually always had one of my demos in my purse. Something my grandma had insisted on. I pulled the CD out of my purse and slid it across the table to him. It probably wasn't very cool of me to accept his offer to help when my plan was to bring him down, but that's how badly I wanted this job. I would go through whatever door opened up to me.

His fingers brushed against mine as he took the CD, and I bit down on my lower lip to prevent myself from gasping. That burning, melting sensation returned wherever his skin touched mine. And he was only touching my fingers. What would I do if he ever touched the rest of me?

Probably spontaneously combust.

Jeannie came back in with the appetizers. Evan stuck the CD in his suit jacket while I contemplated what had just happened. Why did I respond to him like this? Was it residual teen angst? Or something more?

If nothing else, he'd been exceedingly clever to distract me by asking about my career ambitions. That always made me let my guard down.

"Here you go," she said, placing the plates on the table. She announced their French names, but they meant nothing to me. It all sounded . . . disgusting. I didn't recognize any of the so-called food in front of me, and I was too embarrassed to ask her about it.

"What is this?" I asked when Jeannie left the room.

"I don't know. I told the hostess to bring me the chef's signature appetizers."

"You do know that the man studied in France, right? For all we know this could be snail antennas and frog tongues."

"Aubrey said you were a foodie."

"I'm not. I like eating, and I enjoy cooking, but I'm not one of those people who take forty pictures of their meal and put it on Instagram. Or who thinks that life is unfulfilled if you haven't tried yak's milk, ostrich eggs, or hissing cockroaches." I was perfectly happy living a less fulfilled life with normal food.

He leaned forward, his hand near mine on the table. It took all my willpower not to move it away in a pathetic attempt to show him he didn't affect me. "Let's be adventurous and try it."

I never backed down from a challenge. I grabbed the gray stuff in front of me and dished some onto my plate. I took a small, tentative bite. And whatever this slimy meat-like substance was, it was extremely salty. I spit it out onto my plate. My mother would have yelled at me, using my first and middle names as some kind of curse words, if I'd done that at home. "I'm sorry, but that is truly awful. There should be a calorie refund on things that taste that gross."

For some reason that struck Evan as completely funny, and he was laughing with a mouthful of food. He did finally manage to swallow his but only barely. He had the kind of laughter that was contagious, and while I did keep my own laugh in check, I couldn't help but smile.

"Smile Number Four," he said after he'd started breathing normally again. "And you were right earlier. I was trying to impress you."

"Swing and a miss."

"Wrong sport."

"Fourth and ten, then."

Another brilliant smile from him that had my baby-making parts giddy with excitement. I told my glands to chill the freak out. I reached for my napkin, intending to drape it across my lap. Evan was going to think I'd been raised in a barn, given how I'd been acting all evening. My hands were shaking. Why were my hands shaking?

In my effort to be quick, I dropped the napkin ring on the floor, where it rolled under the table.

"I've got it!" he said before I could even react.

He reached for the ring and held it aloft to me, bending on one knee. "Ashton?"

It was such a magnificent picture, him on his knee like he was going to propose, that it took me a second to respond. "Yes?"

He took my hand, and explosive flames enveloped my skin. My heart beat so fast and so hard I was sure he could hear it. He dropped the napkin ring into my open palm, and my fingers curled around it.

"We need to talk. About this long-standing fight we're in."

CHAPTER NINE

Some part of me was weirdly disappointed. That wasn't what I'd hoped he would say. Obviously I didn't want him to ask me to marry him, because that was beyond ridiculous—I still hated the guy. But I wanted him to say something that wouldn't bring me crashing down to earth quite so hard.

"We're not in a fight," I said as he got back in his seat. "That implies us both devoting a lot of time and energy to it, which we're not." *Liar,* my inner voice whispered. "Think of it more as an ongoing, detached distrust of you and everything you say."

"I severely underestimated your anger, and I'm not someone who underestimates anyone. Ever."

Jeannie chose that moment to reappear with our entrées, telling us not to touch the hot plates as she placed them on the table.

Was that what this was about? The quarterback known for his field vision, his tight control on every play and over every player, had finally been blindsided? And he didn't like it? As if I'd somehow bruised his precious ego?

The waitress left, closing the door behind her. My food smelled delicious, but for the first time in a long time, I didn't want to eat.

Evan picked up his fork and knife, and then, like he shared my sentiment, he immediately put them back down. "I didn't think back then about how it all might make you feel. I was too wrapped up in my own drama to think about anybody else. And you were so much younger than we were. I should have taken that into account. I should have been more considerate of your feelings. I am really sorry for everything that happened. But I didn't betray you the way you think I did."

"What do you mean?"

"I mean that I didn't pass your letter around. I thought it was really sweet, even though it never could have happened between us. You were thirteen. You hadn't even hit puberty yet. While I was reading it, Piz found me. Do you remember Piz?"

Aaron Piznarski. He'd been our team's center and one of Evan's best friends. I nodded.

"Anyway, he grabbed the letter away from me and started reading it out loud. He's the one who took pictures and passed them around to everyone at school. He's the one who stole my phone and texted you to come out to the football field. He started all the teasing."

He was going to blame it all on someone else? *What if it's true?* that voice asked me. Even if it was, why hadn't he defended me? "Why didn't you do anything about it? Why didn't you stop him? I'd thought we were friends."

Evan again reached out, like he wanted to hold my hand, but he stopped himself. "We were friends. I loved hanging out with you. You were like the kid sister I never had."

Oh, that was a blow to the old ego. I'd always suspected he'd seen me that way, but it was a totally different feeling having him confirm it. "Then shouldn't you have protected me?"

He leaned back in his chair, running a hand through his dark hair. "I was only fourteen when my parents died. And I didn't have any relatives who could take me in. Coach Edwards stepped up and went through all the hoops so that he and his family could become my foster family."

I reached for my purse at my side and pulled out my phone, unlocked the home screen, then pushed the record button. Evan was talking about his time in foster care, something he never, ever shared with the press.

"And I thought it was because of some bond or connection we had until I overheard him one night on the phone. He said he couldn't have me ending up in a home in a different school district. That I would win him the state championship." Evan let out a self-deprecating laugh. "He was right. I did. Three times. After hearing that phone call, I almost considered quitting."

"Why didn't you?"

He cleared his throat. "Football always made me feel close to my dad. He played college ball, and he had a football in my hands before I even started walking. We used to drill and practice together all the time. I didn't want to . . . I don't know . . . dishonor his memory or something. I did consider throwing some games, just to make Coach Edwards mad, but I couldn't have done that to my teammates."

I glanced down at my phone, making sure it was still recording. "Are you close to the Edwards family now?"

He let out a short bark of laughter. "No. I haven't spoken to them since I graduated from high school. They took me in only to exploit me and my talent. And I did my best when I was living with them to make their lives hard. I acted out. Committed some petty theft, went to too many parties. We even stole a police cruiser once."

Aha! I'd been right about that. "And despite all the partying, you really never hooked up with anyone?"

I held my breath, waiting for his response.

He narrowed his eyes briefly, then smirked as if he found me amusing. "I was acting out to punish Coach, but I think some part of me was doing it with this belief that if I was bad enough, it was like I was daring my parents to come back and discipline me. I know it sounds crazy, and I didn't really think it was possible, but I did have that thought more than once. They were really committed to me waiting for marriage, and it turned out to be the one line I couldn't bring myself to cross. I couldn't disappoint them that way."

I was torn. I wanted to let out a moan of disgust that he was sticking to his story, but I was also touched that he was finally sharing all this deeply personal information with me. In high school our conversations had revolved around football and video games. Very surface-only kind of stuff, not at all deep or meaningful like I'd imagined it to be at thirteen. Which I was realizing now as he was being vulnerable with me. "So you're really committed to this celibacy thing, huh?"

"I am." He nodded. "And the stuff I did when I was younger—it's why I have to be extra careful now. I know the press calls me a Boy Scout and a Goody Two-shoes, but I can't afford to do anything to upset Chester Walton. He knows about my past, and I promised him nothing like that would ever happen again."

"Why would you care what Chester Walton thinks? You could quit tomorrow, and you'd literally have offers ten minutes later from every other team in the league." It was in part what eased my conscience for when I got him fired. Knowing that he'd land on his feet in a different city.

"My grandma lives here, and I don't want to leave her."

"Grandma?" In all the time I'd known him, he'd never mentioned a grandmother. "Why didn't you stay with her after your parents' accident?"

"She had a pretty severe stroke a long time ago, when I was a little kid. She's unable to communicate or interact, and she's living in a nursing home."

I started to feel uneasy. "You could move her."

"I could move her. But I wouldn't want to. Portland is her home. This is my home. I try to get out to visit her every Tuesday morning during the season."

The uneasiness inside me started to bloom into something darker and ickier. The feeling nagged at me, and I had the sneaking suspicion it might be guilt.

Then I got annoyed with Evan for making me feel guilty. "What does any of this have to do with what happened between you and me?"

He picked up his water glass and took a quick drink. "Sorry, I started off down that road but got a little sidetracked. The point of what I was trying to tell you was that when you knew me, my family was gone. I was estranged from my 'substitute' family. The only family I had were the guys on the team. For about six months after the accident, they were the only thing that kept me from throwing myself off a bridge. And I should have been stronger, and I should have stood up to them when they went after you. I was afraid that if I went against them, they would turn their backs on me. I just . . . I didn't want to lose the only family I had left. I'm sorry."

I could understand what he was saying. I didn't know what I'd do without my parents and my two sisters. Losing my grandparents had been hard enough.

I'd been so angry at him for so long for something he hadn't even done. If he was to be believed, and in that moment I did believe him, he didn't have anything to do with the letter or the constant teasing. And I understood why he hadn't stood up for me. How could I blame him for having a very human reaction?

It still didn't let him off the hook entirely. He needed to know what he had done to me. "I appreciate that, and I even kind of get it. But do you have any idea how hard my life was back then? Do you know that for the crime of having a crush on you, I was bullied and tormented and teased to the point that my parents had to pull me out of school? That I suffered from depression because of it? That all my friends ditched me, including you?" My voice cracked on the last word, and with horror I realized I was about to start crying.

A look of deep concern settled on his perfect features. This time he did reach out and hold my hand.

And I didn't pull away.

"Ashton, there is nothing I can say to make up for what happened. If I could go back and fix it, I would. But I can't change the past."

"You could at least have the decency to be haunted by it."

His grip tightened. "I'm haunted by it every day in so many ways. And if you never want to see me again, if that's what I can do for you, I'll do it. I hope it's not, because I'd like for us to be friends again."

"Yeah. Sounds like you still need a kid sister."

A rueful smile twisted his lips, and he let go of my hand. Weirdly enough, I felt sad when he did it. "I won't ask for your forgiveness yet. If you'll let me, I'd like to try and earn it. But for now, how about we dig in before our food gets completely cold?"

My appetite had returned with a vengeance. And something else was different. I felt . . . lighter. Like by letting him explain and apologize, a weight had been taken from me. One I hadn't even realized I'd been carrying around.

Maybe I should have let him explain it years ago.

I had just cut my first bite of filet mignon when he said, "Tell me about your family."

"I have one."

My default setting had been sarcasm for so long it took me a second to register what I'd just said. "I'm sorry, Evan. That was really insensitive of me. I wasn't trying to be mean. Just to blow off your question."

"Which is kind of mean in and of itself."

He didn't seem to be hurt by what I'd said, but now I got to feel like the world's biggest jerk.

"I don't know how to stop being mad at you," I admitted. "I can't just flip a switch."

"Maybe you could pretend I'm someone else. That we're meeting for the first time, and this is our first date. Hi. I'm Evan Dawson. Nice to meet you." He held out his hand, ready to shake mine.

"I appreciate the gesture, but there's too much that's happened to just pretend to ignore it. I probably need some time."

He picked up his lobster tail and studied it, like he was trying to figure out the best offensive move to crack it open. "So we can still work on the reunion committee together?"

"Sure." I could handle that.

"And maybe we could hang out some other times? The last time we played *Madden*, I'm pretty sure I won."

"Your memory is flawed. That never happened. I am the supreme champion of that game."

"Then I want a rematch," he told me with a smile.

And again, I couldn't help myself. I smiled back.

"Number Five," he said under his breath, more to himself than to me. He seemed . . . happy. I was responsible for that. Maybe confessing and apologizing made him feel lighter, too.

Which made me feel guilty all over again. "So you said you don't have to worry about money? If the team cuts you?"

He grinned at me. "Don't worry. I'm not going to stick you with the bill after dinner because I forgot my wallet."

"That's not why . . . I mean, you'd be okay if it did happen, right?"

"My parents left me a pretty substantial life insurance policy, on top of the money the Jacks have paid me." Which was in the tens of millions. "But you know what *NFL* stands for."

"Not for long."

He nodded. "And nothing lasts forever. We're always one injury away from our careers being over. So I've made sure to invest it all wisely and have done really well. I would be fine."

"I bet you'd trade it all in for one more day with your parents."

An anguished look clouded his bright-blue eyes. "I would."

"Me too. I have a trust fund from my grandma that I'd hand over without even thinking if I could see her again. You know, I was named after her. Well, kind of."

"What do you mean?" He was watching me intently, like I was the only person in the entire world, and he couldn't wait to hear what I said next.

It made me nervous, so I, of course, started to babble. "Her name was Evelyn. She was one of those debutante types who developed a love for football, especially the Portland Jacks. And more than anything she wanted to be a sports announcer. But they barely let her do any reporting at all. They wouldn't even let her in the locker room after the games. She did end up writing for the *Portland Blaze*'s sports section by taking her maiden name and her married name. Ashton Bailey. Because it sounded like a man's name instead of a woman's. So the readers wouldn't know. I'm her namesake. Aubrey was named after my mom's mom."

He put down his fork and wiped his mouth with his napkin. "Why did your youngest sister get left out of the *A* naming thing?"

"She didn't. Her actual name is Aurora. My mom claims it had something to do with the aurora borealis, but I suspect that it's for the Disney princess." I grabbed a roll and some butter. Better to stuff my face than to keep saying stupid things.

"I have an *A* nickname. Sounds like I'd fit right in."

I stopped buttering my roll. "My whole family sort of hates you because of the high school stuff. I mean, we're a Jacks family with season tickets, and we cheer for you on Sundays, but they're ironic cheers."

He shot me one of those knowing smiles. "So the Jacks are your favorite team?"

"Obviously." How could anyone live in Oregon and not love the Jacks?

"Which by default would make me your favorite player, right? Seeing as how I'm the QB and all."

"Hardly. And here's why."

I brought up a bunch of different players on the team and their skill sets, but even I had to secretly admit that Evan was the best.

Our conversation just kept snowballing from there. We talked about our college experiences. He told me some funny stories about the other players on his team, trying to make a case for why he should be my favorite. He admitted to his superstition about putting on new laces for his cleats before every game.

If it had been any other guy sitting across the table from me, I would have considered it a really successful date. We had a lot of common interests. We clicked, we bantered, we connected.

But it was Evan Dawson, and it wasn't actually a date. Just the chance for him to say sorry and for us to catch up. For me to think about forgiving him and moving on.

Or, more accurately, a chance for me to get him to admit he was lying to everyone about his personal life.

We had dessert and kept talking and talking. Jeannie brought in the check and said to stay and keep enjoying ourselves. Evan signed it and then excused himself to use the restroom.

Without even thinking, I leaned over and opened up the little leather check folder. I'd always been too curious for my own good. Dinner had been expensive, and he'd left her a $500 tip and included a handwritten thank-you at the bottom.

Of all the things he'd done that night to impress me, the one thing he'd done that he hadn't expected me to see was what impressed me the most.

My phone buzzed with a text message, and I realized it was still recording. I held it up, pushing the stop button.

I'd started the evening off thinking that I could give the recording to Brenda. He'd stayed with his "I'm a virgin" bit, but there were lots of really personal things on here we could use for the show.

Without hesitation, I deleted it.

"Ready to go?" Evan asked. "I'd like to walk you out to your car."

"Yep." I grabbed my flowers and followed him out. He moved quickly through the main dining room of the restaurant, and I realized it was to avoid being recognized. The hostess thanked us as Evan opened the front door for me, putting his hand on the small of my back to guide me through it.

I felt his touch all the way to the cuticles on my toes.

He didn't drop his hand, and we continued to walk quietly toward my car. When we got there, I suddenly felt thirteen again and completely awkward. I pushed the button on my key fob to unlock the car.

I turned to face him, standing in front of my driver's side door. "So, thanks for the flowers and the blackmail and the free steak."

His grin was slow, sexy, and smoldering. I leaned against my car for support. "You wanted to come to dinner with me. You let me win."

"I didn't . . ." But the words died in my mouth. I had totally let him win. I knew it, even in the moment when it was happening, no matter how much I'd tried to convince myself otherwise.

"And I had a really fun time tonight. If you're interested, I'd like to see you again."

See me again? Like he wanted me to stand in his line of vision, or he wanted to go on another sort-of date? He needed to clarify.

"Because call me crazy," he said, putting his hands on the side of my car, effectively trapping me in place. I tried to back up but was met with a wall of metal behind me and a wall of muscle in front. "But I think we're having a moment."

"A moment of delusion?" I croaked, my throat not operating properly since my throbbing heart was stuck in it. "We're kind of friends. That's what we established."

"I can move from the friend zone into the end zone."

It was so cheesy I laughed, and he held up one finger. Now he was counting laughs, too? "You are a very long way off from the end zone."

His eyes flicked over me, studying my face, and my skin went hot, like he was touching me again. Even though he wasn't. "Have you ever seen me drive a ball down a field?"

Of course I had. He was the best at it. Chopping away at the other team's defense, slowly gaining yard by yard until he scored.

I was now greatly concerned. "That's not happening."

"The last time you said that, it did happen."

"Don't flatter yourself."

"I don't have to. You're doing that for me."

How was I doing that? My flushed skin? My rapid heartbeat? My wobbly knees?

He might have had a point.

"I want to make things right. I know words aren't enough. I'll do whatever I need to do to earn back your trust."

Somehow he moved even closer, making my pulse skitter and my nerve endings totally fray.

"And, Ashton? I don't think of you as my kid sister."

He reached up, his large, warm hand totally engulfing one side of my face. His gaze trapped mine before it traveled down to my lips. His breath mingled with mine, and I felt the soft material of his pants against my bare legs.

Evan Dawson was going to kiss me.

Even more shocking? I was totally going to let him because his touch had rendered me unable to resist.

My eyelids drifted shut as he moved in closer, and my breath stuttered when his lips softly brushed against my cheek. I'd been right about the total spontaneous combustion thing earlier. All he'd done was gently kiss me on a place other than my mouth, and my entire body melted. Like my blood was made out of molten lava, and he knew just how to ignite it.

"'Night, Ashton."

He reached behind me to open my door, waiting for me to get in. Not knowing what else to do or how to process this entire night, I got in the car. I was going to wait for him to leave so I could put my head between my knees and breathe slowly, but he stood there, waiting for me to drive off. Presumably so he knew I would be safe.

Despite the fact that my brain was scrambled and my heart was racing and utterly confused and my stomach had twisted itself into a thousand knots, I drove out of the parking lot and headed home to my condo.

It took me a very long time to fall asleep that night with all the questions that kept running through my head.

Had he told me the truth about what happened in high school?

Did Evan like me? Could I like him? And would any of that matter once he found out my main objective in spending time with him?

And when had I lost total control of my body? It was like it was acting without my permission and doing whatever it wanted.

Why had I deleted the recording?

Did I forgive him? If not, would I be able to? Or was it better to hold on to the anger, to keep some distance between us? I'd lose out on my dream job if I didn't find somebody to verify that Evan wasn't celibate.

But the question that concerned me the most was this one: What was I going to do when I saw him again?

CHAPTER TEN

I'd been so dazed by Evan's cheek kiss that although I'd managed to put his flowers in a vase when I got home, I'd forgotten the water. I added it when I woke up the next morning. Which was later than normal, because I had no alarm. And no phone with said alarm. After searching my entire condo for more than an hour, I discovered I had left my cell phone on the front seat of my car, where it had died. I brought it back in and plugged it into the charger.

Although I knew I should dress up for Tinsley's tea party so as to fit in with the natives, I was worn out. Emotionally and physically. So I put on some jeans and a nicer shirt than I might normally wear, put my hair up in a bun, and scrubbed my face clean. (My forgetfulness the previous night had also extended to not washing off my makeup.)

Traffic was light on the way to Tinsley's place. I checked in with her doorman, who nodded when he saw me. "Ms. Bailey! A pleasure to see you again. Mrs. Hale is quite excited to see you. She said to send you right up."

He walked me over to the elevator and pushed the *P* button for me. I thanked him. I'd never lived in a building with a doorman before. Were they all that enthusiastic? It felt a little weird.

On the ride up I took out my phone, wondering why it had been so quiet all morning. Usually by this point I had at least three different reminders from my mom to not forget about Sunday and our season tickets for the Jacks game. The same thing we did every week they played at home, rain or shine. I completely understood why she thought I might possibly forget. Even though I'd been doing it for over two decades.

And although I had recharged my phone, I hadn't turned it back on. A few seconds later it started to beep and buzz repeatedly. I looked at my notifications. There were, like, ten missed phone calls from my mother. I needed some kind of automated response that said, "I promise I'll be there. You can stop nagging me now."

But strangely enough, there was a series of texts from Brenda that all basically said to call her right away, no matter the time.

There was a text from Aubrey.

> Why are you macking on
> Evan Dawson?

What? I had to respond.

> Macking? What does that
> even mean? Is that some old
> person lingo that you expect
> me to know?

I pushed SEND as the doors to Tinsley's penthouse opened. I had more texts and missed calls, but I'd deal with those later.

First I wanted to take my chance to appreciate Tinsley's elaborately set-up tea party. My niece had a serious *Alice in Wonderland* obsession (especially the Mad Hatter scene), and this would have made her giddy. I was about to take a picture for her when I got accosted by Nia.

"What is happening?" She was smiling at me, giving me a hug, but her words came out as a hiss under her breath. "All anyone can talk about is how Evan Dawson is engaged."

Engaged? He'd taken me out to dinner and been all charming and apologetic and hot and sexy, and he was engaged to someone else? "To who?" I demanded.

"To you."

"Me?" I squeaked, completely stunned. "Trust me, I am not engaged to Evan Dawson." I was pretty sure I would have remembered if that had happened.

"Not according to the internet. I've been texting you all morning because it made no kind of sense. How did you two get engaged?"

"I don't understand what you're talking about."

Tinsley waved. "Nia! Bring our guest of honor in here so we can all say congratulations!"

"Seriously, I'm not engaged. I barely even tolerate him." There were still long-standing feelings of hatred that I was trying to get over.

"Everybody here thinks you're engaged. It's being reported on every tabloid, sports, and news site."

This was totally surreal. I did not get it at all. I wanted to turn around and run back into the elevator so I could go home, crawl into my bed, and figure out what was happening.

As if she sensed my instinct to run, Nia slid her arm through mine and led me into the dining room. Where everyone went completely silent as I walked the ten steps from the foyer to the table. "Just smile and nod. After this is over, you need to give me all the details. I'll help you get it all straightened out."

"There she is!" Tinsley proclaimed, walking over to hand me a flute of champagne. She leaned in to do an air kiss, which I had never done in my entire life. "I thought we should celebrate your engagement! How long have you been seeing Evan without us knowing? And at my party you two acted like you barely knew each other. But I saw the looks he gave you. Even though you were supposedly there with Reggie! Sneaky!"

Everyone was smiling at me, and I felt like I really had stepped into Wonderland, because nothing was making any kind of logical sense whatsoever.

My phone buzzed, and as a reflex, I looked down at the screen. Brenda. Again.

CALL ME.

I knew better than to keep her waiting any longer. "Can I use your restroom?"

Tinsley told me to go down the hallway and take the second door on the left. After locking the door behind me, I sat down on the closed toilet lid and dialed my boss's number.

"Where have you been?" she demanded, not even saying hello.

"My phone died, and I recharged it, but I forgot to—"

"Never mind, I don't care. These photos do not reflect what you have been telling me about your relationship with Evan." She sounded furious.

"What photos?"

She sent me a text message, and I put her on speaker to open her attachments. There was a picture of Evan kneeling when he'd picked up the napkin ring. Somebody had shot this from outside our private dining room, out on the patio or at the marina. I didn't remember seeing a flash. But if someone didn't know the context, it absolutely looked like he was proposing.

The next photo made me catch my breath. It had been taken just after the moment that Evan kissed my cheek, and from this angle it looked like we were about to make out. Or like we just had been.

I could see how people might jump to conclusions, but none of it was true. "In the first one, I'd dropped something, and he picked it up for me. In the second he kissed me on the cheek to say good night. Like I was his little sister. Nothing else happened."

"You're sure nothing happened?" Brenda sounded slightly less angry and also a bit disappointed.

"Yes, I'm sure. Seeing as how I was there." Living it and not taking creepy pictures of it. "He apologized, and we reminisced a little bit. Then I drove home in my car, and he went home in his. That was it. I can't believe somebody took pictures of us."

There was a long pause. "I was worried that you weren't being completely honest with me. I had one of our photographers follow you. Just in case."

I gasped. It was such a violation of my privacy. I wasn't a public figure. Or at least I hadn't been before Brenda made me one. "In case what?" I asked. Did she imagine Evan would be so overcome with lust that he would throw me on the table and ravage me? Like we were the R-rated floor show for the other diners at the restaurant? Totally ridiculous. And I was trying to be completely outraged, but parts of me tingled at the thought of Evan grabbing me and kissing me.

"It doesn't matter."

"It matters that the entire world now thinks I'm engaged to Evan Dawson." No wonder my mom had called me so many times. She was probably freaking out.

"Let the world think it."

"What?"

There was a muffled sound, as if she had covered the mic on her phone to speak to someone else. "This is completely perfect. As his fiancée, do you have any idea how much more credibility your story will have when you tell the world the truth about him? You need to stay engaged."

"That's not really a one-sided decision. He hasn't actually asked me to marry him, and I can't exactly just start pretending like we're together."

"We'll strategize on Monday. For now, don't deny it if anyone asks. If you get approached by the press, just say no comment. There has to be a way for us to use this to our advantage."

I agreed to do as she asked, not knowing what else to say. It all seemed so preposterous. The truth was obviously going to come out. It seemed dumb to deny it. But she was the woman who held my future in her hands. I just had to go along with it.

We hung up, and I contemplated calling Evan. But he was probably in team meetings or doing run-throughs in preparation for Sunday's game.

I still had the urge to run home and hide. But I had a room full of women who wanted to celebrate my nonexistent engagement. Time to face the music.

"There you are!" Tinsley exclaimed when I rejoined them. "I was about to send out a search party for you. We thought maybe you'd fallen in!"

Several of the women giggled at Tinsley's stupid joke. I tried to smile. "Sorry about that." *I was just busy discovering that in order to get my dream job, I have to pretend like I'm getting married to a man I've spent half my life hating.*

I wondered what they'd say to that.

But I kept quiet, smiling and nodding as people congratulated me.

"Where's the ring?" someone asked, and I looked down at my bare left hand.

"Did you have to get it sized?" the woman next to her asked. "I had to get mine sized."

"It was definitely too big," I told her, glad I could be truthful about one thing. No way that napkin ring would have fit on my finger.

"When are men going to learn to either take one of your rings or get your sister or roommate to do it?"

"How did you two meet?"

I couldn't imagine how much worse this would be if I hadn't known Evan before. "We met in high school. I was a freshman; he was a senior.

I had a huge crush on him, and he . . . did not feel the same." There were some laughs. "We reconnected recently, and I don't know. Things just happened."

The women sighed and said, "Aw." Nia perfectly arched her left eyebrow at me but sipped at her drink and said nothing.

"I think it's sweet that you feel like you don't have to get made-up. You've got your man, and now you're keeping things casual." This came from a girl at the far end of the table who sounded like she was on her third glass of champagne. It was meant to be mean, but I couldn't get too worked up about it. I preferred to be comfortable, and apparently I was the only one seated at the table who felt that way. "I could never go out without my face on. Not when I know paparazzi are following me."

I was about to ask why anyone would follow me, given that I was one of the most average people on the planet, when I remembered. At the moment I was engaged to Evan Dawson. And he was one of the country's most famous virgins.

Of course people would be interested that a woman he'd never mentioned and never been pictured with was now his fiancée.

"Big sunglasses are your friend," someone added. "When you don't have time to do your hair and makeup, those block most of your face." Several of the women nodded and agreed.

This was how bizarre my life had become in only a few days. Getting tips on how to avoid the paparazzi from the Jacks' WAGs.

"Congratulations again, Ashton," Tinsley said, standing up at the head of the table. "But now it's time to get down to business. Beverly, would you read the minutes of our last meeting?"

Not caring about whatever it was they were discussing, I tuned Beverly out. And tried to figure out how to get out of this mess. If Evan publicly announced that we were not a couple, Brenda would be furious with me. Which was hypocritical, given that it was her photographer who had put me in this position.

My phone buzzed with another text from Aubrey, but I didn't open it. My entire family thought I was engaged and just hadn't bothered to mention it. What was I going to tell them?

"This Tuesday we have our annual Jumping Jacks hospital visits with the kids, and I'd like for each of the participating players to have one of us as his guide and to help out however is needed," Tinsley said, her sharp voice interrupting my thoughts. "Ashton, I'm assuming I can assign you to escort Evan?"

There was no way for me to refuse. "Sure."

"Perfect." Tinsley continued to hand out assignments, and nobody seemed surprised about who they were paired off with. Their meeting closed soon after that, and everyone stayed, chatting in small groups while they ate and drank.

Here was my chance. I could finally chat up some of the women and see what they could tell me about Evan. I introduced myself to a woman named Natalia. She told me she was currently sort of seeing Finn MacNeil. Poor Rory. She was going to be so disappointed that her crush had a semi-girlfriend.

"Kudos on landing Evan Dawson. I didn't think it could be done." She raised her champagne flute to me.

"Oh. Thanks." What were you supposed to say to that? There really wasn't a good response for it. So I decided to dig around for Evan's dirty laundry instead. "I can't be the only woman here who's dated him."

"He and I went out once or twice. Which seems to be about his limit. I don't remember him ever being serious with anyone. Until you, of course," she said. Another woman walked up and elbowed her in the side, shooting me a side glance. And Natalia immediately shut up.

Uh-oh. This was an unforeseen consequence of the engagement story. Unless they were blackhearted and evil, nobody here was going to tell me if they'd slept with him, because now I was his fiancée, and that would be really petty.

Some of them must have been awful and would have been willing, but I couldn't see Evan dating a woman like that.

Could I turn it around somehow? "Oh, come on. There had to have been someone who made it past date three." I tried to keep my voice light and teasing, to show it didn't bother me.

Because it totally didn't.

Right?

The woman who had interrupted us turned to Natalia. "Wait. What about Whitley?"

Natalia's eyes lit up. "Right. He did date Whitley for, like, four months."

Finally! A lead! "Who's Whitley?" I was shooting for casual and not overeager.

"They dated a couple of years ago. She was a Lumberjill who got cut for dating him."

"I thought she got cut for putting on three pounds," the second woman interjected.

"And why did they break up?" I tried to get them back on track.

"Nobody really knows," Natalia said. "Last I'd heard she married some accountant and moved to the suburbs. What was that guy's name? I think I got an invitation to the wedding."

"Something Schultz?"

That was good enough for me. Whitley Schultz. His ex-girlfriend. She had to have some dirt.

I had just excused myself in order to do a quick Google search when a text popped up on my screen.

My lungs stopped functioning when I saw that it was from Evan.

Can we talk?

CHAPTER ELEVEN

I walked off to a corner of the room so that I could respond.

> Aren't you meeting with your team right now?

> We'll be done in about an hour, and then we're headed to the hotel. Could you come by?

"The hotel" was the Davenport, located ten minutes from my condo. The Jacks always stayed there the night before a home game, as did their opposing team (on a different floor). But they had very strict rules, the main one being no women in their rooms. Which included their significant others. And they had a curfew.

I mean, it didn't matter to me one way or the other. It wasn't like Coach Sitake could kick me off the team.

But was Evan willing to risk getting in trouble to talk to me? That gave me a weird, twisty feeling in my stomach that I didn't recognize.

> You do know people think we're engaged, right?

> I do know. And I need to talk to you before you say anything to the press.

Why? Shouldn't he have been like most men, running for the hills and screaming to anyone who would listen that he didn't believe in commitment?

Maybe he was afraid of what I might say and how it could hurt his perfect reputation.

> I have plans tonight.

That my plans consisted of putting on yoga pants, clearing out some DVR space, and working on my knitting was none of his business. I did need the knitting practice—I was truly terrible at it. My loops were always uneven, and so far all I'd managed to make were lopsided scarves that nobody in my family ever wore. Maybe because of the scarves' weird holes.

Plus, I didn't want him to think I was readily available whenever he wanted to see me. Because that would be pathetic.

Almost as pathetic as pretending to be engaged to him just for a story.

> Sorry for trying to change them, but I think it's important.

I shouldn't go. What if someone saw me? Took a picture of me sneaking into the hotel? There would be no clean way of getting out of this then. Even though Brenda wanted me to stay engaged.

It was all really confusing.

And I wasn't sure that I was ready to see Evan again. I had all these conflicting emotions where he was concerned. An anger I couldn't let go of fought with the overwhelming attraction I'd felt for him ever since we'd first met.

If last night had proved anything, it was that I still thought he was the most handsome man I'd ever known, and not even my residual anger could keep me from desperately wanting to kiss and touch him.

I didn't know what that said about me.

As if he sensed my hesitancy, he texted again.

> Come and see me. You know I never give up and I'll just keep asking.

> I know. It's one of the more annoying things about you.

He sent me a laughing emoji, and I let out a deep sigh. My curiosity insisted that I go to find out what Evan was thinking and why he thought it was important to talk to me.

> Won't you get in trouble?

> Not if we're careful.

And it wasn't like something was going to happen between us. This wasn't a secret code for a booty call. He really did want to talk. About our so-called engagement, apparently. Which I needed to keep in order to make my boss happy.

> What time?

That got me a football and a ref doing the touchdown sign emoji. He was such a dork. I was glad he couldn't see me smiling right now.

> How's 8:00? I'll be in Room 2722.

> I'll be there.

The how part of that might give me some trouble. I didn't know if it would be as easy as getting on an elevator and just going to the twenty-seventh floor. Did they have security?

I was about to ask him when he texted me.

> Knock-knock.

> Are you five?

> Just answer.

> Fine. Who's there?

> This.

> This who?

> This is happening.

Both cute and annoying.

The how got worked out quickly. When I returned to the group, Nia grabbed me by the arm and led me off into the kitchen so we could chat.

"Talk. Now," she commanded as we sat down on two of the bar-stools surrounding the island.

So I filled her in on most of the details of my encounters with him after the basketball game and at dinner. I told her the pictures were misleading but that Evan wanted to talk to me about them before any official denials were made.

"He likes you," she said, sounding shocked.

"He does not. He's just trying to ease his guilty conscience or what-ever. He feels bad about what happened between us years ago, and he wants to make amends."

"You keep telling yourself that." Nia sounded like she did not believe what I'd just said. "I think there's something there."

"You mean besides my resentment and inability to forgive?"

At that she just shook her head. "Things can be worked out."

"The only thing I need to work out right now is how to get up to his room to see him."

"Oh, that's easy. Go to the front desk and ask for Mickey. Tell him Nia sent you, and he'll get you onto the twenty-seventh floor."

I raised my eyebrows at her.

"What? Malik and I don't like to be apart. There's a whole work-around for anyone who wants to find it."

"Do you think Evan's had any girls use the work-around?" And for some reason the answer felt desperately important. Not just because of my job. I didn't want to explore why that little jealous emotion had bubbled up.

"Who knows? And why would you care? Since he doesn't like you, and you don't like him."

What I didn't like was her implication, but she was doing me a solid, and I wasn't going to give her a reason to be angry with me.

I currently had enough negative emotions in my life.

Later that evening I drove over to the Davenport Hotel, leaving my car with the valet as I didn't intend to stay for very long. I found Mickey, and just as Nia had promised, he took me up to the Jacks' floor, bypassing all the security.

And I found myself standing outside of Evan's room, not sure if I wanted to knock. I sucked in what I hoped was a calming breath and rapped lightly on the door.

It opened almost immediately, as if Evan had been standing behind it and waiting.

"Hey, Ashton. I'm glad you made it."

His dark hair fell forward onto his forehead. He brushed it back, and I noticed that his bright-blue eyes somehow managed to sparkle in this dim hotel hallway lighting. His shirt was tight, clinging to a row of laddered abs that I remembered all too well.

At that moment Reggie walked by, almost smacking into me because he was once again glued to his phone. He glanced up, looked at me, and then held out a hand to Evan for a high five. "Yeah, Dawson! Get some!"

Had it really only been four days since Reggie had pretended to be my date? Was I that forgettable? I was about to tell him off for being so completely offensive in what he'd just said but realized he wouldn't have heard me since he'd returned all of his attention to his tiny screen.

Evan was trying not to laugh as he held the door open, gesturing for me to come inside.

Not wanting to sit on his bed, I sat on the couch directly across from it. Evan walked over, and I noticed that he was barefoot. And that he had really nice feet. Attractive, even. I'd never particularly noticed a man's feet before.

He sat at the edge of his bed, and it creaked beneath his weight.

"Should we, um, lock the door? Put out the DO NOT DISTURB sign?" I asked.

"No. That sign is a red flag to the coaches that something's going on." And Evan should know something about red flags considering that he was basically a red-flag factory, and I had no intention of signing up to be the shift manager at Red Flags Manufacturing, Inc.

I mean, he came across as trustworthy and honest, but that was part of his public persona. It was hard to give up my distrust of him and his motives.

"So, you said you wanted to talk to me?"

He rubbed the back of his neck and looked pained, as if he didn't know how to say whatever it was he'd planned on saying. "I hate that all this happened. I like . . . to be in control of things. And now this engagement story has happened, and all of it feels like it's very much out of my control."

That wasn't necessarily true. He could deny it, and then it would all be over. I'd be in trouble at work, but I wasn't going to tell him that. "You don't seem like the control-freak type."

"Probably not something I should admit, but I used to be much worse. I would boss my teammates around and act like all of our losses or wins were on my shoulders. I would try to do everything myself instead of delegating, gave a lot of unsolicited advice to people. But the Jacks have a great sports psychologist who worked with me to focus on controlling my emotions and thoughts instead of everything around me."

"Oh." This surprised me. Evan was known for being tightly controlled on the field, but I'd had no idea it spilled over into other parts of his life.

He ran a hand through his hair and let out a self-deprecating laugh. "I always choose the best way to do things. I need to ask you for a favor, and what do I do? Unload my dirty laundry on you. Anyway, first off I just want you to know I didn't have anything to do with those pictures or the stories about us being engaged."

"Oh. Yeah. I know that." Because I knew who was responsible for it. "I didn't, either." And a favor? What kind of favor did he need from me?

"I know. But, okay, I'm just going to say it, and I feel bad even asking, but here goes. So my agent thinks it's a good idea for us to pretend to be engaged."

"What?"

"They've started negotiating my contract renewal. And given how much of a family man Chester Walton is, he will be happy about this, which can only work in my favor. Especially if I'm engaged to a Portland native. It makes me seem more stable and more likely to stick around. On the flip side of that, if I come out and say this was all a big mistake and we're not engaged, it could potentially bring a bunch of negative publicity that I don't need right now."

As one of the people who wanted to bring a bunch of negative publicity down on him, I couldn't help but cringe. "Why would people care if a photographer made an incorrect assumption about you? I'm not really seeing how that would hurt you."

"Because . . ." He let out a deep sigh before continuing. "The world sees you differently when you're like me."

"Like you?" Genetically perfect? Annoyingly charming? Surprisingly smart?

"It's kind of like . . . I'm this self-proclaimed prophet in a completely atheistic society. Either I'm dismissed as some ridiculous impossibility, or I just antagonize people and cause all this anger by challenging their worldview."

The picture started to become a little clearer. "Because you're a virgin?"

He nodded. "And because I'm a professional in a sport where aggression is rewarded. Because I'm famous. Because I'm rich. Because

I'm athletic. Because I'm a guy, and I'm waiting. So because of that, my masculinity is constantly questioned, because how can I be a real man if I'm not hooking up with every random woman in my path? Even Chester Walton, this religious, conservative family man, has made some condescending remarks to me about it."

I had a sinking feeling in my stomach. Whether or not it was true, Evan was committed to maintaining this public persona that he was waiting for marriage. Even in private. "That doesn't seem fair."

"It's not fair. It's also stupid. We complain about toxic masculinity, but people don't allow men to make different choices. Our society doesn't let them be who they are and then makes fun of them when they don't conform to a certain stereotype. Which is why, even though it's nobody else's business, I talk about my choices. Because the silent majority is strong, but it only takes one or two people to speak up to start changing people's minds about what's normal and what's not."

"I can see that." I was making these neutral statements, hoping that he'd keep talking. Maybe slip up.

"Wow," he said with a short laugh. "Listen to me! I'll get off my soapbox now. Sorry."

"No problem. I can tell it's something you're passionate about." But did all that passion come from true belief and action, or was it to keep his sponsors happy?

"I am pretty passionate about it. Especially since people don't ever seem to respect it. There's that adultery website that put a bounty on my virginity. Like it's another commodity the world can buy. I've found naked women in my bed. In my closet. My bathroom. And it's not because they want me. They want starting quarterback Evan Dawson. Or the million-dollar reward."

You wouldn't have to pay me a million bucks. I'd definitely do it for free. I told my inner vixen to be quiet for a second because jealousy smacked into me, hard and strong. I had the urge to find said women and start clawing them up. But the weird thing was, I felt like I'd heard these words from him before. Because he said them so often they sounded a little rehearsed? Or because they weren't his words at all but something he was regurgitating from his publicist?

He looked down at his feet. "Everybody always wants something from me."

His last sentence felt a hundred percent real and honest. Guilt made me wiggle a bit on the couch. I wanted something from him, too. He just didn't know it. "So about this engagement?"

His gaze met mine. "Right. I don't know what it is about you that gets me going off on all these tangents. You're easy to talk to, I guess."

Which was good. And could be helpful.

And also made my heart pound with an emotion I didn't want to examine too closely.

Evan cleared his throat. "Back to what I was saying, hiring starts on January first, but Chester Walton likes to get his contracts ready to go beforehand. So we would need to be together for a few months."

Now my mouth was dry. A few months? "I don't think I'm at a point where I'd be okay dating you." And I was probably the only woman in a thousand-mile radius who felt that way.

His confident smirk made me feel like my thought bubbles had returned and he'd just read my mind. "Don't think of it as dating. Just hanging out. We used to hang out all the time. And I know it's a lot to ask. It's hard for me to even ask for it. I have a hard time trusting people."

The guilt intensified. I was the worst person ever and the last person he should trust. But as I knew from all the time I'd spent watching and participating in sports, the best defense was a good offense. "I don't know that I can trust you, either."

There was a look of pain in his eyes that was quickly gone. "That's fair. Guess I'll just have to do my best to prove that you can."

I was the slime of all humanity. If he was being sincere.

And unfortunately the best way to figure out whether he meant it or it was all an act was to do what Brenda wanted me to do: stay "engaged" to Evan.

He got up and came to sit next to me on the couch. Not too close to make me uncomfortable, but close enough that I could feel his warmth and smell the soap on his skin, and every cell in my body tingled with anticipation of his touch.

"Please give me a dirty look so I know we're okay."

What else could I do but smile?

He held up six fingers and mouthed the word *six* to me.

Which made me want to smile again, but I pushed the feeling down. I didn't know if I could do what he wanted. I was sure Brenda would be ecstatic, but it would be really hard to pretend to be his fiancée. Especially when I had only just started to think about him with something besides hatred. "I don't know . . ."

"It is a lot to ask," he said. "I get that. And I get that there's not really anything in it for you. I could come and do an interview at ISEN and give you all the credit for bringing me in."

That was not what ISEN wanted from him, and the guilt nearly overwhelmed me. "That's not necessary."

"Or how about for the home games I could get your family a luxury box?"

Years ago my father had been invited by a client to attend a Jacks game in a luxury box, and he mentioned it practically every time we went to the stadium. He desperately wanted to go back but couldn't justify the cost.

How could I say no and deny my father that chance?

As if he sensed I was weakening, Evan pressed his case, reaching out his hands as if he intended to grab mine. "The boxes are really nice. I think your family would enjoy them."

I had to say yes. Even though I didn't want to. Not just for my career's sake but to make my dad happy. "Okay." I swatted at his hands. "I'll do it. I'll be your fake fiancée for the next few months."

"That is so great. Thank you!" He leaned forward, his arms moving toward me like he intended to hug me.

In that moment it would have been too much. I was trying desperately to remember my end goals: to stay professional and not let Evan Dawson in. Being enveloped in his strong, manly arms would not help with any of that.

I quickly stood. "I'm going to need a ring. That's the first thing women ask about."

He stood as well. "I'll take care of that. I'll have my assistant grab something. Text me your address so I can have it delivered."

"Sounds good. I should get going."

"Right. I am kind of bummed that people think I proposed to you in a restaurant. I would never do something so cliché." He must have caught my disdain, because he immediately started backpedaling. "Uh-oh. Did someone you know get proposed to in a restaurant?"

"My oldest sister. My mother. My paternal grandmother. I could go on." Clichés were clichés for a reason. We stopped just next to the door.

"Sorry, I have a bit of foot-in-mouth disease when I'm around beautiful women."

"Ha." He was either blind or the liar I suspected him to be. "I know how I look right now."

"What do you mean? I like how you look." His gaze lingered on me, following the contours of my body until he again met my eyes. My skin burned everywhere his gaze touched me.

"Yeah, men say they want someone low-maintenance, but they're always drooling over the Barbies. Would you have talked to me at Tinsley's party if I hadn't been all done up?"

His body seemed to be moving closer to mine. My internal temperature rose about forty degrees. Had the walls started closing in? Or was he edging his way over to me?

"I didn't talk to you because of how you looked. I talked to you because of what you were saying about the game. That you're a knock-out just happened to be icing on the cake."

The flush started, and I was glad it was dim where we stood—hopefully he wouldn't see it happening. I didn't need him to start counting all the times he made me blush.

What I did need was to leave. Now. But he was blocking my only exit, because I was not Batgirl and couldn't do a flying leap off his balcony. "Could you open the door so I could go?"

He put his hand on the doorknob and paused. "Are you coming to the game tomorrow?"

I was having a hard time concentrating. His nearness was throwing off my ability to think clearly. "There's no way I would miss out on my luxury box. My family are season ticket holders. We always go to all the home games and watch the others on TV."

"Isn't it weird to think we've been in the same place at the same time so often? Maybe this is fate."

His intense, blue-flamed gaze was going to make me come apart and confess everything to him. "Yeah. Weird. I'll talk to you later."

Finally getting the hint, he opened the door and stuck out his head, making sure the coast was clear. When he nodded, I had to duck under his arm and brush against that delicious chest of his to get out of his room.

I hurried down the hallway without looking back.

He was wrong. None of this was fate. It was a deliberate choice on my part.

And it wasn't really personal anymore.

It was just business.

CHAPTER TWELVE

This entire day had emotionally drained me. I was relieved that now I could go home, put on some pajamas, and sleep until noon the next day.

I'd just finished getting ready for bed when there was a knock on my door. It was late. What kind of sociopath just stopped by without calling or texting first? I tiptoed over to the peephole and saw my older sister. Maybe if I just stayed quiet she'd go away.

She banged on the door again. She was going to start waking up neighbors, and I would get yelled at. "I know you're in there! Open up, Ashton!"

"What are you doing here?" I asked, opening the door slightly. She barged her way in, throwing her purse on my sofa.

"Do you even know how busy I am right now? I don't want to be here, either, but you're not answering texts and not picking up when any of us call!" Aubrey crossed her arms and glared at me.

There was a reason for that. I had no idea what to say to any of them. I wasn't in the habit of lying to my family. I shut the door behind me. "Do you want something to drink?"

"No, I don't want something to drink! I want you to tell me how you're engaged to a guy who you were calling Satan just a few days ago!"

She sat down hard on the sofa, next to her purse. Everything in her body language said she wasn't going to move until she got the full story.

So I told her about the party, the basketball game, and the dinner and how he'd apologized. I told her the paparazzo following us had made a mistake, assuming we were getting engaged when we weren't, and that Evan had asked me to play along for the sake of his contract renewal.

She wore her scary *I'm going to crucify you in court* expression. "Nope. I'm not buying it. There's something you're not telling me."

"I don't know what you want me to say." I poured myself a glass of water and took a big gulp. Her intense attorney glare was making me nervous.

"The whole truth would be good."

"Is this where I slam my hand on the counter and say you can't handle the truth?"

But my sister did not appreciate my joke. "Out with it."

I set my glass down and leaned against the kitchen counter. "It's . . . complicated."

"I'm not looking for your Facebook relationship status. Just . . . give me a dollar." She held out her hand.

"I'm not giving you a dollar," I scoffed. "You don't need it."

"Give me the dollar, Ashton." She added her "don't screw around with me" voice to her judgy, scary face. Just as it kept her kids in line, I felt compelled to do as she commanded.

"Fine." I went over to my purse, pulled out a dollar bill, and handed it to her as I plopped down on the couch next to her. "Here's your dollar."

She held it aloft. "Now you've officially retained me as legal counsel, and anything you say is privileged and will be kept just between the two of us."

"Where has this been all my life? It would have been very useful when I was in college."

"Come on. The whole truth."

I told her everything. It was a relief to tell someone else. Someone not as cutthroat or ambitious as Brenda. Aubrey didn't care what happened with Evan one way or the other. And I knew she'd always be on my side.

I talked about Brenda's ambitions, how she'd chosen me for the story because of my past relationship with Evan. How I wanted to take him down and destroy him for revenge. Get him kicked off the Jacks.

"Wow," she interjected. "I can't believe you're out to get Evan Dawson. I've never seen anybody pick a fight with the entire state of Oregon before."

"But maybe he's not who I thought he was." I told her about his apologies, about how he claimed he hadn't been responsible and wanted us to be friends. She didn't look surprised at this part, and it made me wonder if she'd already had this discussion with him.

"So it's possible he's telling the truth, and he is a good guy, and you're doing something terrible?"

"Well, when you put it like that . . ."

"What? It sounds true?"

Aubrey didn't get it. "I don't know what's real and what's not. That's what I'm trying to find out. And keeping the engagement going is good for me and my aspirations."

"Yeah, I'm pretty sure this is going to bite you in your aspirations. And I'll take that water now."

I got up to get her a glass, thinking about what she said and trying to find a way to explain myself. "I do need this job. My grandma money isn't going to last for much longer." My grandmother had left us three girls with trusts that were to be used for college and graduate school. It was a set amount that our father had disbursed to each of us. And since I hadn't gone to graduate school, I'd been using that money to live off while I worked for free at ISEN. "It's all about to work out for me. I'd hate to be this close to the end zone and fumble the ball."

She took the water from me and set it on the coffee table. "Some things are more important than money and jobs."

"Says the woman who has both. And a great husband and kids." I put my feet up on the coffee table, turning away from her. "And the money's not the only thing. Can you imagine how hard Mom and Dad would gloat if I lost my one chance to make this job a reality?"

My parents would literally choke on spewing out "I told you so" over and over again. Nobody wanted me to chase this career path. When I'd told them what I planned on majoring in at college, my dad had spent months quoting statistics at me about the unlikelihood of me ever becoming an announcer for any professional team, let alone a network, while my mother tried appealing to my emotional side. Why did I feel like I had to be an announcer? What was it that made me want to call games? Why was it so important? Could I really not imagine myself doing anything else? Wouldn't another job make me just as happy and fulfilled? They both did everything they could to discourage it. And I'd always been the perfectly obedient child. Although I'd never had an issue standing up for myself with peers, for some reason I'd always had a hard time when it came to authority figures. I wasn't the defiant type. But this had been really important to me. So I'd cried all the way through it, but I'd told them it was my money and my choice, and they didn't get a say.

The only person who'd ever believed in me was my grandmother. One of my earliest memories was of sitting with her at a Jacks game, listening to the play-by-play of the announcer over the loudspeakers and her telling me, "Someday that will be you, my little gingersnap."

I was pretty sure if I lost my job my parents would never let me hear the end of it about how right they'd been and how I should have listened to them. And that I'd have to move home would just make the entire situation untenable.

"You also shouldn't be making decisions based on what you think Mom and Dad will do."

Easy enough for her to say. She was the perfect child making all the perfect choices. Our parents bragged about her constantly, and I'd spent most of my life trying to live up to her. "Maybe this is what's supposed to happen. Did you ever think that maybe this is the universe giving me the chance to get my revenge? To turn the tables on him?"

"But you're still sitting at the same table."

Before I could ask her what that meant, she sighed and put her hand on my shoulder. "I love you, Ashton. And I will support you. I won't tell anybody else the truth. All the beans will remain firmly unspilled. But I think maybe instead of listening to this boss of yours, you should start listening to what's inside your heart."

"Oxygenated blood?"

She shoved me lightly, laughing along with me. "And you have to call Mom. Now. She has been freaking out the entire day."

I glanced at the clock on the wall. "Isn't it kind of late for her to be up?"

"Trust me on this one." She stood up, putting her purse over her shoulder.

"What am I going to tell them? I can't tell them the truth." My parents couldn't keep a secret even if I stapled their lips shut. If I told them what was going on and then introduced them to Evan, my dad would be like, "Great game, my daughter's only dating you to do an exposé on you, and could you introduce me to Coach Sitake?"

Our mom was a family therapist, and it was like keeping all the information about her clients private made it so that she had no filter and no privacy setting whatsoever when it came to her kids.

"Oh no. You definitely can't tell them or Rory the truth. It'll be on the six o'clock news by tomorrow if you do that. I don't know what story you and Evan have made up for mass consumption, but tell them that." She held out her arms, and I stood up to hug her goodbye.

"We don't have a story planned out yet. Just that we're going to stay engaged for a few months."

"I don't envy you having to have the parental conversation. But your lie will be blown apart if some press come to talk to Mom and Dad. It will seem weird that the world knows about your engagement but you didn't bother to tell your parents about it."

As I walked her to the door, she hesitated, playing with the zipper on her purse. "So what if he's not lying, and this is who he really is?"

I'd done nothing but consider it since our dinner. "I wish I could let myself believe that, but this Evan feels . . . fake. Like my thirteen-year-old self dreamed him up and brought him to life. So he's saying everything I want him to say and telling me I'm beautiful, and I can't trust it. It so goes against everything I've thought about him for years, and I can't buy into the fantasy."

I thought of Evan's comparison earlier—only I was the atheist who didn't know what to think when Evan showed off his angel wings as he descended from the sky. It rocked my worldview, and I couldn't figure out how to reconcile it with what I'd always believed. All of my interactions with him felt like they were happening to someone else. Because it couldn't possibly be my life.

She stood quietly, not responding. Which I recognized as another lawyer tactic—people felt compelled to fill in the silence. And even though I knew it, I still kept talking. "Not to mention it feels like it's all just an act to win me over so that he doesn't have to feel bad about whatever part he played in what happened to me."

"Well, he is real. You didn't conjure him up, and nobody's forcing him to say or do anything he doesn't want to. If you think he's being fake, I guess you'll find out one way or another eventually. No one can keep up an act like that for forever." Then she hugged me again. "And call Mom."

"I will!" I said and told her good night. As I shut the door behind her, I realized she was right about my parents. I had to call them. Since Evan and I didn't have our stories straight, I was just going to have to wing it. I entered my mother's phone number into my cell.

She picked up immediately. "Are you pregnant?"

"What?" Was she serious with this? "Yes, the most famous virgin in the world impregnated me. It was an immaculate conception. Do you ever even read anything about him? His celibacy is, like, this whole big deal."

"Well, people slip. Especially when they're in love." She let out an overly dramatic sigh. I could deal with my mother's drama. It was her criticisms and suggestions about how I should live my life that made me feel like I couldn't cope. "You had such a crush on him in high school."

"I remember, Mom. Thanks."

"What I can't figure out is why you'd become engaged to Evan Dawson of all people without even telling us you were dating him."

I headed into my bedroom and got under my plush comforter. If I was going to be interrogated, I was at least going to be relaxed while doing it. I could picture her in her kitchen, cutting vegetables to calm her stress. My mother considered herself to be a bohemian free spirit, but nobody had told her about the usual optimism that went along with it. She wore the flowy skirts and chunky necklaces but generally thought the world was always on the verge of ending.

And now she was on a melodramatic roll. "Were you going to tell us? Ever?"

"Obviously I was going to tell you, Mom. It's just . . . things happened so fast. We didn't know people were taking pictures of us. I didn't call you earlier because I had this thing, and then Evan and I had to figure out where we were going from here and what to tell people." All true. Sort of.

"I suppose it's sweet in its own way that you two found each other as adults, but I'd hate to see you get hurt like that again."

"So would I. That's not going to happen." She would assume I meant because he loved me, but I meant it wouldn't happen because I wouldn't let myself get hurt like that by him again. I had learned my lesson in the worst possible way. Even if he hadn't been directly responsible for what had happened to me, he had been a silent bystander. If I had to keep him at arm's length in order to focus solely on advancing my career, then that was what I would do. "Things are different now."

Just not in the way she imagined.

"Well, your father and I would like to meet him."

That didn't sound like something I wanted to have happen anytime soon. "You've already met him."

"Ten years ago. You said things were different now, and it is customary to bring your fiancé home to meet your family."

She skipped right over the rest of her planned guilt trip and headed straight into logical, rational arguments. But it sounded like a terrible plan. If I waited long enough, our engagement would be over, and then my two worlds would never have to collide.

How could I get out of it?

"Oh!" she said. "I know! We can meet him tomorrow after the game."

"Maybe. But he's going to be really busy after the game with interviews and stuff." That wouldn't be happening. If I had to fake a heart attack to get my family to leave the stadium, I would.

I knew that at some point it might happen—I just preferred to delay their meeting for as long as possible.

"Well, Thanksgiving is this week. That would be a perfect time to bring him over."

I was hoping that wouldn't work. Along with the Detroit Lions and Dallas Cowboys, the Portland Jacks always hosted a Thanksgiving Day game. Our family had a long-standing tradition that had begun with my grandma of celebrating the holiday on Wednesday, allowing us to attend the game. It also worked out well for Aubrey and Justin, as they were able to visit Justin's family after the game on the actual holiday.

But Evan had to be busy. He'd have a game to prepare for. Practice and weight lifting and team meetings. "I'll talk to him about it and let you know. But it's late, and I'm going to bed. I'll see you tomorrow."

We hung up, and right before I drifted off to sleep, I decided that this fake engagement to Evan Dawson was making my life more difficult than it ought to be.

Although I wasn't there, I had no doubt that my parents arrived at eight o'clock in the morning to grab their usual tailgate spot, along with all their tailgating friends. My sisters and I used to drive in with them when we were younger; now we typically showed up an hour or two before the game.

Today I intended to wait until the last possible minute. I didn't want to hang out with anyone and have to answer more questions. I headed out to the stadium, which had a long official name involving several different corporate sponsors. But everyone had always called it the Forest, because it was where the Lumberjacks cut down all their opponents.

I found my family as they were in the middle of putting away their folding table and sticking coolers and barbecues back into my dad's SUV. Everybody wore a Jacks jersey as per usual, but I noticed this time they were all Dawson jerseys. Mine was still generic.

"There's my girl!" my father said, coming over to give me a hug. Monday to Saturday he was a normal, serious, rational adult/partner in a law firm. But come Sundays he turned into a rabid, face-painting, flannel-wearing Jacks fan. He also called himself "the Punster," which should tell you everything you need to know about him. "Did you know you made me the most popular guy here today?"

Rory sidled up alongside me. "That's because Dad has spent the last four hours bragging to anyone who would listen that Evan Dawson is his future son-in-law. I think you are the current titleholder of 'Favorite Daughter.'" She gave me a pointed look, as if she suspected that something was up with my very fast engagement, but apparently she didn't care enough to press the point.

For which I was grateful.

"Should we head in?" I asked, helping to put away what was left of their stuff. I kissed Charlotte and Joey hello and let my mom hug me for longer than what would be considered normal.

"My sweet little engaged girl."

"Okay. That's enough, Mom. Seriously." Finally, I gently disentangled myself and again encouraged my family to head into the stadium. Because once that game started, nobody would ask me anything about Evan. They'd all be too caught up in the action.

On our way inside, we passed a group of blonde women who all looked alike due to their hairstyles and makeup. Like my family, they were all wearing Dawson jerseys but for a very different reason. Were they hoping to meet up with him after the game? Did any of them even like football? They were probably the types of girls who thought a Hail Mary was something a Catholic priest said at mass.

I remembered Evan talking about being accosted by women determined to sleep with him and realized these jersey chasers were exactly the kind of girl who would do that.

Which meant I should probably stop and talk to them in order to find out any dirt they might have, but for some reason I couldn't bring myself to do it.

I rationalized that I was here with my family to enjoy an outing, not to work.

But that wasn't what really stopped me.

We waited in line for our turn with the ticket taker. When we got up to the front, my dad handed over his cell phone. The ticket taker scanned my dad's QR code and made a funny face at his screen. "Can you wait here a minute? There seems to be an issue with your tickets."

That was strange. We were season ticket holders. How could there be a problem? I watched as the ticket taker stepped away and got on his walkie-talkie.

"An issue with our tickets? We've never had any trouble getting into a game before," my dad said, and I could see Fan Dad slipping and turning into Lawyer Dad. He was going to demand to see a supervisor in a minute.

The ticket taker returned wearing a giant grin and walking next to a girl who also wore a purple Jacks polo shirt, indicating that she was part of the staff.

"Hi, I'm Cassidy. I've been asked to assist you while you're at the Forest today. Come on inside—Mr. Dawson has arranged for some special seating for you."

CHAPTER THIRTEEN

In my fear at my family's reaction to my engagement news, I'd totally forgotten about the luxury box. Now I wanted to enjoy their surprise and so said nothing.

Cassidy waited for us all to enter through the gates before walking briskly in a direction I'd never gone before.

"Special seating?" Aubrey said to me in a stage whisper, holding Joey as she walked. "Interesting."

I fought back a grin.

We walked through parts of the stadium I'd never been in before, passing multiple security guards who just nodded at our guide. We climbed up and up the gently sloping walkways until Cassidy came to a stop in front of a door. She then slowly opened it, as if trying to build up suspense, revealing our luxury box. "This has been reserved for your family. Mario is working at the bar and will get you anything you need. He can also call for me if you need me."

It was much nicer than I'd anticipated. Maybe too much. We should refuse. "Maybe we shouldn't . . ." My voice trailed off as everybody pushed past me to get inside.

My family entered the box, oohing and aahing over the leather couches, the massive big-screen TVs, and the full spread that waited for them on several dark-wood tables. Instead of having something fancy like sushi, the table was loaded with premium stadium food—like nachos, buffalo wings, mozzarella sticks, pretzels, fried chicken, and sub sandwiches.

There was no way I was going to be able to convince them that we should leave and go back to our regular seats.

I also saw Jacks tote bags on the couches with our names pinned to them. My mother opened hers, and inside were a football, a T-shirt, an umbrella, a tumbler, and a ball cap with the Jacks logo emblazoned on it. "Come over here and look!"

Each football had been autographed by the entire team. The bags for the kids had a shirt in their size, a tiny rubber football, and a stuffed Paul Bunyan, the Jacks' mascot.

It was really, incredibly thoughtful. And nice. And unexpected.

Another chunk of my protective barrier came crashing down.

Cassidy went around the room, putting paper wristbands on everybody. "These will allow you to come and go on this level." Then she approached me. I offered her my wrist, and after she had put the band on, she said, "Ms. Bailey? May I speak to you alone?"

"Yeah, of course." I followed her out into the hallway, and she handed me a small box wrapped in bright-purple wrapping paper.

"Mr. Dawson asked me to give this to you in private."

She walked away, and I waited until she was out of sight before opening it. Inside I found a jewelry box.

And in the jewelry box was an engagement ring. Even though I knew our situation was fake, I still gasped when I lifted the lid. The ring was sweet and simple—a platinum band with a large circular diamond in the center.

The words of the women at Tinsley's tea party echoed inside my head, and I realized I should have thought to offer him one of my rings in order to size it. I hoped it would fit.

I took it out of the box, then slid the box into my jeans pocket. I put the ring on, and it fit perfectly. Like it had been made just for me.

Which didn't mean anything at all. There was no hidden symbolism or metaphor here. Right?

I returned to the luxury box. On the way I threw the wrapping paper into a trash can and slipped the jewelry box into my purse, hoping no one would notice. I wanted to flash my ring for everybody to see but refrained from doing so. I was hoping they didn't notice I'd had it for only, like, two minutes. Maybe I'd pull Aubrey aside and show it to her.

Somebody had opened the big window so we could hear the roar of the fans and the announcers the way they were meant to be listened to—not on a television screen but in real life, thundering in your ears.

My family was gathered around the food table, loading up their plates. They were all smiling and chattering away.

I'd told Evan that my family didn't like him because of our high school situation. He'd offered up this box as some kind of quid pro quo for the pretend engagement, but now I wondered if he'd done it for other reasons. Because it was pretty clever of him to use my family's love of football and free fried food to win them over.

"Dad, you spilled some of the melted cheese from your nachos," Rory complained, trying to dab at it.

My father took the napkin from her and said, "Don't worry. It's nacho problem. I'll get it." We all groaned in response, as if on cue. He picked up some salsa and spooned it onto his plate, next to his nachos. "Hey, I'll have you guys know this salsa was born to be mild."

If he did this for another three hours, I was going to toss him out that window. Most of my family went over and claimed spots on the couches to watch the game. The kids were seated on the floor to eat so their food would have a shorter distance to fall.

Since Aubrey's kids were situated, she came around to my right and stared at the food selection. "This is all so bad for you," she murmured, but I didn't notice her gravitating toward the vegetable tray. "I really love buffalo wings."

"You know what they say. If you like it, you should put a wing on it."

I heard my dad go, "Ha!" behind me.

"Really?" Aubrey asked.

"I'd say no pun intended, but I knew what I was doing." I added some pepperoni pizza to my plate.

"What's happening right now? Has Dad infected you with his cheesiness? I didn't realize it was contagious. Or genetic. Am I going to start saying stupid things?" she asked.

"You made your point," I said, nudging her with my elbow. "But maybe I'm just feeling a little giddy because of this."

I showed her my ring, and she gasped, much as I had done when I first saw it. "Ashton! This is gorgeous! And it's just so you. Nothing too frilly or fancy, you know?"

I did know. I wondered how Evan had known it would be just what I wanted. "Just play it cool. Let's join the others."

We found spots on the couch, Aubrey curling up next to her husband. The announcers, Scooter Buxton and Keith Collinsworth, were chatting about the Jacks. A moving picture of Evan flashed up on the TV screen. I paused, my slice of pizza halfway to my mouth.

"What are we thinking will happen today with Number 4, Evan 'Awesome' Dawson? Do you think his game against the Raiders will be at all affected?" Keith asked.

"What Keith's talking about is the fact that Dawson recently got engaged," Scooter explained to the audience. "We're hearing the lucky lady is ISEN intern Ashton Bailey. He recently cheered her on at a local intramural basketball game."

I nearly dropped my pizza when I saw the clip they put up next. It was a video of Evan at my game, yelling, "Way to go, Ashton!" Somebody had recorded it on their cell phone. It was wobbly and a bit blurry, but there was no mistaking Evan for anyone else.

Why were they showing this? No NFL fan cared.

Present company excluded.

"She's here in the Forest today with her family. Do you think she'll be a distraction for the nearly flawless 'Awesome' Dawson?"

"That's hard to predict," Scooter responded. "We'll have to wait and see."

"Interestingly enough," Keith interjected as they went back to showing the inside of the stadium, "Ashton Bailey is the granddaughter of Harold and Evelyn Bailey, founders of the Jumping Jacks charity, which so many of our players and Lumberjills support. It raises money to help pay for treatment of sick children and for their families to be able to stay on-site with them. The Baileys lost their oldest daughter to bacterial meningitis when she was eleven, and they formed the charity in her name."

I turned, my mouth hanging open, to stare at my dad. He didn't like to talk about his older sister, Jennifer, and her death. My grandma had nicknames for everyone, and they'd called Jennifer their jumping bean, which became part of the name for the charity founded in her honor. My mom had her arm around my dad, her head on his shoulder.

It had never occurred to me that the media would bring my family into this. I had thought it would just be me. But now they were talking about my grandparents and my aunt. Who would it be next week? My parents? My sisters? Charlotte and Joey? I really hadn't thought this through. What would be the effects of me pretending to be engaged to Evan?

"I'm so sorry, Dad." My words felt inadequate. There was no way to make this up to him.

"For what?" He looked legitimately confused. "Everything they just said is public knowledge."

"But what happens when they start sharing not-public knowledge?"

My father contemplated this and then said, "I get to see my little girl happily married and get Evan Dawson as a son-in-law. Which means he'll be part of the Baileys. And we'll figure out a way to deal with it. The Baileys stick together, no matter what."

Guilt, which seemed to be my primary emotion lately, filled my chest and made me feel weighed down. I didn't know what I would do if the media tried to hurt my family.

I needed to talk to Evan about this.

The announcers were discussing the Raiders' starting lineup, and my mom asked Rory how she'd done on her most recent art project while Aubrey and my dad talked about a case they were working on together. Normalcy resumed, and I was finally able to eat my now-cold pizza. Still delicious.

The players took the field, and the stadium went nuts when the Jacks ran out from the tunnel.

Mario came over and began to clear our dishes, which we all immediately protested. We got up and helped clean our own mess with him showing us where to put our emptied plates. He then took our drink orders and reminded us that the game was about to begin.

Then it was time for the kickoff. Everybody else sat back down on the couch, but I wandered over to stand near the windows, not blocking anyone's view. I was not watching the special team come out onto the field.

I was scanning the sidelines for Evan.

Finn MacNeil ran up to kick the football, and at the moment his foot connected with the ball, everyone in the stadium shouted, "Tim . . . ber!" It was thrilling as always to hear seventy thousand people yelling the same thing at the same time.

"Even the way he kicks is hot," Rory said with a sigh.

"Come sit down," my mom said to me.

But I was too anxious. Edgy. And I didn't know why. "I'm fine."

"Don't worry about the Raiders," my dad said. "The Jacks have got this handled."

The Raiders were stopped on their forty-three-yard line and had possession. The defensive line did their job and only let them gain about six yards.

"Fourth down," I murmured.

"I told you the Jacks were a better team," my dad said. "And here's my case in punt."

The Raiders did indeed have to punt the ball, and Evan ran out onto the field with his offense.

And I couldn't breathe.

I had watched him play a million times before. Why was this different? What did I think was going to happen?

I'd only just started to breathe normally again when Evan turned his head, looking up at our box. Was he looking for me the way I'd been searching for him? He raised one hand, and I held mine up against the glass. Could he see me all the way up here?

Evan called the first play, and his team got into position. He had set up to pass the ball, taking his time in the pocket to throw it exactly where he wanted it to go.

One of the Raiders' defensive linemen found a hole in the offense and broke through, running straight for Evan. Evan released the ball and threw it downfield to his wide receiver. Two seconds later the defensive lineman tackled Evan.

I was only vaguely aware of the announcers' voices as I watched the foul being committed. Scooter announced, "Dawson is being rushed, and—oh! Terrance White has got him."

"That had to hurt!" Keith replied.

"Where's the call?" I demanded, yelling out the open window.

"What call?" my brother-in-law asked.

"White took two steps after Evan released the football. Where's the 'roughing the passer' call?"

Scooter said, "Dawson is down but looking none the worse for wear as he gets back on his feet."

I felt this rush of relief when Evan got up and went back over to his huddle, ready to set up his next play.

Still no call for him.

"Come on, Ref!" I shouted, knowing he couldn't hear me but unable to contain my anger.

I used to like watching Evan get sacked. There had always been something cathartic about it. Now? It kind of upset me.

A lot.

They weren't going to call the penalty, and I lost it. "Hey, Ref! Do you know what a football player does when he loses his eyesight? He becomes a referee!" I was literally shaking my fist out of the window. What was happening to me?

"She's going to get us banned from another sport," Rory said.

"You seem awfully protective of the QB," Aubrey added. "Maybe you should go down there and be one of his offensive linemen."

"Hilarious," I muttered sarcastically and turned to see my sisters exchanging satisfied glances.

"We think so."

I whirled around and went back to the food table. I'd get a bunch of carbs and then sit in the corner where I couldn't see the game. Maybe it would be better for my family and my blood pressure if I didn't watch.

I focused on my niece and nephew, who were running in big circles in the open space behind the couch. Aubrey was cuddled up with Justin, and they both looked extremely relaxed. Usually they had to spend most of the game trying to keep their kids entertained and in one spot so that they didn't bother the other fans. But here in this enclosed space, the children could run around to their hearts' content, which they did. They were going to pass out like little blackout drunks on their ride home.

Evan got another first down according to Keith, and I pulled out my phone. Part of me wanted to text him to be more careful. Because stuff like your spleen, rotator cuffs, and knee cartilage? They were useful in your everyday life. But mostly I wanted to thank him. For giving my family this amazing experience. I knew it would be hours before he saw it, but I owed him my gratitude.

> Thank you for the luxury box. My family is loving it. Thank you for the ring. It's perfect. And thanks for the swag. Just . . . thanks.

Just as I sent off the text, I heard that Evan had gotten another first down. I put my phone back in my pocket and headed over to the window. I couldn't stay away. I had to watch.

Evan had been doing what he always did—he slowly drove the ball down the field one play at a time. And it made me think of the night of our dinner and how he'd told me this was his specialty. Wearing down his opponents until he got what he wanted.

I was starting to get the sneaking suspicion that he had been a hundred percent right in his assessment and that it was going to work on me, too.

"Why doesn't he throw it?" Justin asked, and of course my dad was ready with a quip he'd probably been holding on to for years.

"Don't worry. Right now is the calm before the score."

His statement turned out to be prophetic. The very next play Evan handed the ball off to Curtis Mattison, who dodged two defenders and leaped over the goal line to score a touchdown.

It was like I had made the touchdown myself. I was jumping up and down, whooping and hollering along with the rest of my family and almost every person in the stadium.

But while everyone else was watching Mattison doing a lap in the end zone, I saw Evan turn and point at our box. Like he was saying he did it for me.

Little arrows shot through my heart, clearing my personal defensive line.

"That is seriously the cutest thing ever," Rory said. "Good thing you locked that down."

The Jacks made the two-point conversion and went on to score once more in the first half, while the Raiders got one touchdown.

Scooter's voice carried over the loudspeakers. "We're heading into halftime with a score of fifteen to seven in the Jacks' favor. And there seems to be some disturbance down near the Jacks' tunnel."

The cameras focused in on the area where the Jacks fans were lined up, holding out their hands or things to be autographed. A Raiders fan ran along the stairs, yelling unintelligibly. He was followed by three security guards, who were closing in on him. Then the fan turned, squeezed his way past the waiting Jacks fans, and threw something at Evan. A water bottle?

It hit Evan in the head while the security guards tackled the crazy fan. Stunned, I sank onto the couch to watch. It was either that or run out to help Security. Every camera in the place focused on Evan. He wore a shocked expression.

Aubrey put her hand on my arm. "I'm sure he's fine."

He seemed fine. He didn't pass out or anything. I didn't see any blood.

One of the sideline network reporters ran up to Evan with a microphone. "Wow, Evan! That was awful. Are you all right?"

He flashed his blinding grin and turned to face the cameras. "I'm okay. I will say, though, that's probably the hardest I've been hit so far in this game." The crowd in the stadium erupted in cheers at his response.

"I'll give him this. He certainly knows how to work his audience," my mom observed.

Which was part of my problem in figuring out my Evan dilemma. I couldn't tell what was real and what was fake. What was the Private Evan and what was the Public Evan. The lines kept blurring.

My phone buzzed a second later. I checked it and saw a text from Evan.

You're welcome.

It took me a second to place what he was responding to. It was the text I'd sent him in the first quarter thanking him for all the special effort he'd gone to on my family's behalf.

But was he for real sitting in the locker room and writing to me? Shouldn't he be concentrating on the game and whatever the head coach was saying to him?

I can't believe you're texting me right now.

I had a break from work.

That made me laugh, drawing the attention of every single one of my family members. I ignored their curious stares and typed my reply.

I don't want to be a distraction.

Which was true. I didn't want fan forums filled with how much they hated me because I'd ruined Evan's game or to get booed in person every time I came to the Forest. More than one NFL girlfriend/fiancée had faced that particular form of wrath.

I was more distracted by the water bottle that was thrown at my face.

Are you okay?

> The doc says I'll live. The moneymaker is intact.

I wanted to giggle again when my mom's voice stopped me. "Tell him we want to meet him after the game." I realized she was reading over my shoulder. I'd been worried about distracting Evan, but I was the one who had tuned out the rest of the world while chatting with him.

"Mom! Boundaries!"

I got up and moved away from the others, into a corner where no one could eavesdrop. Or eyesdrop.

> You're staying for the rest of the game?

> I will if you promise to keep your head away from unidentified flying objects.

> I make no promises.

> If you can't guarantee your safety, then at the very least win.

> That I can do.

I saw the three dots, indicating that he was still typing. I waited and waited as the dots disappeared and reappeared. Finally, I had another message come through from him.

> Can we meet up? After the game?

It was a good idea since we needed to get our stories straight. How we'd met, how long we'd been dating. The how-did-he-propose question was already taken care of, at least.

> Yeah. Do you want to come by my place?

He already had the address, and it was much closer to the stadium than his huge house out in Lake Oswego.

> There are things I have to take care of after the game, but as soon as I can I'll head over. I'll text you when I'm on my way.

Now I could truthfully tell my family that Evan was too busy to meet them.

And I tried hard to ignore how tingly and excited I felt at the prospect of seeing him again.

CHAPTER FOURTEEN

I wondered if, despite his assertion to the contrary, I had distracted him, as Evan didn't play quite as well in the second half of the game.

The Raiders were able to tie up the score, and as I watched, I alternated between being terrified every time he got hit and being impressed with him in his natural element. The power, the strength, the absolute grace he had while he played . . . why had I never noticed it before?

Then in the last minute of the game, when it looked like we'd have to go into overtime, Evan did something phenomenal. He couldn't find an open man, the defensive line was closing in on him, and so he made a run for it. Thirty yards, all the way to the end zone. He got a touchdown, and the Jacks won by seven points.

I practically screamed myself hoarse watching that play.

Once the game was over, I walked out with my family, wondering what Evan was doing right then. If he was thinking about me or solely focused on his interviews. After lots of hugs and goodbyes, along with a blood-oath promise to my mother that I would ask Evan about Thanksgiving, I was finally able to drive home. I had a quick shower and changed into a T-shirt and yoga pants. I did not shave any body parts, I did not put on any makeup, and I did not get dressed up for him.

Since my internal walls had started to break down, I decided that maybe this was the best way to keep him at bay.

I turned on the TV and switched to ISEN. They were discussing the Jacks game and were showing some footage they'd taken of the players after their win. One of the interviews was with Evan. He'd been approached by a reporter from a local affiliate before he'd even stepped foot in the locker room. The reporter asked to speak with him, and I saw a flash of impatience on Evan's face, like all he wanted to do was take a shower. He nodded and smiled, and I noticed that it didn't quite reach his eyes.

"What was going through your mind when you made that run?"

"That I'd promised my girl I'd win the game, and so I did what I had to do."

I wondered if the camera operator was female, since the person backed up, getting a full-body shot of Evan. He looked a mess—his hair sweaty and the black grease under his eyes dripping down his face, his uniform covered in dirt and grass stains.

But there was something oddly compelling about him. I paused the TV as I tried to figure out what it was.

Was it the way he'd so casually called me his girl? How that had made my heart skip a beat?

Or was it his pads that almost seemed like armor? Like he was a warrior returning home from the battlefield. Or from a battle he'd won in my honor.

I let out a sigh of disgust at my own stupidity. I had a seriously overactive imagination. I turned off the television.

To take my mind away from its crazy path, I decided to make a chicken-and-noodle dish that had been my grandma's favorite. I wondered what she would think of what I was doing right now. Trying to get the dirt on Evan's personal life. Would she be cheering me on, wanting me to get my dream career? Or would she think less of me?

I picked up my phone when it beeped. There was a text from Evan.

> On my way. Will be there soon.

I fought off my natural urge to run to the bathroom and improve my current physical situation. *We're not really engaged, he's not actually my fiancé, and I don't care what he thinks of me,* I told myself.

He showed up about twenty minutes later, and I took in a deep breath before I opened the door. He smiled at me, a real smile that lit up his eyes.

"Hi." Then he leaned in and kissed me on the cheek, like he'd done it a million times before, and it was totally normal and no big deal.

I, meanwhile, had to hold on to the door for a second until the feeling in my legs returned. He didn't have any product in his dark hair, causing it to fall forward onto his forehead. Like he'd taken a shower and rushed over here. He wore a light-blue shirt under his jacket that made his eyes appear even lighter than normal.

"Please, come in. Are you hungry? I just made some dinner."

"The answer to your question is I'm always hungry. I'd love to eat with you. Can I help with anything?"

"You can set the table." I told him where the plates and silverware were as I put the casserole and bread I'd made on the table. We sat down when everything was ready.

"Not quite as fancy as Rodrigo's," I said, feeling a little sheepish. He was probably used to all luxury all the time.

"No. But this is better," he said after he'd taken his first bite.

"Better than steak and lobster?" I asked, disbelieving what he was saying.

"Homemade is always better." He proved his point by having not only seconds but also thirds. I was glad I'd cooked up extra. I had originally intended to have leftovers, but it gave me a strange satisfaction to watch him enjoying something I'd made.

And while we ate I reminded him that we needed to create our love story. So we talked through the details, staying as close to the truth as possible. We'd met in high school, where I'd had a crush on him. We'd reunited a few months ago and quickly fallen in love. It all seemed easy enough. Because it hadn't been a long courtship, people wouldn't expect us to know every detail about each other, and his agent thought social media would love our "meant to be" fast engagement.

"Thank you for dinner," he said, standing up to grab both of our plates, interrupting my musing about our current situation.

"You don't have to do that!" I protested.

He carried all of the dirty dishes from the table to the sink. "Since you cooked, it's only fair that I clean up."

"Your . . ." I let my voice trail off. I had been about to say that his mother had raised him right, but would that be insensitive? Would it hurt his feelings?

And when had I started caring about not hurting him?

After scraping off the leftover bits of food, Evan began to load the dishwasher.

"You really don't have to do that." I felt dumb just sitting there, watching him. Although somehow his doing household chores made him even more attractive.

"It's not hard to stick them in the dishwasher."

"Thanks." I drummed my fingers against the tabletop, not sure what I should do while he washed everything. "And thank you for what you did today. My family had a once-in-a-lifetime experience that they absolutely loved."

He glanced over his shoulder at me. "I didn't intend to make it a onetime deal. They're going to be my family, too, right?"

"For pretend," I quickly corrected him. Just in case he'd forgotten after getting hit in the head one too many times today.

That sexy, knowing smirk of his was back. "Yes, for pretend. But I plan on renting that luxury box for their personal use for every home game. You guys don't have to use it if you don't want to, but it will be there, waiting."

There was no way my family would ever, ever turn down that offer. And they'd kill me if I did. So I just said, "They'll love that. Thanks."

"Where do you keep your dishwasher soap?"

Instead of telling him, I got up to grab some from underneath my kitchen sink. When I stood up, he had moved closer to me, and we were almost, but not quite, pressed together. Which meant that every square inch of my skin broke out in goose bumps as I fought off the urge to lean forward just a fraction so we would be touching.

"Here," I said in a breathy voice and handed him the tiny powder tablet.

"Thanks." His voice was low and gruff, like he was affected by my proximity, too.

He really was a beautiful man with a face so symmetrical that it added to my distrust. So unfair that he was so perfect. But that perfection was currently marred by the large bruise near his hairline. That must have been where the water bottle had hit him. Without thinking I reached up to touch it, and he made a combination hissing/growling sound when my fingers brushed against his skin.

"That must hurt."

"Apparently that guy was pretty drunk. I'm glad it was a water bottle and not a beer bottle. And that he didn't break my nose or something."

Me too. That would have been a little like somebody carving a mustache and eyeglasses on the statue of *David*.

His lips were right there. My own burned in anticipation. I could have kissed him. I wanted desperately to kiss him, and that worried me more than anything else that was happening.

I blinked twice, cleared my throat, and backed up. All the way into the living room. I sat in the corner of the couch, trying to catch my shaky breath. He joined me a few seconds later, which wasn't nearly enough time for me to try and compose myself.

And he sat closer to me than he should have. I had nowhere to run. I grabbed a throw pillow and placed it against my chest, as if it would ward him off.

"What's your schedule like this week?" he asked.

"Why?" I sounded panicked. I needed to calm down. "What are your plans?"

"Work on Monday, the children's hospital on Tuesday, Wednesday off, and then the game on Thursday and a light workload on Friday, Saturday, and Sunday."

"No Thanksgiving plans?"

He looked down at his hands, flexing and unflexing them. "I don't really believe in Thanksgiving."

"Oh, it exists. I've celebrated it."

That made him laugh. "I meant I don't usually do anything on Thanksgiving. Because of the game."

No, it was because he didn't have anyone to celebrate with. Which made me sad.

And I could have dropped it there. It would have been the end of it. Only I didn't.

"My family wants to meet you. Well, you've met my sisters. I should say my parents want to meet you. They were hoping you'd come over for Thanksgiving. On Wednesday. We always celebrate on Wednesday so that we can go to the game the next day. Anyway, my parents don't know that this isn't real, and I can't tell them because they would blab it to the entire world, so they're expecting me to bring you by."

I didn't realize I was holding my breath until he said, "I'm in."

"Are you sure?"

"Definitely. I'd love to meet your family. Did you show them the ring today?" He took my left hand, holding it with both of his as he studied the ring. It made me wish I was a manicure type of girl.

Then I had to close my eyes against the electrical sensation he was causing by running his thumb along the back of my hand. He probably didn't even know he was doing it, but every cell in my body was totally aware.

When I opened my eyes again, I realized he was waiting for a response to his question. "Oh, uh, just Aubrey. She knows the truth about us, but it's cool because I've retained her as legal counsel, and she's not allowed to tell anyone else. I didn't want my family to know how and when I really got the ring."

"I wish I'd been there to give it to you." Now he was basically just holding my hand, my palm lying open against his. Neither one of us moved.

"No, that would have made it . . ." A thousand times more—more embarrassing, more sweet, more awkward, more every negative and positive emotion I'd experienced with him so far.

All things I couldn't say.

"Do you like it?" His question had an odd intensity to it, like it really mattered to him whether or not I did.

"I do. It's perfect. Something I would have chosen for myself."

I was struck with the overwhelming desire to lace my fingers through his. To feel the warmth and strength of his hand enveloping my own. I curled my fingers in and pulled my hand away. "Speaking of Aubrey and my family, I was upset about the way the announcers talked about my grandparents today."

Evan frowned in confusion. "They did?"

"Before you came on the field. It's one thing for me to be in the spotlight, but none of the rest of them signed up for this. I wouldn't want the press going after them."

"Why would they? Do you have some skeletons in your family closet?"

"Not that I know of, but I want to protect them, you know?"

He laid his arm along the back of the couch, his hand next to my shoulder. "I get that. I'll talk to my agent and see what we can do. I can be more available to answer questions. Maybe in exchange for a handful of interviews, we can get some of the more aggressive outlets to promise to leave you and your family alone."

I knew how much he had avoided interviews in the past, and his offer made my heart flip over. "You would do that?" I left off the part I couldn't speak. *For me?*

"Of course." Was that my imagination, or did I feel his fingertips barely skimming my shoulder? "I'm the one who dragged you into this. It's my job to protect you from anything that would hurt you. Just think of me as your own personal left guard. Or right guard. I'll play both positions for you."

It was like he'd shoved a dagger into my heart and twisted it around. Because I was being taken in and felt terrible about what I was plotting to do to him. After all the kind gestures he'd shown my family all day, as charming and fun as he was right then, it was so easy to believe in him. That this was the real Evan. That he was finally offering to protect me the way he'd failed to do all those years ago.

He's engaged to you to manipulate Chester Walton, a voice whispered inside me. Which was true. I had to remember that his motives weren't pure. This wasn't about being attracted to me or wanting to date me. He was using me to get what he wanted from his boss.

Just like I was using him to get what I wanted from my boss.

"So, no big plans tonight? Should you be out with the rookies at some bar, meeting all the single ladies?"

He leaned back on the couch, suddenly looking exhausted. "Now that I'm an engaged man, I don't think that would be a good idea. And that's not really something I usually do. After a game I like to come home, unwind, and check out how the competition did that day on *SportsCenter.*"

"Me too," I whispered. "Do you want to watch it with me?"

Where those words came from, I had no idea.

"Absolutely." He grinned. I got the remote from the coffee table and turned on the television.

Where it was still paused to that full-screen hero/warrior shot of him. I'd managed to turn the television off but failed to put it back to live TV.

"If you wanted a picture of me, all you had to do was ask."

"With an ego that size, I don't know how you were able to fit your head through the front door when you got here." I frantically pushed the VIEW LIVE TV button, and my remote finally cooperated with me.

"Everyone has an ego. Mine is just bigger and better."

I didn't realize I had been smiling until he held up ten fingers. He was going to run out of fingers soon. Would I be getting toe counting next? I switched the channel over to ESPN.

"I'm serious about the photo. I can have my assistant send it to you whenever. I'll even autograph it."

He laughed when I hit him with the pillow I had on my lap.

We watched the recaps of the other NFL games that had taken place today, arguing about and analyzing the teams and specific plays.

"Do you know what I like best about you?" Evan asked me about an hour later. "It's like you're one of my guy friends who loves sports, only you're in a hot woman's body."

"Thanks? I think?" That was random.

"It was definitely a compliment. I love how much you know about sports."

That was the last thing I could clearly remember him saying to me. We were quiet after that, watching the recaps. My eyelids felt heavy.

I woke up hours later, curled up on my couch. Evan was on the other end, lightly snoring, his feet up on the coffee table. He couldn't have been comfortable.

How had we both fallen asleep? The TV was still on. I used the remote to turn it off.

I checked my nearly dead phone. It was just past three o'clock in the morning. I had a blanket from my bedroom on me. Which meant I must have passed out before he did, and he went and got it for me.

And didn't leave.

Which he needed to do, right now. I didn't want him to spend the night here. No matter how boyish he looked while he slept.

"Evan." I shook his arm, my hand resting against his bicep. Good grief, but it was rock hard and solid underneath my hand. I took an extra second to appreciate it before I tried again to wake him up. "Evan, you need to wake up."

He came to and gave me a groggy smile. "What time is it?"

"Three. You should go."

"Sorry," he said, putting his feet on the floor. "You fell asleep, and I wanted to catch the tail end of the show before I left, and I guess I fell asleep, too."

I stood, letting the blanket fall onto the couch. He yawned and stretched, and I had to avert my gaze so I didn't lap up the sight of his muscles flexing along his skin and under his shirt.

He said in a joking tone, "Are you sure you don't want me to stay?"

Yes. I want you to stay. "If there's some paparazzo out there waiting for you, we wouldn't want anyone to question your virtue if you ended up staying here all night."

"Lately I've been realizing that I don't really care what other people think."

What was that supposed to mean?

He checked his pockets and got to his feet. He went over to my kitchen chair and put his jacket on. I backed up, not wanting to be too close. There was something entirely too intimate about us falling asleep together on the couch. We hadn't cuddled up or anything, but still.

I was suddenly struck with a memory of my dad talking about our dog, who would not sleep unless he was with me or my sisters. He'd said we were to take that as a huge compliment because Buster had come from a long line of predators, and by choosing to sleep with us, he was showing us he was willing to be vulnerable with people he trusted.

Was that something my psyche was trying to tell me? That I could trust Evan?

Or that I already did?

I walked him to the door, and the air around us felt charged and heavy, like he wanted to say or do something. Or like I wanted him to.

When I opened the door, he turned to me and said, "Hear that?"

"If you say it's this, or us, happening, I will throat punch you."

He chuckled. "No. I heard the sound of my six a.m. workout crying because it knows I'm going to kill it in three hours. Why would you think I was talking about you? Not everything's about you, Ashton." His tone was light and teasing, and he winked at me as he walked away. "See you soon."

I locked the door and pressed my forehead against it. I hoped that by the time the sun rose, whatever I was feeling right now would go away.

CHAPTER FIFTEEN

Monday morning, I had a text from Brenda asking about my progress, but I told her I had nothing new to report. I'd already mentioned that Evan and I both agreed to keep up our pretend engagement, and she'd been ecstatic. For some reason I didn't want to tell her about the gifts at the game or how he'd stayed over late. I rationalized that they had nothing to do with my story.

Despite my rationalization, I felt an overwhelming relief when there was no picture of him leaving my condo at three in the morning on any website or TV show. Mostly because it meant Brenda wouldn't find out.

I sent a message to Nia about Whitley Schultz, asking if she had any idea how to track her down. It now seemed more important than ever that I discover what Whitley knew.

> Ask Tinsley. I'll bet she has Whitley's address and phone number. She keeps a list of former Lumberjills.

> Do you really think she'll just give it to me? What am I supposed to say? Maybe you should ask her.

Tell her you need Whitley Schultz's address and she'll hand it over. I don't think you know how much power you have now with these sorts of people since you're Evan's fiancée. You're top of the food chain. Tinsley will fall all over herself to help you.

So I texted Tinsley, and just as Nia had predicted, she gave all the info—along with a lot of heart-eyed smiley emojis—to me without question. I texted Nia again.

Got it. I'm going to call Whitley. Wish me luck.

If she's willing to meet up, let me know. I'll come. You may need backup.

I didn't anticipate needing backup in the suburbs, but it would be nice to have Nia there alongside me. I called the number, and Whitley answered. With my heart pounding in my ears, I introduced myself and told her the story that Nia and I had come up with at the tea party—that we were working on a "where are they now" of former Jacks cheerleaders for a possible segment at ISEN.

"I remember Nia. She was always so sweet. And your project sounds like a lot of fun! Yes, please come by. I'm a stay-at-home mom, so I'm usually around."

"Is there any chance you would be able to meet up today?"

"Sure. My son goes down for a nap at one o'clock. Would one thirty work?"

I told her it would, and she gave me her address, which I already had. We said goodbye and hung up, and I texted Nia to let her know about our new game plan. We agreed to meet at Whitley's house since she was about halfway for both of us.

This time I did make an effort with my appearance. Honestly, I didn't want to meet Evan's former girlfriend while looking like warmed-over roadkill.

Nia was already waiting for me when I arrived. She gave me a quick hug. "You ready to do this?"

"I'm ready. Let's go find out the truth about Evan."

We walked up to Whitley's front door together, and I rang the bell. I got a surprise when she opened it, because Whitley could have been my sister. Tall, redheaded, athletic-looking.

I wasn't the only one who noticed. Nia leaned in to whisper, "I just realized that Evan has a type."

"Hey, Nia, how are you? And you must be Ashton. Please come in!"

Whitley led us into a formal living room and asked if we wanted anything to eat or drink. We both said we were fine and sat down.

To keep up the pretense, I asked about her time with the Lumberjills. Her favorite game, best memory, that kind of thing. She was fun and animated. I could begrudgingly see why Evan might have liked her.

Then I moved in for the kill. "And did you quit the team, or were you let go?"

"Oh, they kicked me off," she said with a laugh. "And they said it was because of weight gain, but it was because I'd been dating Evan Dawson. The quarterback?"

I'm familiar with him, thanks. "Right. I'd heard something about that."

"He was a real gentleman. Very kind and thoughtful."

Whitley didn't say anything about me being engaged to Evan. Either she didn't recognize me, or she didn't keep up on sports news. I decided to play dumb.

"A gentleman?" I repeated. Here was the opening I needed. "Okay, just between us girls, you have to tell us. Did you really never sleep together?"

"We did not."

"Really?" This was from Nia.

"I know. Trust me, I get it. He's beyond gorgeous. And it's not like he was overly religious or something. Just committed to his choice. It didn't happen, and then things ended."

"Why didn't it work out?" I asked, hoping I didn't sound overeager.

"He never really opened up to me. We had fun, but I never felt like I knew the real Evan Dawson. There was no . . . I don't know, intimacy between us. Since then I've come to realize that a lot of people mistake physical intimacy for the real thing, but that emotional connection you make, when it's like his soul is communicating with yours, that's what makes a relationship work. It's what I have with my husband, Gabriel. If Evan and I had slept together, it would have just delayed the inevitable. Masked over our other problems, you know?"

"Did you ever think he might be gay? Or asexual?" Nia asked, and I was grateful for it because that angle had completely slipped my mind.

"You'd have to ask him, but I never thought he was secretly gay. And he definitely didn't seem asexual to me. But obviously I can't know for sure. You'd have to ask him."

It suddenly became desperately important to me to know if Evan had liked her for herself or if he'd used her the way he was using me. "Was there a possibility that he dated you to make himself look good? Maybe to impress Chester Walton for contract negotiations?"

She pursed her lips. "No, I never felt that way. I genuinely liked him, and he liked me."

Nia asked Whitley about a mutual acquaintance, and while they chatted, I processed the information I'd just been given. I had honestly hoped that this conversation would go in a completely different direction. That Whitley would tell us that of course they'd slept together and that Evan was a huge lying liar who constantly lied out of his lying mouth, even if I logically knew nothing would be that easy. What if she had ulterior motives? Maybe she didn't want her husband to know? Because any man would question himself if that's who he had to compare himself to.

You're reaching.

I was taking things to really far-out conclusions. I had thought I'd be more open-minded than I was currently being. Even if Whitley was covering for Evan, it didn't matter. This ruled her out as someone who would go on our show and say she'd hooked up with him.

The conversation lasted for another fifteen minutes or so, until Whitley's little boy started to cry upstairs. "I need to feed and change him." She stood and walked us to the front door. "Nia, it was fantastic to see you again, and, Ashton, so nice to meet you."

We thanked her, said our goodbyes, and walked back to our cars.

"Do you know how jealous you looked in there?" Nia asked.

"Take it back," I told her. I wasn't jealous. At all. Even a little. I was totally fine. And I had not been comparing my every flaw against Whitley's every perfection the entire conversation.

"I'm sorry for saying you're jealous just because you are." Nia paused and winced, holding on to her stomach.

"Are you sick?" I asked.

"Nope. Just a little pregnant."

"Nia!" I hugged her tightly. I could see how happy she was, and I was thrilled for her. "That is so fantastic!"

"Thanks. We've been trying for a really long time, and we haven't really told people yet because we don't want to jinx it."

She got teary-eyed, and I decided to cheer her up. "Better you than me. Whenever I see a cute baby, I always think, 'Man, I really love sleeping through the night.'"

It worked, and Nia laughed, clearing up her hormonal tears. It had been my best tactic with Aubrey during her pregnancies, too.

Speaking of the task-driving devil, I had a text on my phone from my sister.

> When are you coming over to finish up your reunion list?

I didn't have many more phone calls to make, and I replied that I'd be by that night. "My sister needs me," I explained to Nia. "I need to take off. But seriously, congratulations. That is really, really exciting."

We hugged and then each drove off in our cars. When I came to my first stoplight, I found myself wondering what it would be like to be pregnant. To have a baby of my own.

Why was I picturing that baby with Evan's blue eyes?

While I was working at Aubrey's, Evan texted me.

> What are you up to?

> Whatever my evil sister forces me to do for your stupid reunion.

> Ha. I already finished my list.

> Yes, you're amazing and us lesser mortals are happy just to bask in your glory.

As long as everyone knows it. I was going to ask if you wanted to meet up and play Madden so that I could have my rematch.

Can't. But, when you play that game, do you play as yourself?

Obviously. And I always win.

You are the definition of vain.

It's not vanity if it's true. Are you smiling right now?

I was, but he didn't need to know that.

As if.

I'm still counting it. And I guess I'll see you tomorrow. I'm looking forward to it.

Strangely enough, so was I.

The next day I had to be at the children's hospital at nine o'clock in order to "escort" Evan. Which I didn't understand. I was pretty sure he could figure out the layout of a hospital map just as easily as I could.

When I got out of my car in the hospital parking lot, I realized I had severely underestimated how big of a deal this was. As a family, we typically only participated in the administrative side of the Jumping Jacks charity. There was a total media circus happening in the front of the hospital. There were news vans from every station, including one from ISEN, lining the streets. Tons of people, along with security to keep the fans away from the Jacks. Evan was already there, signing autographs and taking selfies with everyone who asked.

A small stage had been set up, along with a podium and microphone. Someone from the Jumping Jacks organization was speaking, and I made my way through the crowd, trying to get close. Tinsley saw me and waved me over, telling the guard to let me pass by.

I didn't want to interrupt Evan, so I hung back.

And may or may not have admired the view.

The speaker said, "You've heard more than enough from me. Let's get Evan 'Awesome' Dawson up here to answer some of your questions. Evan?"

Evan handed the Sharpie pen he'd been using to one of the security guards and then paused when he saw me. I waved, and he held out his hand. Without thinking I walked over and joined our fingers together. My pulse skittered and jumped when our skin touched.

He leaned in and said in my ear, "This is one of those give-them-what-they-want-so-they-leave-us-alone situations."

I nodded and followed him up to the stage. The cameras and lights were overwhelming. Evan tucked me against him, holding on tight. The whole right side of my body felt like it was on fire, pulsing in time to my quick heartbeat. Like I was going to be the lead story on the six o'clock news because of the impending spontaneous combustion.

"How is everyone?" Evan asked into the microphone. "I hear you have some questions for me."

The media in front of us erupted, and Evan had to point to specific reporters so they'd speak one at a time.

"How did you and your fiancée meet?"

"We were friends in high school, and we reconnected at a party a few months ago." The lie fell easily out of his mouth, which was more than a little disconcerting.

"How did you know she was the one?"

Evan turned to look at me and smiled. "It's hard to explain. At first I didn't know, but I couldn't stop thinking about her. And the more time we spent together, the more I realized that there was nobody else on earth I wanted to hang out with more than this woman. That I was falling in love with her. In love with who she was and who she is now. She's amazing. Smart, funny, beautiful, talented, and caring."

My heart beat so hard there was a rushing sound in my ears. Lies, right? Total lies? I knew they were lies, but he sounded so honest when he said them. How was I ever supposed to trust anything he ever said to me or about me?

"And she deflates my ego every chance she gets," Evan added, leading to chuckles and some laughter from the group.

"Let's see the ring!"

I held up my left hand, close to my face. Was I supposed to say something?

All thoughts of how I should be performing in this moment went out the window with the next question.

"Evan! Are you still waiting for marriage?"

"Of course," Evan answered immediately, and it shushed the entire press corps, which made him laugh. "You guys weren't expecting that answer, were you? I made a promise to someone important a long time ago, and I aim to keep that promise."

"Do you feel like you struggle with your choice at all? Especially now that you're engaged?"

Evan's blue eyes burned into mine. "Definitely."

My knees went hollow at his expression and his low, rough voice, and I was very glad he was holding on to me so that I didn't collapse.

"How about a kiss for the camera?" A few other reporters cheered the request.

My mouth went completely dry, my heart pounding in my throat.

Evan turned so we faced each other. He leaned in to whisper in my ear, "Is it okay if I kiss you?"

Yes, yes, a thousand times YES! "You probably should. We have to sell it, right?" Did I sound nonchalant? I desperately wanted to sound nonchalant.

He put both of his hands around my waist, pulling me in close, holding me in place as if he was afraid I'd run off. "You won't think less of me?"

"That would be impossible."

He laughed, and I could still feel the laugh on his lips as they pressed against mine. Stars exploded behind my eyelids at his first sweet, tentative touch. This was not how my thirteen-year-old self had pictured my first kiss with Evan. That had involved riding on a unicorn under a rainbow while being serenaded by a boy band.

He pulled back slightly, as if he'd intended to only give me a quick peck, but I could see in his smoldering eyes that something had changed his mind. I didn't know whether it was the way my body shuddered against him, or the whimpering sound I made, or just the feel of the fiery chemistry that exploded between us in that one brief moment, but our kiss wasn't over yet.

Evan shifted his arms, wrapping them around me completely, as if he meant to shield me from everything surrounding us. My arms wound around his neck, needing his strength to stay vertical. My heart sputtered to a stop and then quickly restarted as his lips came back down on mine.

And this, a real kiss from Evan Dawson, was so much better than anything I'd envisioned when I was thirteen. It still felt like a combination of unicorns, rainbows, and boy bands but in a completely mature and awesome way.

There was some hesitancy at first, like he was worried I might stop him. How could I when all the tension fled my muscles, turning me pliant and more than willing? And even when he grew more confident, given my enthusiastic response, he kept the kiss sweet. Tender. Gentle.

And altogether too short.

Heat flooded through me. It felt like slipping into a deliciously hot bath at the end of a long hard day—my bones melted, and my entire being sighed as the warmth of his kiss infused every cell of my body with longing for more. A lot more.

He ended the kiss, and I had to fight not to whimper in protest. My lips were still parted, my eyes slightly out of focus. It took me a second to get back to reality. He leaned forward and planted a teasing kiss on the tip of my nose. "I've wanted to do that since the night of Tinsley and Jamie's party."

What? Kiss my nose? Or was he referring to the much better kissing that had just taken place?

The press cheered for us, causing a blush so deep that I could literally feel my cheeks burning. At first the sound startled me, as Evan had made the outside world disappear in those brief moments. I had forgotten there was a crowd of people recording and photographing us. Their applause made me feel a little like a trained seal, performing just for the prize at the end.

Though if the prize was more kisses from Evan, I might consider it.

He took me by the hand and gently pointed me toward the exit. I walked away while Evan said into the microphone, "As you can see, I'm a very lucky man."

I only barely registered the laughter behind me. Nia met me as I went offstage, and she wore a superior-looking smile.

"That was such a great kiss. That boy has a huge grin on his face."

"I'm glad two-thirds of us enjoyed it," I muttered, still unable to process all the overwhelming sensory input that had just happened.

"You are a liar. You enjoyed every second of that."

"Okay. I did. A little." A crap ton, actually.

And despite the fact that I still hadn't figured out what Evan and I actually were to each other, whether I could trust him and believe in him, I knew one thing.

Despite my blustery objections, I definitely wanted to kiss him again.

CHAPTER SIXTEEN

By the time Evan had finished with the press, I had regained control of my mind and body. Mostly. Things got a little hazy when he first approached me, but I redirected my thoughts to the business at hand—visiting sick children.

I spent hours watching him with those kids. All those little bald heads just about broke my heart. Evan paid special attention to each one, even the kids who had no idea who he was. I would hand him a gift bag for each child, and he not only autographed each piece of Jacks swag but also made sure to find out the kid's name to personalize it.

Several times throughout the day I caught him smiling at me, like this was something we were sharing together. He seemed to be genuinely enjoying himself. Again, I found myself wanting to believe in this version of Evan. Given the stats on NFL players, some of the men in this room were guilty of domestic violence. Of anger management issues. Or were alcoholics. Just because they put on a great face in public didn't mean they didn't have major issues in their personal lives.

I thought of Aubrey's words—that no one could keep an act up for that long. Was that true?

Evan tried to include me in what he was doing. I attempted to tell him that nobody here wanted to meet me, but he kept introducing me. That burning, sinking guilty feeling returned each time he used the word *fiancée*.

We shook a lot of hands and gave a lot of hugs. I knew the board would be pleased with how much attention and media coverage the charity received today. It would enable them to solicit more funds and help more kids.

When we were finished, Evan turned to me and said, "Dinner? My treat."

I opened my mouth, and no words came out. I didn't know what to say. I felt like I needed a break from Evan. How was I supposed to judge my perceptions and feelings when he seemed to always be around, scrambling everything up?

My nonresponse earned me a small frown, which quickly disappeared. "Or I can just see you for Thanksgiving at your parents' house. You look like you need some 'me' time."

"Yes," I said gratefully. "I'll see you tomorrow. Eleven o'clock."

"I'll be there."

He looked at me like he wanted to say something more but held it back. I thought he might kiss me goodbye. Or hug me. But instead, he just raised one hand and walked back toward the hospital.

I didn't know whether to feel relieved or disappointed.

As I made my way to the parking lot, I wondered: Was my problem that he was always around, or did it just seem that way because I couldn't stop thinking about him?

On Wednesday morning I got up early and laid my clothes and shoes for Thanksgiving out on my bed. My mom liked us to dress up.

My plan was to drive over to a nearby high school track and do a few miles. Maybe running would give me some clarity for my current situation.

Part of the problem was that although Evan talked a good game about us and his supposed feelings for me, other than that one night at dinner, he hadn't really let me know what he wanted out of this . . . whatever it was. Only a friendship? Just because he'd said I was hot didn't mean he wanted to be serious with me. Did he want something more? And had that all changed when we'd been forced into this situation?

Maybe I should ask him today. Find a clever way to work it into the conversation so that it would seem like no big deal, and I didn't care one way or the other if he was interested.

But if he was . . . was I? Did I want to date him? Being combustibly attracted to him wasn't enough to sustain a relationship.

In the middle of my running and pondering, my phone beeped with a text. It was from Brenda. I came to a stop to read it.

> You need to come into the office ASAP.

> On my way.

I glanced at my phone's clock. I didn't have enough time to go home and shower and get changed. Every minute I delayed would be a minute that Brenda would get madder. I thought about reminding her that I had the day off, but lots of people would be working at ISEN all throughout the holidays, given the high number of sporting events that needed to be covered.

If she was demanding that I come in, she was going to have to take me as I was. Thankfully I wasn't too gross because I hadn't been trying to break a sweat. Just to clear my head.

On my way over I decided it was a good thing Brenda had called me in. I was having so many doubts about this whole situation that I was considering putting a stop to it all. There had to be a way to back out gracefully and still be able to get a full-time job with the station come January.

When I got up to the intern floor, it was dark. I went into Brenda's office, and she had her lights off as well. She was facing away from her desk, toward one of the TV screens in her office.

It was totally creepy and intimidating.

"Have a seat, Ashton."

Her voice sounded ominous, and my heart beat double time as I sat down.

She used a remote to turn on her TV. She had a clip of Evan and me from the previous day's press conference, paused at the moment just before Evan kissed me.

"Do you see this?" she asked, pointing with her remote. "Do you see that pathetic, sappy look on your face? I can actually tell the moment when he won you over. When you started to fall for that American pie, Fourth of July, football fantasy that Evan Dawson sells."

I started breathing hard, anxiety overwhelming me. I didn't do well when people in authority spoke to me this way.

"Watch this." She pressed PLAY. "It is so obvious that the two of you hadn't ever kissed before that moment. It was actually painful to watch. Look at how staged it is! Like somebody had to coach you through it beforehand."

Even though she was berating me and making snide comments, the kiss wasn't painful. It was . . . amazing. And watching it made me feel all over again everything I'd felt when it was happening.

Maybe it was sad that a pretend kiss was easily one of the best kisses of my entire life, but I didn't think it looked staged or fake.

And I hated that she was trying to ruin this for me.

"What if Evan's telling the truth? What if he is just a nice guy?"

"What if he is just a nice guy?" she mimicked me in a mocking, nasally tone. "Really? You're being suckered into this? I thought you knew better. I thought you had some revenge you needed to inflict. If

I'd assigned Rand to this story, he wouldn't be all moony-eyed over Evan Dawson. You're one of only two female interns in this office. Do you know how much harder we have to fight? How much more is expected of us?"

I was responsible for the perception of women for the entire company? That didn't seem fair, but I was way too freaked out to say as much.

Brenda was on a roll. "Do you know why I hired you? Because you reminded me of myself. Strong, ambitious, driven. Willing to do whatever it took to rise to the top."

Getting told off like this tended to make me shut down, which was what was happening right now. I kept trying to regulate my breathing, but it wasn't working.

She stood up and turned off the TV, plunging the room into darkness. She flipped a light switch, and I blinked, blinded by the sudden brightness.

"Evan Dawson is using you," she said. "For his contract renegotiation. So he's going to say whatever he has to say and do whatever he has to do to get you on his side. To play along until he doesn't need you anymore, and then he'll dump you."

Brenda moved to the corner of her desk, positioning herself on the edge while she stared down at me. "Are you really that girl? The one who is this close to having the career she's always wanted, but you're just going to give it all up and walk away for some guy? Choosing a relationship over a job? With a guy you can't even trust? Have some self-respect, Ashton."

I nodded, blinking back the anxious and angry tears that were making my vision watery. I would not cry, because Brenda would never let me live it down.

"Go home and think about what kind of employee you want to be. What choices you want to make. Your job is very much on the line here. I expect for you to have the information I want soon. A top reporter would have had this story to me days ago. This is your chance to impress me, and I have a roomful of interns dying to do just that. You need to decide if you're going to deliver on the potential I see in you or accept that there's only room at ISEN for reporters who can deliver."

I heard the dismissal in her voice and quickly stood, then made my way out of her office and to the elevators. I felt nauseous, and my limbs were shaky and cold. I had to get out of the building. When the doors slid open and I stepped into the thankfully empty elevator car, I finally allowed myself to sob all the way down to the lobby.

I'd been wrong. There wasn't going to be a way to get out of this Evan story and keep my job. I'd be held up in my family as the Poor Example of a Daughter, who had failed to take her parents' advice and now wouldn't be able to afford to live. I would have to start all over at a different branch of ISEN or with a different network. Which meant I'd be living at home since I didn't have the money to fund another internship. And then I'd have to get a second job just to pay my expenses.

I walked out to my car and stumbled to a halt when I realized the front driver's side tire had gone flat.

And I already had my spare tire on one of the rear wheels.

"Could this day get any worse?"

Although the tears were blinding my vision, I picked up my phone and dialed.

"Hey, Ashton, what are you up to?"

"Evan? I need your help."

He must have heard something in my voice because he went from fun and flirty to totally serious. "Are you okay?"

"I'm . . . stranded. I was out running, and I had to stop by my office, and now I have a flat tire, and I don't have a spare, and everything is just terrible." My throat felt thick as I tried to hold back my tears.

"Whatever you need, I'm there. Tell me where you are."

It was why I had called him. Somehow I'd known he'd show up, no questions asked. I gave him the address. "There's something else. I'm going to have to call a tow truck and wait for them. Which means I'll be late to Thanksgiving, and that means I'll get attitude from my mother. Can you go by my condo and get my change of clothes and shoes that I left on my bed and then come and pick me up?"

"Absolutely. How am I going to get into your condo?"

"The front door is unlocked." It was a bad habit of mine. My roommates in college had constantly yelled at me about it.

He paused for so long that I thought the call had dropped. "Ashton, why would you leave your front door unlocked? You live in the city. Do you know how dangerous that is?"

"Yes, I'm obviously too stupid to live and will get murdered in my sleep."

"Just . . . it'll be okay. We'll talk about it later. When you will promise me to never leave your front door unlocked again. I'll be there soon. Everything's going to be all right."

And when he said it, I believed it. We hung up, and I called the tow truck company, which arrived much faster than I'd anticipated. I had them take my car to the mechanic I usually went to, and then I called the mechanic to let them know what I needed. They promised to have the car back to me on Monday, given that it was almost the holiday weekend.

I left the parking garage and went to wait on the street for Evan to arrive. It occurred to me that when I was upset and needed help, I hadn't even hesitated. Evan had been the first person I called. Not my parents, not my sisters.

Evan.

While I mulled over what that meant, he arrived in a big black SUV, darting across two lanes of traffic to pull up to the curb. He rolled down the window and pointed to my clothes in the back seat. "Do you want to go inside and get changed?"

I absolutely did not want to go inside and get changed. I didn't want to be where Brenda was. "Holiday traffic getting out of the city is going to be awful. We need to get on the road. I'll just change in the back seat."

I opened the rear passenger side door, and an empty bottle of the Gatorade flavor that Evan endorsed fell out. The flavor was called, of course, Awesome Dawson. It was purple, and I'd always thought it tasted like douchebag and lies. The entire back seat was a complete mess. I had to move a bunch more empty bottles to get in. "It's like a Gatorade graveyard back here."

He pulled back into traffic, driving a bit faster than what most people would consider, you know, legal. "The psychologist said to let something be messy in my life."

"So you chose your back seat?"

"I'm working on letting go."

If only he knew what a mess my boss was trying to make of his personal and professional life, he wouldn't worry about the back seat.

I considered telling him, but now was not the time. "In case you didn't know, your flavor is truly terrible," I said, holding up one of the empty bottles before I dropped it.

"It's an acquired taste. Like me." His eyes met mine in the rearview mirror for a moment before he concentrated on the road again. "Hey, are you sure you want to get changed back there? I could pull over somewhere. Or you could wait and change at your mom's house when we get there."

"Just trust me, it is not worth the grief my mother will give me if I show up in workout clothes." I took the sweater and skirt off their hangers. I suddenly realized that I'd forgotten to have Evan grab me a bra and underwear. Not that I wanted him pawing through my personal things, and it was too late now. I'd be in a sports bra and underwear that I could floss my teeth with. I desperately needed to do laundry. Other women wore their nicest/sexiest underwear first. I was the opposite. After I'd cleaned my clothes, I wore my most comfortable underwear first, and then I wore the stuff that would make my mother blush if I had nothing else left.

And I did not want to flash any of that at Evan.

"I can change back here," I told him. "As long as you keep your eyes pointed that direction." I had changed in the girls' locker room in seventh grade and had been a master of staying mostly covered up while switching between outfits. This was no different.

I pulled my arms out of my tight mesh shirt, leaving it hanging over my chest while I slipped the sweater on. When I popped my head through the top, I caught a glimpse of Evan's gaze in the mirror again.

"Eyes forward!" I told him. Not that there'd been anything to see, but the idea that he couldn't help but look was . . . interesting. And a little bit thrilling.

"Sorry." He didn't sound sorry.

"That doesn't seem very virginal of you," I said as I put my arms through the sweater sleeves and pulled the extra shirt out through the top.

"I'm celibate, not a saint."

I slid my skirt up over my running pants, turning it around so I could do the back button. When that was finished, I yanked my pants off and left them in the back seat. Then I climbed into the front seat next to Evan.

I glanced at him, and he looked, as always, ridiculously handsome. He'd swept his hair up and away from his face, had shaved, and was wearing a light-blue button-down with a darker blue tie and a navy sweater. He cleaned up very, very nicely.

Meanwhile, I looked like I'd just been running. I pulled down the visor and checked my reflection in the mirror. I'd need to do something with my hair when I got to my mom's house, but I didn't currently have a brush. My eyes still looked bloodshot. You could tell I'd been crying. Hopefully Mom had some eye drops, too. I flipped the visor back up and then put on my seat belt.

Once I was settled, he asked, "Do you want to talk about it?"

Brenda's face filled my mind, her sneering taunts and harsh judgments. In the few minutes I'd been with him, I'd forgotten. But instead of saying no, I said, "Not yet."

"Okay. But I'm here if you want to." He took my hand, and a nervous tingle ran up the length of my arm when he squeezed. He let go to turn on his satellite radio. It was set to KPRD, our local sports channel. I wondered if they were hiring.

Because I could be out of a job very soon. Brenda's words echoed in my head like they'd been seared into my brain: "Are you really that girl? Choosing a relationship over a job?"

Maybe Aubrey was right. Maybe there were things more important than money and a job.

Evan took my hand again, comforting me without saying anything.

Of course I didn't want to be that girl.

But I also didn't want to be the girl who missed out on her chance at something that might be pretty wonderful.

I didn't want to be the girl who misjudged Evan and punished him for something he hadn't done.

CHAPTER SEVENTEEN

When we arrived at my parents' house, I asked him to wait a minute before he came inside. Whether that was to give him a chance to prepare or to give my family a second to get ready, I wasn't sure. I let myself in the front door, and everybody pounced on me at the same time. Like they'd all been standing in the foyer, waiting on us.

"Where's Evan?"

"Did you not bring him?"

"I'm going to run upstairs for a second," I told them. "Can you please act like humans today and not embarrass me?"

My mom turned to the others and said, "You heard her. Today we are pleasant and totally normal."

"What's *normal* mean, Grandma?" Charlotte asked.

Good question. My life hadn't felt "normal" in a long time. I went into my parents' master bathroom and brushed my hair. The brushing motion was soothing. Maybe I'd asked Evan to wait not for anybody else's sake but for mine. To prepare for my two worlds to collide, hard. Like a dinosaur-killing asteroid smacking into Earth.

I redid my ponytail quickly and flew back down the stairs just as Evan rang the doorbell. I opened it to see him standing on the porch, holding a large bouquet of flowers and a paper grocery bag.

"I'm sorry in advance," I told him in a low voice as he came inside. He kissed me on the cheek, and I wondered if it was for show.

"Mr. Bailey, Mrs. Bailey, thank you for having me over. This is for you." He handed my mother the flowers and the bag.

"Oh, thank you, Evan. You always were such a thoughtful boy. Brian, will you put these in water?"

My dad took the flowers and held out his hand to shake Evan's. "So. You're the Evan Dawson."

"It's just Evan, sir. I usually leave out 'the.'"

My dad laughed as they shook hands. "Pleasure having you here, son." Only he didn't move to get water for the flowers. He just stood there, grinning at Evan.

"Hi, Satan," Charlotte said, tugging on Evan's hand. Charlotte had always been adept at figuring out words to make adults uncomfortable, and she said them as often as possible.

"Pretty soon that will be Uncle Satan to you, kiddo," Rory said, waving at Evan.

And we all stood in the foyer, staring at one another.

Evan cleared his throat. "How is everyone?"

"Pleasant and totally normal," Rory responded, her eyes dancing. She was enjoying herself. Much like her niece, she was also a fan of mischief.

Finally, realizing how uncomfortable the atmosphere had become, my mother started handing out marching orders. She told Rory to take Charlotte and Joey into the other room, reminded my dad to get water for the flowers, and asked Aubrey and Justin to start setting the table.

"Are they always like that?" Evan asked me in a whisper, his words tickling the outside of my ear.

I tried to ignore the shivers that skated across my skin. "No. Sometimes they're weird."

He grinned at me, and I couldn't help but smile back.

"Ice cream?" my mother asked as she reached into the bag Evan had given her.

"It may have started to melt a little. But there are multiple flavors with everything that goes on top. I hope you don't mind, but on Thanksgiving my family always had ice cream sundaes for dessert."

For some reason that made my eyes well up, and I noticed it had the same effect on my mother. "That's very sweet. We would love to honor your family's tradition. Ashton, would you come help me put these away? Evan, would you mind giving Rory a hand?"

I offered an apologetic smile to Evan before following my mother. My dad filled a vase as quickly as possible, not even bothering to cut off the cellophane wrapping before sticking the flowers in. He rushed out, presumably to rejoin Evan and resume his hero worship.

The kitchen smelled amazing, roasted turkey and pumpkin and sweet potatoes with marshmallows all filling the air. Delicious scents that always made me think of home.

I wondered what my mother was up to as she unloaded the bag. She didn't need my help to stick ice cream in the freezer. Was this about to turn into a Guantanamo-level interrogation, or were we going to board the SS *Guilt Trip*?

Turned out to be neither.

"You know, I'd forgotten that Evan's an orphan. You two will be here for every holiday. That's every mother's dream." Her face was bright and happy at this revelation. She was disturbingly and uncharacteristically giddy. It was disconcerting.

"What? To get an orphaned in-law? You are certifiable," I said, taking out the toppings, which included hot fudge, caramel, and sprinkles, and placing them in our pantry. There was no countertop space, as the mess for Thanksgiving covered every square inch. "I mean, I love you, but that's crazy."

Usually when I threw around words like *crazy* or *certifiable*, my mom would launch into a long explanation of why I shouldn't use those kinds of terms because they were hurtful and not clinically quantifiable. Not today. "You'll understand someday when your children start to get married."

"You're not going to, like, kill Justin's parents, are you? Because now I'm going to have to testify against you so I won't be prosecuted as an accomplice."

"Who's going to kill Justin's parents?" Aubrey asked as she entered the kitchen.

"Mom. So she can be the only grandma."

My mother rolled her eyes until Aubrey said, "Justin's using the wrong silverware, and he won't listen to me."

That caused our mom to practically sprint into the formal dining room. She liked the table to be perfect for the holiday. Everything had to be as Norman Rockwell as possible.

"So I caught your little burlesque show yesterday."

"What?" I asked as I looked in the fridge for a spot to put the whipped cream.

"The video? Of you and Evan kissing?"

"Oh." I was glad I was standing in front of the refrigerator so it could cool off my cheeks. I took out the vegetable tray and set it on the counter to make some room. "That kiss was just for the reporters."

"Okay." She said it with a tone that made it clear she didn't believe me.

"What's that supposed to mean?"

Aubrey grabbed a carrot from the tray and dipped it in some ranch dressing. "You used to be in love with Evan Dawson, and I don't think it would take much to get you back to that point. If you're not already."

What was that I'd been saying about being crazy and certifiable? The delusional apple didn't fall far from the lunatic tree. "I don't . . . I didn't love him. I had a crush on him."

She popped the carrot in her mouth. "That's not how I remember it."

It didn't really matter how Aubrey remembered it. "I wasn't capable of loving him at thirteen."

"Juliet was thirteen in *Romeo and Juliet*."

"Clearly she's not my role model and shouldn't be a role model for any teen girl."

"But she was the same age as you and fell madly in love. Evan was your first love. And you never forget your first love."

Now she was just talking nonsense. "Of course I can't forget him. He's sitting in the family room playing with your children. And speaking of forgetting, you said you wouldn't interfere with my love life."

Aubrey had moved on to the celery. "That doesn't sound like me at all. Did you get it in writing?"

"Stupid lawyers," I muttered. "No wonder Hamlet said to kill you all."

"That wasn't Hamlet. It was Dick the Butcher."

"How do you even remember—never mind. The point is . . ." I let my voice trail off as I opened the dishwasher. Someone should get this thing running before we sat down to eat and made a bunch more dirty dishes. Like Evan said, if somebody else had done the cooking, the least I could do was some of the cleaning.

It also gave my hands something to do while I worked through my Evan thought process. "I don't know what I think about Evan and what's happening with us."

"Explain."

"There are so many possibilities with him. One, he is who he says he is. He's genuine and a nice guy."

"That's my choice."

I paused with some silverware in my hand. "You haven't even heard the other ones yet."

Aubrey sat down on one of the barstools, still going to town on the veggies. "Tell me the others."

"Two, he's trying to ease a guilty conscience for how he treated me ten years ago."

Justin wandered into the kitchen, presumably having been chased out of the dining room for not setting the table right. "Who's trying to ease a guilty conscience?" he asked.

"Evan," Aubrey said. "Ashton thinks he feels bad about what happened in high school."

He looked confused. "You think he's hanging out with you now for something that happened ten years ago? As a man, allow me to tell you that guys don't do that. Unless they're in rehab, they're not worried about making amends. We're very good at compartmentalizing and moving on."

"Yeah. What Justin said."

"I don't need you both ganging up on me. Don't you two have some cooking or ballroom dance class to sign up for and never go to?"

Charlotte shrieked from the other room, and Justin said, "I'll check on her." Then he gave Aubrey a sweet but lingering kiss that made me feel like I was missing out on something by not being in a relationship.

"Ugh. Get a room," I told her after he'd left.

"Maybe later," she said with a twinkle in her eye. "But back to your list of why Evan's doing what he's doing."

"Three, and I know there's truth to this one because he said as much, he's using me and this engagement to keep his boss happy while he renegotiates his contract."

"You're using him, too, so that one balances out even if it is true."

I shot her a dirty look while I put a bunch of plates on the bottom rack. "Thanks for the reminder." Like I'd been unable to forget that fact at all recently.

"What about option four?" Aubrey asked. "The one where he is a nice guy, he actually likes you, and he's taking advantage of his contract situation as an excuse to spend time with you. A guy who's using you would not subject himself to all this," she said, gesturing around the room.

"Do you even hear how crazy that sounds?" As if Evan was pretending to be engaged to me because he liked me. Why was my heart fluttering so hard in my chest? Like a hummingbird wanting to break free from a cage?

Because I want her to be right.

Aubrey frowned. "Why do you have to overanalyze everything?"

"Because that's how my brain works," I said. "It is literally what I want to do for a job someday. Watch and analyze and give everybody the play-by-play."

"No wonder Mom and Dad tried to stop you. It's super annoying."

I started the dishwasher up, then dried my hands on a towel. "I don't know why you're so interested in Evan and me. You don't get a trophy for setting people up. Just in case you weren't aware."

"What I would get is the chance to see my little sister happy, and that would make me happy."

I still thought Aubrey was wrong with her earlier assertion. That I used to love Evan. He had definitely been like a religion to me, but I hadn't been capable of love at that age. Had I cared about him? Had we been friends? Yes. But love?

"Even if what you're saying is true, and I used to have some kind of feelings for him, that doesn't really matter now. I don't know that I can go there with him. I can't care about him like that again and get my heart ripped out. I wouldn't be able to take it."

I hadn't realized I felt that way until I said it. And I would most definitely end up heartbroken if we dated and he found out about Brenda and the story.

I'd already fallen hard for the guy once. I didn't need it to happen again.

"Well, I've already told you this before, but I think it bears repeating. Stop trying to be logical and rational about everything, and listen to that oxygenated blood in your heart."

The last time I listened to my heart where Evan was concerned, it got ripped to shreds. "The oxygenated blood just wants more iron."

"Maybe I should talk to him," she mused aloud.

"Don't Evan think about it," I said.

Both of her eyebrows lifted in delight. "Do you hear yourself? You just said, 'Don't Evan think about it.'"

Had I? "I did not. I said, 'Don't even think about it.' That you can't hear is on you."

My mother returned to the kitchen and started handing us food to carry out to the dining room. I hoped I was done with the sisterly interference for the day. When I put the mashed potatoes on the table, I glanced up to see Evan sitting with Charlotte at the tea party table my parents kept at their house specifically for her. His knees were practically in his face as he accepted a cup and saucer from her.

I put my hand over my chest because the sight of them together was doing funny and inexplicable things to my heart.

"Ashton!"

I hurried back to the kitchen to grab more food, and before long my mother was calling everyone over to eat.

The twisty heart palpitations got worse when Evan came in, holding Charlotte's hand.

"Everything looks wonderful, Mrs. Bailey."

"Thank you. And please, we're just Brian and Stacy."

The one saving grace was that she hadn't invited him to call them Mom and Dad. Although I was sure that was coming at some point.

Our seats had been labeled with name cards, and my mom had put Evan on my left, right next to my dad at the head of the table. Rory was on the other side of me with Aubrey's family across from us. I went to sit down, and Evan was there, helping to pull out my chair for me.

Aubrey elbowed Justin and said, "Why don't you do that?"

I thanked him as I scooted back in, not missing the knowing glances between the women of my family.

My father said grace, and then everyone started serving themselves.

"So, how long have you two been married, Brian?" Evan asked.

Dad patted his stomach. "I'd say for about forty or forty-five pounds."

That made Evan laugh, but he was the only one. It was not the first time we'd heard that joke.

"They've been married for almost thirty years," I told him. "They're actually going on a Disney cruise with Aubrey's family in a couple of weeks to celebrate their anniversary."

"I'm going to see the real Alice!" Charlotte announced, standing up in her chair. Aubrey got her to sit back down, telling her to stay put and eat.

"I'd rather talk about last week's game, if you don't mind," my dad said. "That final run of yours at the end, that was amazing!"

As the two men started talking football, I felt Rory nudge me.

My hope that the sisterly interference portion of the evening was over had been misplaced.

"Did you see your fiancé in there with Charlotte and her *Alice in Wonderland* tea set?"

When my heart had melted into a million tiny puddles? "Yes. It was very cute."

Rory let out a slight gasp. "Is the world ending? You just called Evan Dawson cute, and I'm pretty sure that's one of the signs of the apocalypse."

"Oh, ha."

I took the green bean casserole from her and turned to offer it to Evan. He smiled as he accepted it, brushing my fingers with his, and I nearly dropped the whole bowl due to the electric shock of his touch.

Rory, who never missed anything, saw it but thankfully said nothing about it. "So, what did you two crazy kids *not* do last night? Aubrey sent me the clip. Talk about steam."

"I didn't see him last night."

She picked up her napkin and wiped some gravy off her lip. "I don't know how you keep your hands off him. When he walked in tonight, I was all 'Mother, may I?'"

"Gross. Don't bring Mom into this." I glanced up at the woman in question, and she was busy helping Joey cut his turkey into smaller bites.

"Aubrey also told me he doesn't take any of your crap. Which is good. For you to have someone who stands up to you. What was the name of that last idiot you dated? Brett? Anyway, he let you walk over him, and you didn't respect him."

"Thanks for the random observation." Which may or may not have been true, in regard to both Evan and Brett.

"Here's another one. Thanks for bringing Evan tonight. You've seriously taken the heat off me this year. Mom hasn't asked me a single question about my love life, and I had so many great responses prepared, but I'm happy to not have to talk about it."

"Like what?"

"That I'm not single but in a long-distance relationship with my boyfriend, who lives in the future."

"It might confuse her for a minute, but she'd regroup."

"Last month she asked me if there were any 'hot singles' at my gym. I figured if she went there again, I'd tell her the only hot singles in my life are made by Kraft and go on bread."

Hearing my mother use a phrase like "hot singles" would be a permanent mood killer. Having been there myself, I felt bad for Rory.

I heard Evan saying my name, and he placed his hand on my knee. Which made me buck my legs straight up, ramming my knees into the edge of the table. Hard.

Glasses wobbled, silverware rattled. Everyone stared.

"Sorry," I mumbled.

I didn't need to worry about my family embarrassing me. I was doing an excellent job of it all by myself.

CHAPTER EIGHTEEN

Thanksgiving ended up going much more smoothly after that incident. There was the slight issue of me being left-handed, and I kept bumping into Evan while I ate, but even that I got accustomed to.

After everyone had their fill, we all sat around the table and talked. Whatever initial awkwardness had existed when Evan first arrived seemed to disappear. He chatted and joked with my family like he'd been a part of it for years.

He fit like he was a jigsaw piece sliding into the right spot.

And I didn't know how to cope with that.

Then he took off his sweater, which was understandable as the room was getting a little warm. I'd assumed it was Evan causing all the sweltering heat, and it surprised me that he was feeling it, too.

He looked so nice in his shirt that I played with the leftover food on my plate so I wouldn't stare.

My mom announced it was time for dessert, and I volunteered to help her out. Avoidance seemed to be my drug of choice lately. Evan was sitting next to me all handsome and funny, and now that we'd kissed, I found myself reliving it at inopportune times. And it was still difficult to reconcile all of that attraction with my fears about him and a possible relationship between us.

The different kinds of pies—pumpkin, pecan, chocolate silk, and apple—were already sitting on a sideboard in the dining room. I helped my mother with the whipped cream and gathering up all the stuff that Evan had brought over with him. We set his ice cream sundae ingredients next to the pies.

"Do you know what this is missing?" my mom asked.

"Medication for type 2 diabetes?"

"No. We have some maraschino cherries on the top shelf of the cabinet next to the stove. Can you grab them for me?"

"Sure."

I found the cabinet and reached up on tiptoe to see the contents of the shelf.

"Do you need a hand?"

Evan's voice behind me scared me so much that I jumped and yelped. "Don't sneak up on me like that!"

"I'm sorry. But I can reach that top shelf for you."

"So can I," I said, reminding him that I wasn't the kind of woman who needed a stepladder in the kitchen. I couldn't see the cherries, but I felt around for the jar and found it. Triumph. "Aha!"

"Isn't there anything manly I can do to impress you? Vanquish a spider? Take the trash to the curb? Mow the lawn?"

I tried to twist open the top of the jar, but it wasn't budging. "I can do all those things, too, thanks." What I couldn't do was get the cherries open. In the past when I'd had a stubborn jar, I'd just smack the side of the lid against a countertop corner, but I wasn't allowed to do that anymore since my mom had the kitchen remodeled.

"Now do you need some help?" I could see he was trying very hard not to smile.

"I'm only doing this for the sake of your delicate male ego," I said, handing it over to him.

He twisted the lid but came up against the same issue I'd been having. He bore down, really putting some of his strength into it.

"And I even loosened it for you." I had to bite my lip so I wouldn't laugh. I was also enjoying the sight of his muscles straining against the fabric of his shirt.

Evan got a determined look on his face, and there was a popping sound as he forced the lid off. Problem was he'd used so much force that it surprised him, and he splashed himself with cherry juice.

He put the jar down and surveyed the damage. "This is one of my favorite shirts. I guess you can't take me anywhere."

"Yep, you're a real menace to society. Come on, let's go up to the laundry room, and I'll get it in the washing machine before the stain sets."

He followed me upstairs, and I suddenly realized the issues with this plan when we got to the very small laundry room. He dominated the space all around us, his presence overwhelming.

And as he took off his shirt, he wasn't quick about it. No, instead, he watched me the whole time as he slowly undid each button. By the time he'd finished, I was breathing so fast I worried I might pass out.

There was no undershirt, just Evan's chest in all its ab-tastic, muscly fantasticness. I hadn't appreciated it nearly enough the first time I'd seen it.

He still had a rainbow collection of bruises on his exposed skin, and without thinking I stepped forward to run my fingers against some of the more prominent ones. I loved the way his body felt, his rock-hard muscles wrapped in soft skin.

Evan flinched, and I went to pull my hands away. He stopped me, keeping them in place.

"Does this hurt?" I asked, worried.

"Nothing hurts right now," he said in that gruff, deep voice that made me forget my own name. He moved a step closer. "Now that you've gotten me out of my clothes, what are you planning to do next?"

He was teasing, but there was a serious undercurrent to his words.

"I . . . I'm not . . . I wasn't . . ."

"Why are you so afraid to get close to me?" he asked as he reached up with his free hand to run his fingers along the side of my face. "Why do you jump every time I touch you?"

Because that kiss yesterday had set my calves on fire? And I hadn't known that was even possible?

"Maybe I don't want to tempt you." I was aiming for light and jokey, but I wasn't pulling it off. Instead, even I could hear the shakiness in my voice and how fast I was breathing.

"Too late."

I don't know what made me suddenly want to be truthful with him, but I did. I averted my gaze. "It's because of how you make me feel when you touch me."

He reached under my chin, forcing my eyes up to meet his. "I feel it, too. So what are we going to do about it?"

Rory walked by us in the hallway, coming to a stop when she saw what we were doing. Her eyes wide, she mouthed, "OMG!" to me. She was holding Charlotte's hand, and the sight of my impressionable niece helped bring me back to my senses. I pulled my hands away and reached for his shirt.

"I'm going to, um, wash this now. In that thing we have for cleaning clothes."

"The washing machine?" he asked, the amusement evident in his voice.

"Yep. That's it. The washing machine." I got the stain remover and soaked the red juice on his shirt with the spray. My mom's machine had one of those little drawers for small loads, and I put Evan's shirt in, along with some laundry detergent.

"Stay here," I told him when the machine started. "I'll see if I can find one of my dad's shirts."

I ran into my parents' room and stopped short when I saw Rory lying on their bed, watching *Alice in Wonderland* with Charlotte. They were both eating pieces of pumpkin pie. Well, Rory was eating. Our niece was totally focused on the movie, and Rory jumped up to talk to me. "Hey, so what's up with you and Ab Lincoln?"

"Nothing. He spilled something, and I'm cleaning it." I went into my parents' master closet and tried to find a shirt that would fit Evan. I settled on one of my dad's Jacks T-shirts. It would probably be too loose on Evan in some places and too tight in others, but I couldn't let him keep walking around the house without a shirt on. I wouldn't want him to be the reason my mother and sister left their husbands.

He was already the reason I couldn't catch my breath or get my heart to stop frantically trying to beat its way out of my chest.

"You know, you've always talked about what an awful jerk Evan is. But today he seems so . . . shirtless. That was Mike with some extra magic."

"Rory, I can't do this with you right now. I am freaking out and barely holding it together." There was a slightly hysterical edge to my voice.

Her eyes narrowed in concern. "Okay. Calm down. You'll be fine. Even if Mom and Dad are oblivious, I can see what's going on with you and Evan. And I don't know why you're pretending to be engaged."

I tried to protest, but she held up her hand.

"I'm not stupid, Ashton. You almost have a heart attack every time he touches you. And I can only imagine how his truly magnificent chest probably just short-circuited your nervous system."

I nodded. "It's a long story, but I guess all you need to know is that we're only friends, and this is all a little overwhelming, and I'm not sure where to go from here or how I'm going to get through this." Yep. Just friends. Apparently the kind of friends who admired each other's perfectly sculpted bodies.

"Friends." Rory drew out the vowels in the word. "Right. I couldn't really tell, given the way you look at, talk to, and touch each other. You don't have to give me the details, but you two are more than just friends."

"Okay." I wasn't in the mood to argue. "I have to get this shirt back to him."

"Such a shame." She sighed, rejoining Charlotte on the bed.

When I got to the doorway, she said, "Hey, Ashton?"

"Yeah?"

"You should remember the most important thing from this movie." She pointed at the TV screen.

"Never trust a headless cat?"

"No. Before Alice got to Wonderland, she had to fall hard down a dark, deep, scary hole. But it was worth it, right?"

It was probably the most profound thing Rory had ever said to me. And then she wrecked it. "And by Wonderland, I mean his body."

"Thanks, I caught your drift."

"Uncle Satan was naked with Aunt Ashton," Charlotte announced, not taking her eyes off the TV screen. Crap. That was going to get repeated in front of other people.

Rory patted her on the back. "That's because your aunt Ashton is a very lucky girl."

I went back to the laundry room and handed Evan the shirt, being careful to avoid getting my retinas scorched by his chest again. "Here."

And my dad's shirt fit just as I'd expected, but unfortunately it didn't diminish Evan's sexiness even a little.

"We should go back downstairs." I took off without seeing if he was planning on following me.

When we got into the family room, Aubrey and Justin were off in a corner arguing. It was one of those intense and scary whispered arguments married couples have right before they kill each other.

"What's going on?" I asked.

"Mom and Dad went to take some pie to the Barris family, and I wanted to go on a walk with Justin, and Rory's already watching Charlotte, and Joey's tired and needs a nap, and I don't want to take him because he'll just whine the whole time." Aubrey's voice rose slightly higher with each word.

"We can watch him," Evan offered behind me.

We? What was this we business?

"Really? That would be great." Aubrey grabbed Justin's hand and hustled him out of the house before I could object or Evan could change his mind.

Joey realized his parents were gone and threw a tantrum worthy of a supremely spoiled reality star who'd just been told an airline couldn't upgrade his seat. I thought his shrieks were going to burst my eardrums.

"I've got this," Evan said. "I think I know what he needs."

"An exorcism?"

Evan got on the floor and started playing with some of Joey's cars, ignoring his fit. Eventually Joey realized that no one was responding to him and started to watch Evan. Then he got up and sat in Evan's lap, and they played cars together.

About fifteen minutes later, Joey nodded off, curled up against Evan.

It was tea-party-with-Charlotte adorable, and my heart lurched again.

"Tomlinson has three kids, and he told me once that this was how to deal with tantrums. Joey just needed the chance to calm down."

I wished that kind of thing would work for me. But I knew if I crawled into Evan's lap, it would probably have the opposite effect. "You're like the toddler whisperer. I would say you should write a book, but you don't need the money."

Evan cocked his head to the side, running his fingers over the top of Joey's hair. "Kids always seemed scary to me because everything about them is so out of control."

"As just witnessed here."

He looked up at me. "Do you ever think you want one of these?"

"My own personal demon spawn?"

"Kids. Babies."

The floor shifted out from underneath me, and I sat down hard on the couch. "You know you have to have sex first for that to happen." I had to retreat into sarcasm. It was my only defense.

He ignored it. "I've been thinking that maybe I'm at a point in my life where I'm ready for all of it. Crazy in-laws, possessed two-year-olds, a cranky wife."

The smile he gave me was full of meaning and promises I wasn't ready to see. I heard the front door open.

"We're back!" my dad called out.

And even though it was my family's home and my nephew was on Evan's lap, I darted out into the backyard.

I headed to the gazebo my dad had built my mom for their twentieth anniversary. In the spring and summer, it was covered in climbing honeysuckle, but now it just had barren branches. The firepit in the center was filled with wood and a starter log. I found a lighter on the arm of one of the Adirondack chairs and lit the paper covering the starter log. I rubbed my arms, trying to ward off the cold.

My mini freak-out had to do with the fact that this was all moving so fast. One minute I hated Evan Dawson; the next he was in my childhood home making my entire family fall in love with him.

Making me fall in love with him.

Aubrey had been right. Tears ran down my face, despite my wanting to laugh at myself. I was falling for a man I'd spent half my life detesting.

A man who was honest and kind and thoughtful and didn't deserve all the bad things I'd thought about him.

Who didn't deserve to be the center of a witch hunt led by my boss. I had to tell him.

But when I told him, this would be over. He'd never look at me again with delight, or tease me, or keep track of my smiles or laughter.

I'd never get to kiss him again or feel the warmth of his skin against mine.

Those thoughts gutted me.

How could I have finally figured out that I had serious feelings for Evan, had probably had those feelings for the last ten years, only to have it all blow up in my face?

As if I'd summoned him, Evan walked across the dark backyard and joined me in the extra chair. I wiped my face with the backs of my hands, hoping he couldn't see that I'd been crying. He'd put his sweater back on over my dad's ill-fitting shirt.

"Where's Joey?" I asked.

"Your dad took him upstairs to the guest bedroom." He leaned against the chair's backrest, studying me intently. "Can I ask you a question?"

Oh no, this was it. We were going to have a serious heart-to-heart, and it would destroy everything.

But I couldn't be a coward forever. "Sure."

"Why does your niece keep calling me Satan?"

The relief I felt was so strong it was almost tangible. "I may have called you that once." Or fifty times.

"I should have known." He drummed his fingers against the armrest. "Your mom was in there telling me all about their anniversary trip. You're not going?"

"No." I laughed, rubbing my nose against my sleeve. "I love my family, but nothing about that trip sounds appealing to me."

The wooden chair creaked as he shifted his weight. "To be honest, it's weird to see Aubrey married with kids."

"Why?"

"In high school? She was kind of wild."

"Aubrey? My sister, Aubrey?" Was he sure he had the right person?

"She used to sneak out all the time and could drink the defensive line under the table."

This was mind-boggling information. "I've spent so many years in her perfect shadow." I felt . . . cheated, somehow. "I've always been trying to either measure up to Aubrey or be better than Rory."

He reached over, taking my hand. And the same pleasurable warmth filled me; I just didn't feel so skittish this time. "Why don't you just be Ashton? Because she's pretty wonderful."

How could that make my heart sink and be filled with hope at the same time? "Really?"

"I spend an inordinate amount of time thinking about you," he confessed.

I gripped his hand harder. "That's a big word. *Inordinate.*"

"I went to college, thanks. But I wouldn't spend that much time thinking about somebody who wasn't worth it. You're amazing, Ashton. And I know this engagement is pretend, but I think there's something here. Something worth exploring. Something very real. What do you think?"

What did I think? At the moment I couldn't think at all.

So I did the only thing I could.

I burst into tears.

CHAPTER NINETEEN

"Whoa, hey. I didn't know the idea of dating me would make you cry." He got up out of his chair and crouched down in front of me, his arm resting on my knees, the other going to wipe away my tears. "I have to admit, it's kind of a blow to the ego."

I laughed in between sobs. "It's not that. It's . . . my family loves you."

"Yeah, the same family that you said hated me, right? I mean, if that's what happens to guys they don't like, I'd hate to see how they act with people they love."

He didn't understand what I was trying to say, so I ignored his snark. "Even my mom, who is basically a pessimist, is excited about you. They adore you."

"I'm . . . sorry? I don't know how to make you feel better about that. I could go back inside and insult your dad and hit on your sisters if that would make you feel better."

He joked, but he wouldn't if he knew what I'd been trying to do to him. "There are things you don't know about me. Things I haven't told you."

"Do you like me?"

His question shocked me. I had expected him to pump me for information, asking me what I was keeping from him. "What?"

"Are you attracted to me? Do you like being with me? Do you think about me the way I think about you? Because if the answer to those questions is yes, and my answer is yes, which, to be clear, it is, then nothing else matters to me right now."

It didn't matter right now. But it would at some point.

I wanted one stolen moment with him before that happened. The chance to be held and kissed and desired before it went away.

To believe in unicorns and rainbows and boy bands again. For one brief instant it wouldn't matter that I'd been spending my time doing something awful behind his back. To believe we could be here, right now, just the two of us, and nothing else in the world could possibly interfere.

"Yes." After I said the word, I threw my arms around his neck and pressed my lips against his. I heard a surprised sound in the back of his throat, but the reflexes that had made him an NFL superstar had him quickly responding.

He stood up, pulling me with him, my body pressed flush against his. My feet weren't even touching the ground as he held me aloft. I wrapped my arms around his neck and let out all my pent-up attraction, kissing him over and over again.

And he did the same.

While yesterday's kiss had been cautious and sweet, this one was the opposite. I made sure of it. I threw off my armor, my restraint, and let myself just . . . be.

Let myself enjoy the way that even the slightest brush of his lips against mine sent waves of tingles coursing through my body. How a blazing river of fire burned through my veins at every touch, the way his fingers pressed against my back, seeking, holding.

He pulled his head back slightly, and I heard the harsh undertone of his breathing. "Your family is right inside."

"I don't care." And I didn't. I ran my fingers up into his hair, and his eyelids drifted shut as I applied pressure and played with the silky strands.

"One of us should care." His voice sounded so rough and exciting. The man who didn't get winded easily was sounding a little short of breath.

"Not yet." I didn't explain what I meant and instead started brushing kisses along his jawline. His five-o'clock shadow felt rough against the softness of my lips, but I liked it.

"Ashton," he tried again, sounding like I was strangling him. Pleading.

But I wasn't interested in stopping.

I followed the curve of bone until I came to his neck, pressing hot kisses against his skin. His Adam's apple bobbed hard when I reached it. I ended my trail in the hollow of his throat, and he suddenly grabbed me by my rib cage, lifting me up so that our faces were level.

His strength was beyond thrilling.

And his eyes burned, intense and overwhelming. He said my name again. "Ashton." Only this time it sounded like a promise.

Then he kissed me, his mouth devastating mine. It was an onslaught of sensation: the sound of his broken breathing, the smell of soap and cologne on his skin, the feeling of his muscles rippling and flexing underneath my fingers, the taste of his lips.

Now he was as hungry as I was, as if I'd infected him with the fire that still roared out of control inside me. My mind went totally hazy, and I floated dizzily in the pervasive sensations he caused with his intoxicating, delicious mouth. I didn't know if the weightlessness I was feeling was due to me losing total control or because he was still holding me up off the ground.

His body shuddered beneath mine as I tried to get closer to him. As if I could burn my way into him, branding us both. Leaving behind pieces of myself that would never be removed. So that he wouldn't be able to forget me even if he wanted to.

But it meant I might not ever feel whole again, as if a part of me was always missing, unless I was kissing him just like this.

"Okay." He broke off the kiss with that word, like it had been ripped from his chest. "We have to stop. Now."

He tried to let go of me, but my feet gave way. "I think you disconnected my legs."

"Then you should keep holding on to me."

"That's not a good idea if you want this to stop," I told him with a breathy sigh, more than ready to start that kiss back up again.

"Can't resist me?" he asked with a wink.

"No. I can't."

I both heard and felt his sharp intake of breath. He moved me over to my chair, helping me to sit down. Which was good, since my head was still spinning. Evan might have been celibate, but it did not extend to his lips. That man knew how to kiss. I put my fingers against my mouth, still able to feel him there.

He stood against one of the gazebo pillars, his arms crossed. "You know, we don't have to kiss like we've got to get all the kissing done today."

"Why not?" Getting all the kissing done today sounded like a fantastic plan.

"Because we'll kiss again tomorrow. And the day after that. And the day after that."

"And what if there is no tomorrow?" What if he found out what I had agreed to, and this was my one and only shot to kiss him? It would be so much worse now that I knew what I'd have to give up.

"There will be a tomorrow for us. And the tomorrow after that. Unless you have Black Friday plans. Which I never really understood. Celebrating and being grateful for everything you have and then literally one day later trampling other people to get the best sales."

"We used to go out and shop, but you're right. It's kind of turned into one of those dystopian movies where there's one night of lawlessness and no such thing as crime. I do it all online now." Bantering felt safer. Normal. Made the feeling in my legs return.

But now that I knew what a real kiss between us was like, I was torn between wanting to protect the fragile thing we'd just discovered and telling him the truth and dealing with the consequences.

"Earlier, there was something I wanted to say—"

He cut me off. "We probably both have a lot of things to say. Just like we don't have to get all the kissing done tonight, we don't have to have all the conversations, either."

"I think this is different."

"Spend time with me this weekend. Let's just hang out, have fun, keep it light. See what's between us. Nothing serious. What do you say?"

"Yes."

I said it exactly the same way I'd said it earlier, before I'd attacked him. His hungry gaze shifted to my lips, and he took a step toward me.

"Hey, come inside!" Rory stepped onto the back porch and waved us in. "The movie's starting."

Every year my mom bought a newly released movie for us to watch in the evening after Thanksgiving dinner. They wouldn't start it until we joined them.

Evan offered me his hand and helped me back to my feet. Where I happily discovered that my limbs had started functioning again. He put his arm around my shoulders, hugging me to his side as we walked back.

"So, good kiss, right?" he asked.

Good kiss? Great kiss. Spectacular kiss. Life-altering kiss. "I suppose."

"What you're saying is I did something right?"

"Law of averages," I told him. "It had to happen eventually."

He laughed and kissed the top of my forehead, and I felt a sparkling lightness that I hadn't felt in a long time.

Right as we reached the sliding glass doors, Evan said, "For those people keeping score at home, I'd like to point out that that was Kiss Number Two."

I hoped it was the second of many more to come.

My family and I went to the Jacks game on Thursday (the Jacks won, thirty-seven to nine) and got to watch from the luxury box again. Evan and I had dinner together after at my place. Where he left well before either one of us could fall asleep.

We spent the weekend in a kind of bubble away from the real world. I pretended like Brenda and my issues at ISEN didn't even exist. I let myself talk to him, confide in him, tell him things about myself that I'd never told anyone else. We went out to dinner, watched movies, played some video games (where I maintained my number-one spot on the leaderboard).

There were also a couple of times we shot some hoops, and Evan committed a world record number of personal fouls against me. Mostly of the holding variety.

I didn't mind.

In general, we hung out the way a dating couple would.

And our physical chemistry? Off the charts would be underselling it.

He invited me over to his house for dinner on Sunday night. He was anxious about it, maybe even a little nervous, and I wondered why. We'd been alone together more than once.

I texted Nia to let her know I would be in the neighborhood, thinking maybe I could stop by before or after my date with Evan.

Don't worry about it. You have fun.

His house was even more impressive up close than it had been the one time I'd driven past it with the Owenses. Like it had probably had a moat at some point.

I knocked on his door, and it took a bit for him to answer it. "Hey. I'm glad you're here."

"Me too. Thanks for inviting me."

He kissed me quickly and then let me inside.

Even though he made more money than any one person probably should make, his home didn't have that designer-y feel to it. It wasn't cold or modern at all. It felt very homey and cozy. Almost like the inside of a giant cabin.

The kitchen, however, was totally state-of-the-art. "So you made me dinner, huh?"

I was a bit worried about it because during a previous conversation he'd said to me, "I was banned from using the stove or oven for years. And I'm not going to tell you the whole story, but it was justified."

He shrugged. "I wanted to do something nice for you."

"But you cooked instead?" He laughed at my teasing. I laid my purse on the counter and went in to see what he was working on.

"It's chicken stir-fry. The YouTube video made it seem easy enough."

It was endearing to see him fussing over a frying pan, and I jumped up on the island counter to watch him. "Do you need any help?"

"I've got this. The table is already set, and it looks like dinner is almost done. I just need to get a serving spoon . . ." He turned around and walked to me. He picked me up by the waist and moved me over two feet in order to get into the drawer under my legs. Like it was no big deal.

I loved this feeling—where a man could lift me like I was a bag of flour that needed to be shifted over.

It was . . . heady.

"Let's eat!" he said.

I jumped off the counter and followed him. He pulled out my chair for me when I went to sit down. It was something I was becoming accustomed to.

Evan served me first and then filled his own plate.

"It smells really good," I told him with a smile.

Then I took a bite.

And I chewed it. And chewed it. And chewed it.

The chicken was rubbery, and I was worried whether it was cooked all the way through. And the more I thought about it, the more grossed out I became. But I couldn't exactly spit it out because he was watching me, and it seemed so important to him that I like it.

Then the spiciness hit me. He had put in way too many hot peppers. It was burning my esophagus, and my eyes teared up.

My only saving grace was when Evan put a forkful in his mouth, and I could tell he was having the same reaction. "This is really awful," he said, spitting it out into a napkin.

Relieved that I could finally do the same, I got rid of my mouthful and then drank down the entire glass of water on the table.

When I finished, I said, "It was really sweet of you to cook. And it wasn't . . . that bad." Even though it totally had been.

"You have to stop doing that."

Did he mean the lying? "Stop doing what?"

"Saying things that make me want to kiss you."

"Me saying your cooking wasn't that bad even though we both know it was makes you want to kiss me?"

He leaned forward and kissed me slowly, lingering, savoring me. The way I wasn't able to enjoy his dinner. "I'm discovering that everything you say makes me want to kiss you."

Oh. I was okay with that.

"I'm going to order some pizza. Any preference?"

"I like just about everything."

He raised his eyebrows playfully at me, and I cleared the table while he made the call. "It'll be here in half an hour . . ." Evan was staring at his phone, and he'd seen something that upset him.

"What is it?" I asked.

"I just saw a message from one of my college teammates. About our old coach, Coach Oakley." Evan had had a full ride to a Division 1 school—with the best college football team in the country. "He was just fired from his position."

He sat down hard on one of the barstools, the shock evident on his face.

"Do you know why?" I asked him. Those kinds of decisions were not made lightly.

"This article says that he claims some of his players were at a party and tried to take advantage of an unconscious girl, and the coach stopped them. He was planning on kicking all the players off the team. And rather than cut the school's entire starting lineup, they fired him instead. Can you give me a minute? I'd like to text him."

"Sure. I'll just clean all this up." I threw the completely inedible dinner out and put all our dirty dishes in the dishwasher. I wondered if Evan cleaned up after himself or if he hired someone to come in and do it, because I didn't see a speck of dust or a dangling cobweb hanging off the twelve-foot-high ceilings.

After I finished cleaning, I found him sitting on a dark-brown leather couch in his family room. I came over to sit next to him to wait.

A few minutes later, he said, "It turns out that he's moving up to Seattle. He took a job at a junior college there. He says the story is true. But the girl was his daughter. Somebody put something in her drink, and she called her dad before she passed out. Apparently, he laid a couple of the players out."

"That's really terrible," I told him, shaking my head and shuddering with disgust. That poor girl. What a nightmare.

"I feel really helpless. I wish I could do something. I wish I'd been there. Maybe I can go up to Seattle after the season is over and see if he needs any assistance. I don't know what I'll be able to do. Maybe help with his new team?"

I didn't know what else to say to tell him how bad I felt for his coach and his daughter, so I ended up asking some random question in response to the last thing he'd said. "Is that what you want to do when you retire? Be a coach for an NFL team?"

"No. During the season NFL coaches don't see their families. Players have a pretty regular schedule, but the coaches have beds in the offices down at the stadium for a reason."

He was uncharacteristically quiet and sad.

"I feel so bad for her. That must have been really scary. I'm sorry it happened to her."

Evan nodded. "I've always been the kind of person who learns from other people's mistakes. It's another reason I chose celibacy. One of our tailbacks has a higher number of children with different mothers than the average first grader can count to, and his life is pretty hard. And the guys who do stuff like this, getting drunk and going to parties where they treat women like objects. They could have ruined that girl's life. And is she the first?" He put his head in his hands. "I'm glad this kind of thing isn't part of my life right now."

"I can see that. It still must be hard, though. The waiting." As soon as I said it, I felt guilty. Like there was some part of me that wanted to make Brenda happy and was still searching around to make sure I had the total truth about Evan. I wished I could take it back.

"I'd be lying if I said it wasn't. I think about it a lot. Like when you're on a diet and all you can think about is brownies? Because you know you can't have brownies?"

"I love brownies. Does it bother you that I've already had brownies?" I found that I was holding my breath. Once my feelings toward him had started to change, this was a topic that had occurred to me from time to time and concerned me. Would he look at me differently?

"Of course not." His reply was immediate. "Why would that bother me?"

Relief flooded through me. "Some guys are possessive."

He absentmindedly kissed me on the forehead. "All that matters to me is who we are together, right now. And the past may not matter, but the future does. I want my relationships to be real. Someday I want to fall in love with my best friend. I read this study that said the level of emotional connection you have when you start having sex with someone is the level you stay at. And I know that I will want an incredible marriage, and I'm willing to do what it takes to get it. I guess my parents spoiled me. I want what they had. I want to love a woman the way my dad loved my mom. For who she was inside."

"Inner beauty doesn't get you free drinks," I joked, as the air had become incredibly heavy and serious around us.

"It doesn't. But it can get you a lifelong commitment with the right man. But that desire helps me to stay focused on other things. I focus on what I can do instead of what I've decided not to do."

"But don't you worry about marrying someone and then finding out the sex is bad? Like you wouldn't buy a car without test-driving it first, right?"

He shrugged. "I think if you love someone, have a high level of attraction, and are committed to honest communication, you'll figure out the other stuff. And you can tell whether or not you have sexual chemistry with someone. Like what we have."

Was it hot in here, or was that just Evan? "Oh? You think we have chemistry?"

"The kind an evil scientist would use to blow up a small country. It's why I hesitated to invite you over tonight."

"Were you afraid I was going to attack you and you wouldn't be able to fend me off?" I teased.

"You'd be surprised at the kind of stuff that happens. Like a couple of years ago, I had a woman over to hang out, and I went into the kitchen to get us some drinks while she used the bathroom. When she came out, she no longer had any clothes on. She was not happy with me when I asked her to leave. My home has always been my sanctuary. You're the first woman I've had over since that incident."

That was incredibly sweet. And made me feel very, very special. I kissed him to show him how that made me feel.

"What was that for?" he asked when I was done.

"For being you."

"Well, I'm me all the time, so if you want to come back over here, I won't complain." He yanked on my legs, pulling me in closer. He leaned his forehead against mine. "And it's so sweet that you were willing to burn off your taste buds for me."

"That's just the kind of girl I am."

"I know. And I love . . . I love that about you."

What? *What?*

CHAPTER TWENTY

Even though Brenda had told me I didn't need to bother coming into work, I now felt compelled to show up. Although I knew I'd probably lose my shot at a full-time job with ISEN, I didn't want them to be able to say that I'd quit or just stopped coming in. I knew that I should start looking for another job. Because I believed Evan and thought there was no story there. Unless he was the most amazing actor and best liar alive, he was a virgin. No matter how badly my soon-to-be-ex-boss didn't want him to be.

I wouldn't be able to give her the story she wanted.

On my way in I texted my sisters and Nia to figure out what his "I love," pause, "I love that about you" meant. Was it just a casual slip? Or had he wanted to say something more and thought maybe it wasn't time? Or we weren't ready?

The general consensus from their replies was that they didn't have enough information to proceed. Nia told me she had to throw up, Rory advised me to get with all that as soon as possible, and then Aubrey said:

Do you want to grab lunch today and discuss it in person?

Definitely.

Walking into the office was one of the hardest things I'd had to do in a very long time. Everyone on my floor stopped and stared as I went over to my tiny cubicle and sat down. I had just switched on my computer when I heard my name being called.

It was Brenda. "In my office."

"You're in trouble!" Rand said with a smirk and a singsong voice, his feet upon his desk and fingers laced behind his head. I considered pushing on his shoulder so he'd fall backward but refrained.

"Well?" Brenda asked as soon as I entered the room. She sat at her desk, glaring at me. "Do you have any updates?"

There was nothing I could say that would make her happy in this moment, but I had to give it a shot. "I've talked to Evan, and—"

"I'm not interested in what Evan Dawson tells people. I'm interested in the truth, and you're not going to get that from him when he has an image to protect."

"Then no, I don't have any updates for you."

She crossed her legs while she glowered at me. "I wasn't joking about your job being on the line."

I'd never thought she had been. I had taken her very seriously. "I just don't think . . ." I took in a big breath. This was hard for me, standing up to her. "I don't think there's a story there. I think Evan's telling the truth."

Brenda just stared at me like I was the stupidest person alive. She did it for so long that when she spoke again, it startled me. "But you're still pretending to be his fiancée. He's getting something out of that. Shouldn't you?"

"I don't know what you mean." I didn't say that it was feeling less and less like pretend.

"You're not some shrinking virgin, too, are you?"

It so surprised me that she'd said it that at first I wondered if I had imagined it somehow. But, given the look on her face, I knew I hadn't. I'd have to check with Aubrey at lunch, but I was pretty sure that was illegal for Brenda to ask. And it wasn't like I could go to HR. Her cousin was the HR manager. I knew he'd take her word over mine, and trying to file a complaint would just get me kicked out faster. I wanted to tell Brenda it was none of her business but couldn't make myself say it. Instead, I just sat there, mute and unable to defend myself.

She let out a sigh of disgust. "I guess I have to spell it out for you. If you're dating him, I'm guessing it wouldn't be too hard to seduce him."

It was like she had slapped me. After all of my conversations with Evan about this subject, it would be a total violation of him and what he stood for. "I . . . I can't. I won't."

She frowned at me for a really long time. "Then I don't know why you're still assigned to this story. You told me you'd be willing to do anything to bring Evan Dawson down. You're forcing my hand, and I'll have to assign someone else. Someone who can get the job done."

Someone who wouldn't have a problem seducing him? Was that her endgame? If Evan really was celibate, then she'd find somebody to make him not be?

Brenda pushed a paper across her desk. "This is an official reprimand form. On it I have noted your refusal to fulfill tasks that are assigned to you."

Was she serious? "Did you also note that you just told me to have sex with someone for a story?"

"I don't know what you're talking about, Ashton. I never said anything like that. It would be against the law and company policy."

Shock made my mouth drop open. It had literally just happened. But I saw from the expression on her face that she was serious, again. She would deny that she'd told me to seduce him, and everyone at work would believe her and not me. Especially her cousin.

"Given that you're Evan's fiancée, and that you seem much more devoted to him than you are to this network, and how you've accused others in the workplace of jealousy, do you really think anyone will ever believe you?"

All of that was untrue. Brenda had the experience, nepotism, and connections that I didn't. She was feared and respected. I was just some nameless intern. She was right. Nobody would listen to me. They would all choose her side.

Why wasn't I like one of those women in movies who had their phones out recording when the bad guy made an incriminating speech?

There was a big lump in my throat, and I swallowed it down. "I'm not . . . I'm not signing that."

"I'll note your refusal to sign along with the date. That's all, Ashton. You may go."

I seemed to be operating solely from muscle memory. I walked back to my desk, not really seeing where I was headed.

"Aw, is your love affair with Brenda over?" Rand asked as I sat down.

"Shut up, Rand," I told him, the words sounding vicious even to my ears. I could not deal with him right now. I wanted to lay my head down on my desk and sob. Over being on the outs with Brenda. Losing my job. Worrying about what they might do to Evan. And instead of being able to cry, I had to get to work and pretend like nothing bad was happening. The sharks on this floor would smell blood in the water.

Catching up on my email kept me busy until lunchtime. I grabbed my purse and coat and fled, all too happy to escape. I let out a deep breath of air when I got outside. Even the overcast sky felt less dark and oppressive than ISEN.

I headed for the Asian fusion restaurant in the building where Aubrey worked. She looked as upset as I felt, collapsing into the chair across from me. "There are days when I really, really hate my job."

"Really? You know, there's a support group for that. Its membership includes everybody, and their group meetings are at the bar after work."

"Ha. Have you ordered yet?"

I told her I hadn't, and we figured out what we wanted to get so that when the waitress stopped by our table, we were ready.

"I don't know why you're all up in arms about your job," I said. "It's not like Dad's going to ever fire you. If I were you, your home life would stress me out more. I don't know how you do that all the time, every day."

"Well, wine helps. And the fact that I adore my kids more than my own life. It's different when they're yours."

I could see that. I definitely thought Charlotte and Joey were superior to every other child on the planet.

"But we're not here to talk about my kids. We're here to talk about Evan. Tell me everything that's been going on."

So I filled her in on our activities up to the present day, obviously leaving some private details out of my recap.

"Are you still mad at him?" she asked.

"No. I was really angry in the beginning, and then it just kind of flared up occasionally. Like herpes. And now . . . I enjoy being with him."

"Sounds like things are going well," Aubrey said, leaning to the left so the server could put her dish on the table.

"They are. Today it's Brenda who is making me miserable. What is the penalty if you accidentally murder your boss?"

"It's pretty bad. You don't want to know."

"Even if it's justified?"

"Even then. What did she do?"

Aubrey already knew the basic gist of what Brenda wanted, so I laid out every detail of her evil plans, including today's interaction.

She sat and listened, not eating, not saying anything. Her eyes got wider and wider until she vaguely resembled an anime character.

"You have to quit. Right now. You have, like, Stockholm syndrome or something."

"What?"

"You've always been competitive. You want to be the best, and you have this really unrealistic dream that will be really hard to attain, and this woman is using that. 'Just do what I say, and I'll give you everything you've ever wanted.' And you did what she said. I know you felt justified in the beginning because of how mad you were at Evan, but that's passed. It sounds like it's time to move on."

"But this job, this opportunity, it's everything I've ever wanted."

"Is it? Or is it all Grandma wanted? And it sort of became your dream?"

My brain internally gasped. No one had ever said that to me before. It had always just been my dream that my grandmother shared. But how could that be true? What four-year-old wanted to be a sports announcer someday? She'd settled on being a reporter since she knew she'd never, ever become an announcer. That opportunity was denied to my grandma in her career, and she spent my entire life telling me I should want it.

Did I, though? Was it something for me, or a mantle put on my shoulders by somebody else? I couldn't tell where my grandmother's hopes began and my dreams ended. It was all blended together.

It was like when I tried to stop being angry with Evan in the beginning. I didn't know how to let go of it. Just like I didn't know how to let go of wanting to become an NFL announcer.

I'd never questioned my ambition before.

It was something I'd need to think more about.

"I don't know," I finally told her. "I do know that at some point Brenda's going to fire me, and that devastates me."

Aubrey finally began to eat, and she spoke in between bites. "Let her fire you. People get fired. It happens. And somehow the world keeps spinning."

"You don't understand how this feels because you'll never be in this position."

"That doesn't mean I can't point out that you're being stupid. Not to mention that you wouldn't have to worry about Evan finding out. If you're someplace new, it doesn't matter what your old boss asked you to do. You don't necessarily have to tell him all of the truth."

"Right. Because who wants a relationship based on communication and honesty? Gross."

"I just mean that if you're worried the Brenda stuff might be a deal breaker, because I would be freaking out about that if I were in your shoes, this is a way to avoid all of it. Your options are to either come clean to him or just look for a new job."

I picked at the lo mein with my chopsticks. "Do you think I should tell him?"

Aubrey just shook her head. "I can't tell you that. It has to be your decision. I will say that from the moment he came back into your life, even though you've acted annoyed or put out, you've been excited. Besides this job stuff, do you think about anything else besides him?"

"Not really."

"Tell me you're not developing real feelings for him."

"I . . ." The word died in my mouth. I couldn't lie to Aubrey. She was a lawyer and had mom-level liedar. She would see right through me. "Okay, I have feelings for him. Maybe I'm even falling in love." It was the first time I'd said it out loud. "But it's too soon, right? Too fast?"

"Who's to say what's too fast? And you guys have a history together and a former friendship. It's not like you're just meeting him for the first time. And I'm the wrong person to say that something is happening too soon because I knew the first night I met Justin that we'd be together forever."

This whole conversation was twisting my stomach up in knots, especially since Brenda's words about being "that girl" came back to haunt my psyche. "But if I quit, isn't that like choosing a man over my career?"

"No," Aubrey scoffed. "It's choosing to not work for a deranged sociopath who has violated, like, ten different laws. The way she treats you is neither normal nor acceptable. It's not my area of expertise, but let me know if you want to start a hostile work environment lawsuit. I have a friend from law school who can do it."

That was all I needed. To sue ISEN. Then I'd definitely never work there again.

Our server returned to refill our water glasses, and I asked her to box up my food for me. I'd have to eat it later when my stomach had settled.

Aubrey leaned in and lowered her voice. "Speaking of awful things your boss said, between us, you have wanted to take things further with Evan, haven't you? The thought has crossed your mind?"

"Well, yeah. But I'm not going to." In large part because I respected him and his decision, but some tiny egotistical part of me refrained because Evan had such fantastic self-control that I didn't want to suffer through the humiliation of being shot down. "But to be honest the delayed gratification and all that restraint, the anticipation, it's actually kind of hot. I think kissing is way underrated. I'd forgotten how much fun it could be when it can't lead to anything else."

It was almost like my teenage self actually was getting to date Evan. I'd discovered that being with him was about the journey and not the destination. And so far we'd spent a fair amount of time dedicated to the journey.

Which was awesome.

Aubrey and I chatted some more as she finished up her lunch and then graciously paid the check. I thanked her, and we hugged goodbye after we walked out of the restaurant. She headed for the lobby and its elevators, and I went back to the ISEN building.

My sister was right. I needed a new job.

But whether or not to tell Evan? That was a whole big processing/ freak-out for another day.

Over the next few weeks, Evan and I settled into an easy routine. We played basketball, and he went to his football games while I cheered for him (either in the Forest or from home). We played our video games, watched movies and TV together, made out a lot, and generally spent as much time together as possible around his schedule.

I got cute and funny tweets from him while he was on the road, playing in different cities. Like:

> Did you hear QB Dallas Witten can't get into his own driveway? Someone painted an end zone on it.

Or:

> How's my favorite tight end?

> Whoops, meant to send that to Sanchez.

> Are you smiling?

> No.

> Yes, you are. I'm counting it.

He also took me to meet his grandmother, and she was just as he'd described. Awake but unresponsive. She didn't speak or interact with us in any way. It made me feel so sad for him, that he was so alone, and some feminine instinct in me wanted to fix all of his broken parts.

When he was away, I kept assisting Aubrey with the reunion stuff. I tried to convince her that I should be let out of my Reunion Minion contract. "I don't think I should have to help anymore. This was conditional on me getting the story on Evan, and obviously that's not happening now."

"No," she corrected me. "The promise was conditional on you being introduced to Nia. I actually feel like you owe me more because I got you both a new friend and a boyfriend out of it."

She was kind of right. So I sucked it up and kept doing whatever she told me to do. And then I was the only one doing any work. Evan helped out sometimes, but he was busy, and Aubrey left with her family and my parents to go on their cruise.

I attempted to lure Rory into working with me under the pretense of offering her baked goods. But we'd been sisters for too long.

Whatever it is you want, I can't! With the cats being away, I'm off to Cabo to play!

Cabo?

Don't you have like class and homework?

Mom? I thought you were on a cruise. How did you get Ashton's phone?

PS - Kiss that lumberjack in shining flannel for me!

Rory said she'd be gone for about a week. Whatever. It was her life. She could burn it down to the ground if she wanted to.

I just needed to keep reminding myself that Evan was worth all the ridiculous grunt work Aubrey was forcing me to do.

Speaking of feeling like I was forced to do things, work was the worst part of my life. Brenda spoke to me about once a week to ask if I had an update for her yet. When I said I didn't, she had another reprimand form for me to sign, which I continued to refuse to do. I didn't know how many forms I could get before her cousin in Human Resources called me in to let me go, but I knew I had to be close.

Or maybe I wasn't. Maybe Brenda intended to keep me around and torment me endlessly with her reprimands and dirty looks. They weren't paying me, so it wasn't like it affected her bottom line.

She also wasn't assigning me any tasks. When I asked the other interns if they needed help, I got rejected at every turn. Like they didn't want to be tainted by associating with me. Which I understood, but I was really bored.

Sometimes I wondered if Brenda hoped that I would break. If she was waiting to see if things with Evan and me would end and then she could manipulate me into saying whatever she wanted because I'd be all heartbroken and angry again.

I attempted to look for other jobs, but nothing was happening on that front. I thought my best bet would be to try and transfer into another department at ISEN. I checked the company job postings daily. I would have been happy in any position—anything to get me out from under Brenda's thumb and keep me on the right career track.

Unfortunately, the people doing the hiring weren't interested in talking to me because I was Brenda's intern. No one was willing to cross her by "stealing" me away.

Which probably meant that in order to keep pursuing my dream, I'd have to move to a different city.

And leave Evan behind.

It felt like there were no good solutions. And the stress of my situation was making me sick. I had some awful flu-like symptoms that I managed with over-the-counter medications. I kept warning Evan to keep his distance—the last thing he needed right now was to fall ill, but he insisted on cuddling with me and kissing me regardless. He told me he had an incredible immune system, and it seemed to be true.

About a week after my lunch with Aubrey, he came by after practice and collapsed on my couch. On his more physically intense days, we just quietly watched a show together and relaxed. I wondered what it would be like to be with him in the off-season. Obviously he'd still work out and train, just not at this same intensity.

My throat had been scratchy and raw the last couple of days, and I was trying to drink some herbal tea with honey to soothe the inflammation. But every time I swallowed, it only seemed to get worse. I tried forcing a cough, but that just made me feel like my throat lining had both caught on fire and was being stabbed simultaneously.

Evan noticed my distress. "What is it?"

"I don't know. I'm in a lot of pain in my throat."

He leaned over, as if he meant to examine me, and I backed up. "No way. This might be strep throat, and I'm not giving that to you."

"If you've had it for a couple of days, then I probably have it, too."

Oh no, I really would be one of those girlfriends who cursed her significant other's football career.

That pain spiked again, somehow more intense this time, and Evan looked even more concerned. "That's it. We're taking you to the hospital."

"I don't need to go to the hospital." Money wasn't the issue; I was still covered on my parents' insurance. He just seemed to be making a fuss over something that wasn't that big of a deal. He felt my forehead, as if his hands doubled as thermometers. "I can go in and see a doctor tomorrow."

Another wave of pain hit me, and I almost doubled over. It was getting worse.

And more frequent. The pain slammed into me even harder.

"If I have to carry you and put you in my car, I will."

And I knew he could do it. Maybe he was right. I nodded and went to put on some shoes and grab my coat. Evan locked the door behind us, giving me a pointed look, and then helped me out to his SUV.

He might have broken the land speed record, but I wasn't sure since I could focus only on how much I hurt. A throbbing headache was starting to blur my vision. My head felt like I could detach it from the rest of my body, like it might float away.

After parking the car, Evan basically carried me into the ER. The pain in my throat was constant now and getting worse. He called for help, and some medical professionals came running over.

I was aware of lights being flashed in my eyes and the doctor looking down my throat. I nearly vomited when he touched the back of it with some kind of swab.

"Are you family?" someone asked Evan. I didn't know how much time had passed.

"I'm her fiancé."

"She's had some complications from an illness, and now she is going to need an immediate tonsillectomy."

Then I heard words like *severe infection*, *abscesses*, and *peritonsillar*. None of it was making any sense.

There was a poke of a needle in my arm, and a heavy darkness started to descend.

The last thing I saw was Evan's worried face as he squeezed my hand tightly.

CHAPTER TWENTY-ONE

I came to in a hospital room. I felt a little disoriented and realized I had an IV in my arm. It took me a second to remember what had happened. I wasn't in pain at the moment, but my throat definitely felt weird. Like something had changed.

Evan was asleep in a chair, the scruff on his chin making it obvious that he hadn't shaved.

I said his name, and it came out as a croaky whisper. But he immediately responded.

He rushed over to the side of my bed and took my hand. "How are you feeling?"

"I'm okay."

"That's good. When you first came to, you were really out of it and kept asking where you were and tried to rip your IV out."

"Did I really? I don't remember."

"You've actually been eating and drinking today and going to the bathroom, too. Do you remember that?"

I had vague flashes after he said that but nothing that was clear. It was so weird to think that I'd been doing things like using the restroom and having food and couldn't remember it. "No."

"You asked me if they'd given you your tonsils, and I told you the tonsil fairy wasn't real." Why would I want my tonsils? I must have really been loopy. He went on, "You also texted your boss and told her you were in the hospital."

Panic gripped my chest, my heart squeezing hard. Like I was ready to have a heart attack. At least I was in the right place for it. But I had texted Brenda? What else had I said about her or my job while highly medicated? What had she said? Had Evan seen any of our messages? "Where's my phone?"

He pointed to it on that long, rolling table that hospital rooms always had. I grabbed it and checked for my message to Brenda. I'd told her I was having emergency surgery and was in the hospital.

"Did she reply?"

"She didn't." Did she not believe me? Not care? Would she use this as an excuse to get rid of me? Claim she'd never gotten it and say that I had failed to report for work?

"Do you want me to call her?" he offered.

"No!" I said the word so forcefully that it actually hurt. "No, thank you. I'll take care of it."

"I guess it shouldn't really surprise me that you don't remember all of that stuff because you've been in and out all day. Hopefully you're more awake now."

"What time is it?" I asked, both wanting the answer and to change the subject. Like I didn't have my phone in my hands and couldn't check for myself.

Thankfully, he didn't seem to notice. "It's seven o'clock at night. You've been here for twenty-four hours." Then he leaned over and kissed me softly, and it was nearly as good as my morphine drip. "I was really worried about you," he said. And there was a look in his eyes I hadn't seen before. More than just affection or concern.

Something more like . . . love.

My heart fluttered in my chest.

A nurse came into the room. "Ashton, I'm glad you're awake. I'd like to go over your postsurgical care with you."

She had papers and a couple of medicines that she said they'd filled at the pharmacy next door. Evan took the papers and began to read through them while she talked to me.

The nurse told me to eat very soft foods, that I would probably prefer to have ice cream and Jell-O. I needed to stay hydrated and to take my pain medications as described every two to three hours. "Trust me," she said. "You don't want to be chasing your pain and trying to fix it. You want to stay on top of it. Which means you'll probably need to set an alarm on your phone."

"I'll take care of that," Evan said with a nod. She showed him the prescription bottles and told me when I could have the next doses, and he wrote it down on his phone.

"And take it easy when you get home," she said. "Stay in bed, and let this guy pamper you. It's hard to predict how you'll recover—teenagers take about a week, but the older you get, the harder it is. Sometimes as long as three or four weeks. Days four and five are generally the worst. You'll need to contact your work and tell them you need a week off, minimum. Hydration will help with the pain, so make sure you keep drinking. The doctor's number is on the bottom. Please call us if you have any questions or problems."

She went over to a large cabinet and pulled out a drawstring plastic bag that she placed at the foot of my bed. I recognized my clothing inside and looked down to see myself in a hospital gown. When had that happened?

Then she took my IV out and finished by placing an adhesive bandage on me. "Sorry about cutting you off from the good stuff," she joked. "I'm going to go grab you a wheelchair and get the last couple of pieces of your discharge paperwork, and you'll be good to go."

I wondered how long it would be before the IV pain drugs wore off. My mouth felt dry, and I reached over to take a drink of water. It really, really hurt to swallow.

Which Evan noticed. "This sheet says we can try some ice chips. Maybe that will help. I'll get you some when we get home."

I noticed his casual use of the word. He was taking me back to my apartment. Where he didn't live. It was like he was saying that wherever we were together was our home.

And I didn't feel panicked or worried or freaked out. It just felt . . . right.

I leaned forward into a sitting position, and Evan put his hand on my back, helping me up. I swung my legs over the side of the bed as I grabbed my clothes. "I should get changed."

"Sure." But he just stood there, until it dawned on him. "Right! I'll be just outside. Call for me if you need me."

It was a bit slow-going to get the gown off and my clothes back on. I was able to slide my feet into my shoes, but the backs stayed bent down against my heels. I decided I didn't care. I walked over and opened the door, and Evan hurried back inside, putting his arm around my waist to help me sit back down.

The nurse returned with a wheelchair, and Evan helped me into it. Then he ran out ahead of us to grab his car. When he picked me up and put me into the SUV, I tried to tell him I wasn't an invalid but decided I was too tired to care. I texted Brenda again, telling her that I would need at least a week off work.

I kept expecting my phone to beep with her response, which I expected to be something along the lines of "then don't bother coming back."

But instead, she stayed silent. I would call her cousin in HR first thing in the morning and let him know what was happening, maybe forward some of my medical documentation over.

We arrived at my condo, and despite Evan's protests, I did make him let me walk inside. The nurse had told me to walk around to avoid getting blood clots, and I figured now was as good a time as any to start. He got me into my bedroom and helped me take off my shoes when I sat on the bed. He left so that I could change into some pajamas and returned a few minutes later.

"You can take one of your Percocets now. Which will probably make you sleepy. I'm going to get the foods on this list for you to eat," he told me after I was settled. I nodded and held out my hand for the pill. I put it in my mouth and then took a big drink of water from the glass he'd left on my nightstand, figuring I might as well try to get some fluids into me if I was going to be swallowing anyway.

Still hurt. But the pain medication definitely made me drowsy.

I woke up to the sound of Evan in my kitchen, and I got up to use the bathroom and to see what he was up to. Almost every countertop was covered in a grocery bag.

"Why are you out of bed?" he asked.

"Why did you buy the entire inventory of the store?" I croaked.

He ran a hand against the back of his neck. "I don't know. I just wanted to make sure you were covered. That you had everything you needed."

"Apparently all I need is water and medication. I'm like a house-plant with more complicated pain sensors."

"Do you want something to eat?"

"Not if it means you're the one who's going to cook it."

He rolled his eyes at me and smiled. "I was thinking something more like ice cream or frozen yogurt. I didn't know what flavor you liked best so I bought them all."

"You . . . bought them all? You have seen the size of my freezer, haven't you?"

"I'll go back tomorrow and load up on whichever flavors you want around. It's not a big deal."

It kind of was a big deal that he'd basically bought all the ice cream in Portland for me because he didn't know which flavor to get. Wasteful, but sweet. But he'd go back tomorrow? He had practice. He shouldn't have missed today's practice, either. I was both touched by his sacrifice and a bit panicked at what it meant that he would miss practice for me.

"I'm good with the basics. Maybe not stuff like cookies and cream that has chunks in it. And . . . don't you have to go back to work?"

"I'm sticking around for as long as you need me."

Now I was really confused. "What about the game on Sunday?"

He was in the middle of loading as much chocolate, strawberry, and vanilla ice cream into the freezer as he could. "The Jacks can play one game without me. We have a backup QB for a reason."

The reason was not because I'd had emergency surgery. And it was one thing to miss a couple of practices for my sake, but an entire game? That felt . . . serious. Loaded. Like it really meant something. Panic won out over feelings of tenderness and gratitude. "What about your contract negotiations?" Wasn't that the point of all of this? How mad would Chester Walton be if Evan just skipped a game?

He gave me a look that had a very "screw the contract negotiations" vibe to it. "I'll cross that bridge when I come to it."

"You don't have to stay with me. I'll just call . . ." My voice trailed off as I realized there was no one else who could help me. My parents and Aubrey were on that cruise, and Rory had sneaked off to Mexico.

"I'm here. And I plan on being here for as long as you need me."

The moment felt heavy and important, and I mentally wasn't equipped to deal with it. "Well, if the Jacks lose to the New York Giants because you're here with me, I'm never speaking to you again."

That made him laugh. "Got it. You never did tell me if you want to eat."

"I'm not really in the mood. I think I'll just go back to bed."

And even though I was perfectly capable of walking under my own steam, Evan insisted on escorting me, his arms around me to keep me from falling.

I suspected that it was too late. I don't know if it was just the drugs talking, but I knew I'd already fallen.

Hard.

Evan stayed that week with me, initially sleeping on my couch. The first few days he woke up every three hours to make sure that I had my pain meds and drank my water. He got all my food for me and generally made my life easier. It amazed me that somebody so tough and masculine could be so gentle and caring. I was beyond touched at all he had sacrificed just to make sure I was okay.

I tried telling him I was fine and that he could go, but the truth was I wanted him to stick around. I felt guilty about him missing so much work, but there was such a comfort and relief at knowing he was always there. And could get me peanut-butter-and-chocolate ice cream anytime I wanted it.

I called Human Resources to let them know about my emergency and the doctor's advice that I take at least a week off. Evan scanned my medical paperwork and sent it in for me. I continued to feel better, despite the gross scabs I sometimes spit up.

Evan tucked me into bed, as he insisted on doing every night. He kissed me gently on the lips, and I found it frustrating that my accident kept us from kissing the way I wanted to. As he pulled away I grabbed his wrist.

"Stay with me."

A million different emotions flashed across his face. "What?"

"Just to sleep." I didn't want him to leave. I needed him next to me, to curl into him and his strength.

He studied me for a moment, looking as if he was wrestling with his conscience. Then he slid his shoes off and tugged his sweatshirt over his head. My heartbeat throbbed loudly in my ears as he got into bed next to me. I scooted over, making room for him. He raised up his arm, and I rested my head against his shoulder as he pulled me flush against him.

"Good night, Ashton."

For the first time since I'd gotten sick, I wasn't able to fall asleep quickly. I snuggled against his side, wrapping my arms around his wide chest. His slow, even breaths let me know that he'd passed out. I reveled in his warmth, in the way his strong arms held me tightly.

Although I'd imagined the fun and physical aspects of sharing a bed with Evan on more than one occasion, what I hadn't thought about was this. Lying in his arms. Having this feeling of belonging. Of being made . . . whole. Complete.

Realizing this was what I wanted in my life. Evan by my side, always.

And the idea didn't terrify me.

The following Monday we both went back to our jobs, despite Evan's protests that I should take off more time. "I've already missed a whole week. I can't miss any more work."

"You can, actually. You have this thing called a doctor's note, and it means you get to stay in bed and heal."

"Would you take two weeks off if you'd been the one who had a tonsillectomy?"

He paused. "That's different."

"It's not."

"It is," he countered. "I get paid to be at my job." Then he laughed when I chucked a pillow at his head.

When I got into the office, I expected Brenda to yell for me, but she ignored me and instead sat in her office ranting about bumping up the ratings. Since she still wouldn't give me any work to do, I spent my time sending out résumés to other companies, hoping someone would call me in for an interview.

It didn't happen. I'd confided in Evan about my job worries, that my boss had asked me to do something unethical and was angry I wouldn't. And that I suspected I'd be out of work soon and would have to move back home. Or to a different location entirely.

He'd asked if I wanted him to make some phone calls for me, but I told him not to. I didn't want to be another person in his life trying to take advantage of him.

That I had once very much tried to take advantage of him was something I wanted to forget.

Today I was tempted to take him up on his offer to help as I could feel the sand running out of my hourglass.

Evan called me on my lunch break, sounding completely exhausted. I guiltily wondered if that was partially my fault since he'd spent so many nights taking care of me. "So what are your plans this week?" he asked.

"Fetching and carrying for Aubrey, and then the reunion is this Saturday." Everybody had returned from the cruise late last night, and I swear the first thing Aubrey did when her plane landed was text me with updates about the reunion. I had to help with decorating and the food. Evan was planning on going as well. But he hadn't asked me to go with him. Maybe it was just supposed to be understood, given that I was his sort-of fiancée?

I was, yet again, pathetically waiting for Evan Dawson to ask me to a dance.

"Keep tomorrow evening open. I have a surprise for you."

"A surprise? Of the clothing-free variety?"

He laughed at my teasing. "No. And I'm not telling you anything because it's a surprise, and that's how surprises work."

I was glad he didn't tell me anything beforehand.

Because it turned out to be the best gift anyone had ever given me.

He took me to the Forest on Tuesday evening. "What are we doing here?" I asked.

"Just wait."

There were a surprising number of cars in the regular parking lot and some people sitting in the stands. "There's a game," he told me. "Some kids who play football and got on their school's honor roll were given the chance to come tonight and play against the Jacks. Including me."

"Oh. You brought me here to watch?" It was sweet but not really my idea of a surprise. I'd seen him play plenty of times.

"Not exactly. There's someone I want you to meet. Come on."

Evan took me into a part of the stadium I'd never been in before, and I didn't understand what was going on until he opened a door into the broadcast booth, and there sat Scooter Buxton.

I couldn't speak. Which probably meant I wasn't making a very good impression.

"Hey there, Ashton, right? Evan told me that you hope to be an NFL commentator someday." He offered me his hand.

My head began to nod of its own volition, and somehow my right hand shook his.

"Have a seat," Scooter said.

I didn't even register when Evan left the booth to go down to his mini game. I finally regained the ability to speak, and what I said was, "I grew up listening to you."

Scooter let out a little laugh. "There's a way to make a man feel old!"

But it was true. He'd been the voice of the Jacks for KPRD since I was a little girl. He'd never even seemed like a real person to me. Just this phantom voice who was doing what I'd hoped to do.

"Tell me about yourself. Did you grow up here in Portland? Have you always been a fan of the Jacks?"

Scooter Buxton wanted to talk about me? I wanted to talk about him! But instead, I answered his questions, and we chatted for a few minutes, and he did tell me a little bit about his background and family.

"You're probably wondering why I asked you about yourself," he said. "Chemistry is the most important thing in the booth. It helps when the two people working together know a little something about each other."

Then Scooter showed me the control board and gave me a pair of headphones for when the game started.

"You . . . want me to announce with you?" I felt an actual anxiety attack coming on. "I haven't had any time to prepare!"

Had it been two professional teams, I would have had a board created with names, numbers, and positions so that I knew instantly who I was talking about. I would have watched game films to get a sense of their pass game and run game, what their specialty teams did, their defensive maneuvers, the sack reel, things like that.

And while I knew none of that mattered because it was just a pretend game, I didn't like flying blind.

He picked up on my nervousness. "I understand wanting to be prepared. The thing is, if you do too much of it, you'll want to share everything you learned. Which can be boring for the audience. Just follow the action. Let the game itself dictate what you should say. I think they're getting ready to start."

Scooter put his headphones on, and I did the same. I looked over the list Scooter had given me with the names and numbers of the elementary-age kids who were here to play with their heroes. I wanted them to have their moment in the spotlight; hopefully I wouldn't mispronounce everything.

I couldn't believe how panic-inducing this was. I'd called plenty of games live but never any of them in a professional stadium next to one of my personal role models.

"This is Scooter Buxton, and I'm joined today by Ashton Bailey. Say hello to our crowd, Ashton."

"Hello, everyone! I can't even tell you how excited I am to be here."

He gave me a warm smile and introduced the players who were out on the field. The next hour seemed to just fly by. I did as he suggested and followed the game, and we quickly fell into a rhythm of who should talk and when.

It was everything I'd dreamed it would be. My throat didn't even bother me, and I wasn't sure whether that was due to finally recovering or all the adrenaline pumping through my system.

The mini game ended, and I faced Scooter as he turned off the microphones. "Thank you so much. You have no idea how much of a dream come true this was for me."

"Well, Evan Dawson asked for a personal favor. And who can say no to Evan?"

"I certainly haven't." My eyes went wide as I realized how that might have sounded. "I mean, except for that one thing. And I'm not the one who says no." Gah! I was making it worse!

Scooter laughed and removed his headphones. "Evan gave me your audition CD. I was surprised to see you have real talent. Good instincts. Which you also showed me today. If this is your dream, I say keep chasing it."

He walked me to the door while I kept shaking his hand and saying nonsense about what a pleasure it had been and how much I'd enjoyed it. At least, I think that's what I said. I was possibly delirious with excitement and could not be held accountable for what came out of my mouth.

I'd only gone about ten feet down the hallway when Evan almost barreled straight into me. He picked me up in a bear hug and swung me around. "You did so good! I was so proud of you! I had a hard time concentrating on what I was doing because I just wanted to listen to you."

"Thank you," I told him, out of breath from his hug and his excitement for me, from the pride he took in what I'd done. It did something strange to my stomach, making it flip over a million times in a row. "You don't know what this means to me. Literally the best gift I've ever gotten."

He released me and set me back on the ground, but I didn't let go. I wanted to be close to him.

"When I asked you about your plans this week, there was something I forgot to ask." He kissed my forehead softly, and I sighed.

"What did you want to ask me?"

"I wanted to ask you if you'd go to the reunion with me."

"Really?" I squealed. Just when I'd thought this day couldn't possibly get any better. "Yes! I mean, who didn't have a fantasy of showing up to a high school party on the arm of the quarterback?"

"I never did."

That made me laugh and tighten my arms around him. "So arrogant."

"Maybe. But I feel like this is a topic we should spend more time exploring."

"Your inflated ego?"

"Fantasies," he answered with a wicked grin. "Specifically yours."

"Shut up," I told him, but even I couldn't keep the smile off my face.

I was going to the ball with Prince Charming.

My life was pretty awesome at the moment.

I should have remembered that when you believed everything in your life was perfect, that was the moment the universe liked to cut your legs out from underneath you.

CHAPTER TWENTY-TWO

It ended up being easier than I'd expected to decorate for the reunion. The hotel did most of the work with the tables, chairs, and tablecloths. Aubrey and I, along with a handful of volunteers, came in to finish up the details. Balloons in the school colors, red and black, some strung lights, the floral centerpieces. All tastefully subdued and in line with Aubrey's ultimate vision for the best reunion ever.

When I got back home, I called my younger sister to come over. Rory had already offered to lend me a dress that she'd said "will look amazing on you because it looks amazing on me," and stuck around to help me get ready. It was a royal-blue cocktail dress that I thought would clash with our hair color, but she was right. It looked amazing when I put it on.

"It makes your skin glow," Rory said, going through my lipsticks to find a good color. And it didn't wash out my hair. If anything, it made it seem an even deeper red.

The dress was tight, as Rory was a bit shorter and smaller than me. I probably wouldn't be able to breathe, but it was a small price to pay. It was bare on one shoulder and had a cutout in the short sleeve on the other. "Whatever you paid for this dress, it was worth it," I told her as she helped zip me into it. There was a cute diamanté belt around the waist that I hadn't noticed before.

"Really suck it in," she told me, and I pulled in my stomach, holding my breath, and she managed to get the zipper all the way to the top. We both exhaled when we saw that it would fit. I added a pair of black open-toe high heels, again loving that I could wear these with Evan and still be shorter next to him.

"Are you worried about seeing all your former tormentors tonight?" Rory asked as I slipped my shoes on.

"Not really. I should probably be having, like, PTSD flashbacks or something, but all those years of therapy did do me some good. I'm not going to allow any of those kids to have any control over me or my life. I'm going to go enjoy myself, and they don't get a say in whether or not I have a good time." I had put most of that high school trauma behind me, and part of that was due to Evan. How protective he was of me, how much he believed in me. I didn't have anything to fear from any of those people.

They couldn't touch me.

"Have fun. But not too much fun because Evan's not into that," Rory teased, kissing me on the cheek. "I'm going to get out of here before he shows up. Unless you need a chaperone. And you might once he sees you in that dress."

"Get out of here," I told her, listening to her laugh all the way to the front door. There was a knock about thirty seconds later, and I figured she'd forgotten something.

"Rory, what—" My voice cut off when I saw that it was Evan.

Who was staring at me like I was the Vince Lombardi Trophy.

He looked amazing—I loved him in semi-formalwear. So clean-cut and sexy. Tonight he had on his dark-gray tailored suit and a tie that looked surprisingly close to the color of my dress. Like we were about to go to prom. My teenage self gasped in excitement. Then I wondered if Rory had sent him a text.

"Wow," he finally breathed. "You look so hot that I'm afraid I'm going to burn my fingers if I touch you. You are stunning."

"Back at you."

He stepped through the front door and put his hands on my waist, gripping me tightly. "Are you sure we can't skip the reunion and just stay here?"

"Do you want Aubrey to issue death warrants for the both of us? I have to do whatever menial tasks she has planned, and you are the star attraction. We have to be there."

He nuzzled my neck. "Are you sure I can't change your mind?"

If he kept doing that, he definitely would. "No. We have to go."

With an exaggerated sigh, he let go and took my hand. On the car ride over, I told him all about Aubrey's excessive attention to detail when it came to the decorations. "Like, they're balloons and Christmas lights. It's not that big of a deal."

He picked up my hand and kissed the back of it. "I can't wait to see it."

I couldn't wait to walk into the reunion on Evan's arm. If Aubrey had allowed it, I might have even worn a custom T-shirt that said HERE WITH EVAN DAWSON.

And when we arrived at the reunion, it was every bit as awesome as I'd imagined it would be. We stopped at the registration table to get name tags for both of us, which seemed silly for him. Like everybody at the reunion wouldn't know exactly who he was. The two women running the table gave me a whole lot of side-eye, as if they couldn't figure out why I was the one there with Evan.

Living well really was the best kind of revenge.

Aubrey had left a name tag for me, and I stuck it onto my dress. When we went into the ballroom, Evan nodded. "You guys did a good job. It looks nice."

"Don't let my sister hear you say that. It can't be just nice. It's the best reunion ever. Make sure you say that to her. At least five or six times. I need to check on the food real fast. Will you find somewhere for us to sit?"

"Yep." He kissed me hard and fast, and he left me breathless for more.

The food table looked fine; I didn't know why Aubrey wanted me to monitor it. The catering staff were doing an excellent job of keeping the trays filled and the punch bowl topped off. I picked up a pair of tongs to move them over a couple of inches. It was the only thing I could think to do so that I could tell Aubrey I had helped.

"Ashton, you clean up nicely."

I turned my head and nearly dropped the tongs I was holding. It was Rand from work. "What are you doing here?"

He had on a name tag that said Archie Abrams. "Oh, you know. Just came by to say hi to the old gang. Is your fiancé, Evan Dawson, here? I'd love to chat with him. Brenda filled me in on the specifics of your relationship. Your pretty boy doesn't know, does he?"

Just like that, my life literally flashed before my eyes. This was it. I was done. Rand would expose me, and Evan would hate me.

I'd been living in denial that this day of reckoning would come, and now it was here.

"That you only dated him in order to get dirt on him? I should get my phone out. I'd love to film his reaction."

"Stop it," I hissed at him. "What do you want?"

"Well, since you turned out to be such a terrible reporter, I'm here to get the story you couldn't. I figured talking to Evan's old high school friends would be the best place to start. Somebody here has to have the inside scoop."

I couldn't let him talk to Evan. Rand would ruin everything. "What will it take to make you leave?"

"How about you going on the record saying you've slept with your fiancé?"

"I haven't."

He let out a bark of laughter. "Right. No wonder Brenda wanted to replace you. You're not even a very good liar."

"Just go," I said.

He seemed to be considering this. "Pass. And you can stop your scared-bunny routine. I'm not going to out you tonight and make a scene. I want people to talk to me, so I need to fly under the radar. I'll mind my business, and you mind yours." He walked away with a smirk. How had I ever liked hanging out with him? Such an ambitious, sneaky jerk.

I made my way back over to Evan, not sure if I could trust in what Rand had said. I could absolutely see him torpedoing me just to get Evan's reaction shot. It would be a good runner-up story once Rand realized that Evan was exactly who he said he was.

"Let's dance," I said, pulling Evan out onto the dance floor with me. The song was a slow one, and I wrapped myself up in his embrace, letting him be my shield against the rest of the world.

I was going to have to tell him. I'd hoped I could slink away from ISEN and pretend that Brenda's story and my involvement with it had never happened. But I was beginning to realize that it might not be possible. I had to warn him what Brenda, and now Rand, were up to.

Evan had an away game this weekend. I'd tell him on Monday, when he came over to hang out after practice. I wouldn't want him distracted for the game.

That would give me a few days to build up my courage and figure out how to tell him.

Aubrey danced up alongside us with Justin and yelled, "What do you think of the reunion?"

"Best reunion ever!" Evan and I responded at the same time, laughing as we did so. Aubrey didn't seem to notice. She just gave us a satisfied nod and returned her attention to her husband.

After we'd danced to both fast and slow songs, Evan asked, "Do you want to get something to drink?"

I nodded and followed him to the refreshments. Which were still operating just fine without me. He poured me a glass first and handed it to me.

I had just raised it to my lips when a man approached us, putting his hand on Evan's shoulder. "Dawson! How have you been?"

"Piz?"

Aaron Piznarski, Evan's best friend in high school, stood there with his arms open, ready to hug Evan. People like me always tell themselves in high school that the jocks and cheerleaders would get fat and/or bald, but Piz was still in shape and had all of his hair. And that cocky smirk I'd always hated.

Evan shook his hand instead and gave him an appraising look. "Do you remember Ashton Bailey?"

Piz's eyes flicked over me, and I didn't see any recognition. "No. Should I?"

"We used to hang out at her house. She's Aubrey's little sister?"

That blank stare continued, and he frowned slightly. "I remember being over at Aubrey's, but not her family."

It was odd to stand there with the man who was responsible for my teenage trauma. I'd been mocked, humiliated, and ostracized, and he couldn't even remember who I was.

My pain and I were totally insignificant to him.

He held out his hand to me. "I'm Aaron. Everyone calls me Piz."

I couldn't bring myself to shake his hand and instead took a step behind Evan, letting him be a barrier between me and his former best friend. I should have been laying into Piz, forcing him to face what he'd done. Here I'd thought I was totally over all my issues and problems, and instead I was cowering instead of confronting him.

And Evan seemed completely tuned in to how I was feeling. "She knows who you are. And instead of introducing yourself, I think you should probably apologize to her."

"For what, man?"

"For hurting her. For making fun of her and being cruel. You bullied her and humiliated her when we were seniors. How can you have forgotten that?" he asked. It made me wonder how many other girls Piz had tormented, given that he couldn't place me.

"I'm sorry?" It sounded more like a question than an actual apology. And it didn't mean anything because he obviously only said it because Evan had told him to. "What exactly did I do?"

Evan rattled off a quick list of what Piz had done to me, and I saw the recognition the second it finally dawned on his face.

Then his reaction was not what I had expected. I'd thought he might apologize. Tell me he'd grown and matured and regretted how he'd treated me. Instead, he said, "Oh right! You're Stalker! Look at you. From not to hot in just ten years. Too bad I didn't lock you down in high school. Although," he said with a gross, suggestive leer, "you could come home with me, and we could make up for lost time."

I drew in a sharp breath. It was like Evan was always such a gentleman to me that I'd forgotten men could be this way. Crude and vomit-inducing. Disgust slithered through my intestines. I felt tainted just by standing near him.

"Are you serious?" Evan's face turned dark. My hand was on his arm, and I felt his muscles tightening, saw his right hand clench into a fist.

He was going to punch Piz. I set my cup of punch down on the table.

Not that Piz deserved saving, but I stepped in between the two men right after Evan shoved Piz. "It doesn't matter. Let it go," I told him.

The veins on Evan's neck strained, as if it was taking everything he had to hold back. I could only imagine how much professional trouble he'd be in if he hit somebody at a high school reunion. He didn't need to be fined tens of thousands of dollars because of some male-pattern dumbness. I put both of my hands on his shoulders. "Come with me. Let's go out into the hallway."

And cool off, because he needed it.

"What is your problem?" Piz asked, apparently not realizing how close he was to a beatdown.

"You're my problem!" Evan retorted.

I pushed against Evan lightly, but it was literally like trying to move a wall. I tried again to get him to listen. "If you hit this idiot, you are going to ruin Aubrey's reunion, and then she'll kill us both, and she knows how to get away with murder. She went to law school."

The tension in his shoulders relaxed slightly, and he nodded. I took him by the hand, intending to lead him away.

"Yeah, run along. Listen to your stupid girlfriend." Piz didn't actually say *girlfriend*, although I wished he had instead of his other word choice, because that's when Evan almost went nuclear.

Evan reached out and again shoved Piz with his free hand. Then some choice and colorful words were exchanged, and it wasn't until I said, "Evan, please," that he finally broke things off and went out with me into a quiet hallway.

He started pacing, the fury still evident in every line of his face. "Can you believe that guy? How was I ever friends with him? If he thinks he's going to insult the woman I love, he's got another—"

"Wait, what?" I couldn't breathe. All the oxygen had left the planet, and I was going to suffocate.

In that moment, Evan realized what he had said. The anger left him as he crossed over to take both of my hands in his.

"The woman you love?" I repeated, still unable to believe he'd said it. "That's me, right?"

"Of course that's you. I know I haven't said it yet, and that probably wasn't the best way, but I do love you." He let out a self-conscious laugh. "I've never said that to anyone I wasn't related to before."

Which made it more special. I'd said it once before to another man, but I shouldn't have. Because what I'd felt for him seriously paled in comparison with what I felt for Evan.

I had to tell him the truth. I couldn't tell him I loved him until I'd been completely honest with him.

Even though telling him about Brenda and the story might mean I'd never get to say those three words to him.

I was worried it might hurt his feelings when I didn't say it back, but now that he'd turned the faucet on, he didn't seem to want to stop talking.

"When you got sick, I realized how serious my feelings were for you. That I was in love with you, and something bad happening to you was the worst thing I could imagine." He let out a deep breath. "There's been something about you from the very beginning. Some spark that I couldn't look away from. Some invisible thread that keeps tugging me closer and closer to you."

My heart turned completely liquid, melting its way through my body, filling me with a heady warmth. Even though I'd been fighting it at the time, the same was true for me. Always had been where Evan was concerned. There was something about him that kept me coming back even when I didn't want to.

Like my heart had always known what my head was too stupid to figure out.

"And it's more than just loving you, Ashton. I want to build a life with you. I can't imagine a future without you in it."

The shock of his words hit me like a bucket of ice water. "What . . . what are you saying?"

Was he saying what I thought he was saying?

"This isn't really the place or time," Evan said. "I don't know if you see us like that, too, but we can talk about it later."

Right. Later. Later we would discuss *if we had a future and whether or not we should get married.* That was where this was going, right?

A future we wouldn't have when I told him everything. The idea of finally spilling my guts made me start to hyperventilate.

I did the only thing I could do. Distract and change the subject. "You were going to punch somebody for me."

"I'd punch a hundred guys for you."

"Aw . . . that would so land you in prison."

He laughed and kissed me.

"Let's get out of here," I said. We'd put in our time, and I didn't want Evan to go back into that ballroom and lay Piz out.

I also didn't want to share him anymore that evening. I wanted to stay in the happy little bubble of "I love you" for as long as I possibly could.

"Let's go," he agreed. We ended up going into a fast-food place in our very nice outfits and getting a couple of hamburger meals with chocolate shakes. We had to leave when he started to draw attention, but it took about fifteen minutes. Like nobody could believe that Evan Dawson would descend from the heavens to mingle with mere mortals.

A feeling I understood all too well.

As he drove me back to my condo, I thought about everything that had happened that night. My instinct was to stay quiet, to not let him know exactly what I had tried to do to him and his career. But I couldn't stand on the sidelines and let him take the hit when I could protect him. If I did, it would be like what he'd done to me in high school. Where he'd stood aside and let his friends attack and hurt me because he was too afraid to lose them.

Ironically enough, now I knew exactly how he'd felt back then. I couldn't keep the truth from him any longer. I had to warn him. My heart raced inside my chest, nearly choking me. As if it was trying to keep me from speaking.

"Hey, do you remember how I told you that my boss was doing something unethical?" How was I supposed to phrase this? How could I do the least possible damage to our relationship? "They want to come after you. For a story."

"Wouldn't be the first time. It's one of the reasons why I don't like reporters," Evan said, lifting my hand to his lips and kissing it. He flashed me a brilliant smile. "Don't worry. I'm a big boy, and I can take care of myself."

"I don't think you understand. My boss is determined to ruin you."

"Lots of people are trying to ruin me, Ashton. It comes with the fame and the money. People want to knock you down a notch."

He pulled into a spot in my parking lot and got out of the car before I could explain more. I followed quickly and again tried to think of the best way to tell him what I had done. What could happen to him and his reputation if Brenda had her way.

But my mouth refused to cooperate, especially once he'd laced his fingers through mine.

Maybe it could wait one more day. Or until after his game, like I'd initially planned.

He loved me, I loved him, and I wanted to have some happy part of that before everything completely fell apart.

Evan walked me to my door, and after I unlocked it, I left it open for him to follow me inside. I kicked off my shoes and put my keys on the table. "Maybe we could watch a movie or something."

Anything to delay the inevitable confession I was going to have to make.

But he stayed outside, silhouetted by the hallway lamp. "That's probably not a good idea."

"Why not?" I asked, walking back over to stand in front of him.

He shoved his hands into his pockets. "I have no field vision when it comes to you. I don't know what's going to happen or what I should do."

"That's because this isn't a football game, and I'm not a two-hundred-and-ninety-pound defensive lineman coming at you." I reached for him, but he took a step back.

Which surprised me.

"I can't come in because . . . I'm worried that if I walk in there right now, I won't be able to walk back out."

CHAPTER TWENTY-THREE

The air between us turned heavy and thick, electrically charged with the emotional and physical attraction we were both obviously feeling in that moment.

His words thrilled me in a way I didn't know was possible. Like I had this power over him he could only barely resist.

I knew the right thing to do in that moment would have been to tell him good night. To remind myself that playing with fire got people burned.

Apparently somebody was going to need to sign me up for the burn trauma unit. I moved closer to him. He didn't react, like a perfectly sculpted statue. Only his eyes managed to skate across my skin.

"How do you do that?" I whispered, my stomach quivering. "Make me feel like you're touching me when all you're doing is looking?"

I wanted to touch him, but it had to be his choice. I wouldn't push him.

"Are you sure I can't convince you to come inside?"

His eyes closed, and I saw the slow bob of his Adam's apple. "What is it you want, Ashton?" He practically growled the words.

And it filled my head with the things I'd imagined for weeks now. Things I'd wanted to take place between us. "There are a lot of things I want. Ice cream that doesn't make you fat. A job I don't hate." Somehow

I got just a tiny bit closer. I could feel him on me, even though there were still micromillimeters between us. "To feel desired. Like it's all a man can do to keep himself in check because he wants me so badly."

"Do you think that's not happening here?" The words exploded out of him. "Because trust me, it is. I'm choosing not to act on it. I have thought about what it would be like between you and me. How amazing it would feel. But I drew this line in the sand, and I can't cross it no matter how much I want to."

His words managed to make parts of me feel strong and other parts go weak. My entire body had become one desperate ache, dying for his touch. "Sand is a terrible place to draw lines. They'll keep getting washed away."

"Ashton." I loved the way his voice hugged the consonants in my name.

"I need your help." Some part of my brain registered that it was a cheap shot. So far Evan hadn't been able to resist whenever I'd called on him for assistance. I did want to respect him and his choices. He was always so kind and giving with me. The very least I could do was keep my mindless hormones in check. But want and desire overwhelmed me, flipping off my ability to think rationally. All I knew in that moment was that I had to have his hands on me, and I didn't care what I had to do to make that happen. "I can't unzip this dress by myself." I turned around, presenting him with my back, walking forward a few steps.

It was only kind of a lie; I probably could have undone it, but it would have involved a MacGyvered metal hanger and me cursing the universe for making it so hard to do.

I felt him walk up behind me, his breathing harsh in my ears. He closed the door, and my entire body lit up with excitement the moment I heard it catch.

Shivering in anticipation, I didn't dare move as he came closer.

"Do you know how badly you make me want to lose control?" he asked, his words hot against my bare shoulder. I literally couldn't uncurl my toes. "I want to feel your skin against mine. To be that close to you."

I wanted that, too.

He kissed the base of my neck, which sent delicious swirls through my limbs. I wanted to back up, press myself against him, turn around, and convince him that control was highly overrated.

His hand went to the top of my zipper. I felt like I was standing at the top of a high hill, running down with total disregard for my safety. Feeling off-balance and as if I was always one step away from plunging down.

Evan tugged at the metal tag, inching it down so slowly that my heart started keeping time to it. *Thud-thunk. Thud-thunk. Thud-thunk.* The backs of his knuckles brushed against my skin, leaving tiny pools of fire everywhere they touched.

"You're so soft," he said against my earlobe, and I almost collapsed against him at the sensation. "Are you this soft everywhere?"

"Yuh-huh" was my artful reply. Now my heart had sped up, and my earlobes, fingers, and feet throbbed in time with it.

The zipper kept going down oh, so slowly, and my veins ached in response to how he was drawing this out, torturing us both.

He took it all the way down, and I gasped when he touched the small of my back, wrapping his hand around the curve of my hip. I could feel my body rise and fall beneath his fingers, and I was ready to shatter from the tension.

It was too much. I couldn't take a second more without reacting. I whirled around, and before I could even make a move, his mouth was on mine. Hungry. Desperate. Wanting. Kissing me in exquisitely hot and intense strokes.

His kiss made my entire world shrink down to that point. So that the only thing I could feel was how my body went fluid against his, my softness crashing into his strength. He was all I could taste, all I could feel, the only thing that seemed real to me.

My stomach tightened and swirled with heat, the need for him growing stronger and stronger with each passing moment. My heart transformed itself into a hummingbird, wings flapping faster and faster inside my chest.

His arms crushed me to him, making it impossible to breathe. I didn't care. Who needed to breathe when you could be kissed like this?

Evan said something that might have possibly been my name as he moved from my lips to just under my jaw. He left hot, feathery kisses there, and it shorted out my knees. I grabbed at him, trying to stay upright. His kisses inched down along my throat, and the rest of my limbs gave way. He hit the spot beneath my ear that made me insane, then kissed his way down to my shoulders, tasting and kissing me there.

His other hand was on my one sleeve, pulling at it. That one action started a tiny warning bell in a corner of my mind.

I wanted this. I wanted him. I loved him. It seemed like the most natural thing to do.

But there were so many reasons why we shouldn't. I couldn't think of a single one at the moment, but this needed to stop.

"Evan, wait." I backed up, putting some much-needed distance between us before my body could overthrow my brain and put us right back where we'd been a second ago.

His gaze was unfocused, hazy. He was panting, hard. So was I. My chest was heaving as I tried to both catch my breath and slide my sleeve back into place.

Then the reasons returned. Evan wanted to wait. And I couldn't do something like this, be that intimate with him, when I was still keeping a secret from him. I had to tell him the truth.

Although I was in no condition right now to do that. He needed to leave before I lost myself in him and his touch.

"We can't," I said. He looked regretful but nodded. "I don't want to be the reason you break a commitment you've made to yourself." I said it as a reminder to both of us.

"Right now you seem like a pretty good reason." His voice was low and sexy, and I only just stopped myself from jumping back into his arms.

Then I felt bad for my impulse. I knew he wanted to wait, and here I was, throwing down gauntlets. "I'm . . . I'm sorry. I shouldn't have pushed—"

Evan cut me off. "Don't apologize. You weren't alone in any of that."

Would I ever breathe normally again? "You should probably go."

"Yes, I should."

He opened the door, and I didn't know how he'd managed it. Nothing in my body felt like it was currently under my control.

Evan paused in the doorway. "Lock your door."

"Are you still worried I'm going to get murdered?"

"No. I'm worried I'll change my mind."

Evan had to travel to Cincinnati for his next game, and I was actually glad for the time apart. Because part of me worried that I would attack him again the second I saw him.

I tried to focus on what needed to happen next. I had to tell him everything about Brenda and the story and my involvement in it. When I watched the game on Sunday, I couldn't even enjoy his performance. My stomach felt like it was feeding on itself. Twisted and knotty and not good.

Because I knew the fallout from this would be epic. I could only hope that he loved me enough that it wouldn't matter.

When he got home late on Sunday, I texted him to go home and go to bed. Not only because I knew he was tired, but also because I wanted to delay what I knew was coming. We made plans to get together Monday after practice.

Coincidentally enough, we were scheduled to see each other at the same time my whole world would end.

The next day at work, Brenda called me into her office for her regular but brief interrogation.

Only she didn't ask me if I had any information on Evan.

"Follow me."

I did as she commanded, and she led me onto the set of *Sports Today*, our evening news/sports show that had all the recaps and scores of the games that day. The two hosts were sitting behind a big desk, getting their makeup touched up.

Brenda held a paper on a clipboard out to me. "Sign this. You're going on air."

"I'm not signing a . . ." My voice trailed off as I realized what she had handed me. It wasn't a reprimand. It was a release form.

One of the crew members came up and put a wireless microphone on my lapel.

"What is happening right now?" I asked.

"You are officially out of time. Either you're going on *Sports Today* to tell the world you've slept with Evan Dawson, or you can go back to your desk and pack up your things."

"This has to be some kind of joke," I said, even though I knew it wasn't. My outrage that she wanted to hurt Evan overrode every instinct that told me to be quiet and suffer through whatever she said. My authority-figure anxiety could suck it. Time to stand up for me. And for Evan. "Do you really think I'm going to lie, throw away my integrity just because you want me to?"

"Oh, sweetie, you left that in Evan's bedroom along with your scruples and morals."

She looked crazed. Like a Disney villain during the final act of the movie. She forced a pen into my hand and then put her own hand on top of it, as if she was going to make me sign. I dropped the pen and the clipboard.

"Honestly, Ashton. You are such a child," she hissed. "When I gave you this assignment, I thought, 'Finally! A kindred spirit!' Someone who knows what it's like to be rejected by Evan Dawson and who wanted revenge. Only instead you fell deeper under his spell, like a little idiot."

This was not what Brenda had been selling me all along. She'd made it about ratings and, I don't know, like, girl power and glass ceilings. Now she was saying it was personal? Why? "Revenge? What did Evan do to you?"

I didn't expect her to answer. But it was like she'd become unhinged. "We dated. You think you're the only one who ever dated Evan 'Awesome' Dawson? We met at an ISEN event, and he invited me back to his place. Where I assumed he'd finally drop the charade. That we were both grown-ups and that his invitation meant what it means to every other man on the planet."

Understanding smacked into me, hard. "You're the naked girl in the bathroom. He told me about you."

That only made her outrage worse. "I walked out into his family room with nothing on. Do you know what he did? He put a blanket around me and asked me to leave. Threw me out like I was trash. He said he'd call. He didn't. Do you have any idea how humiliating that was?"

I didn't really know what to make of this. Brenda was clearly obsessed. I'd spent so much time seeing her as this scary professional that I'd never even thought about her personal life. Or what psychological disorders she might be suffering from.

"If you do not go on this show and tell the world that you and Evan have sex, your career is finished. I will personally guarantee that you never work in sports again."

"I feel sad for you," I said, and it was true. In part because I'd been where she was. So consumed with exacting revenge for a slight that I thought had been caused by Evan that I had been willing to be unethical. To lie. To do whatever it took to get the story.

I wasn't interested in being that person anymore.

"Ten minutes to air!" someone called out. The show was about to begin. There was no way I was going on camera and lying, just for my job. I'd never been willing to do that. I would have gone to just about any length to find out the truth, and I probably should have quit my job when I'd realized Evan was telling me the truth.

It was a job I'd known for a long time that I would have to give up.

I should have made that sacrifice for him. And for myself. I should have admitted I couldn't have my cake and eat it, too.

"I don't need your pity!" Brenda said.

She might not have needed it, but I was still going to give it to her. Sort of. "I'm sorry you got your one feeling hurt, but that's not Evan's fault. He's a good man, and I won't help you do anything to ruin his name."

If I hadn't been able to stand up for him before, I was certainly going to do it now. She was not going to use me to hurt him. It was so petty and selfish. And . . . stupid. Who did something like this?

You did, that little internal conscience of mine whispered.

It disgusted me that I'd been willing to wallow in the muck with her. I'd put my head in the sand, prioritizing my career and my fears over doing what was right. I'd put them above Evan, a man who loved me. The man I loved.

I'd betrayed Evan and what we shared, and that realization made my stomach plummet down to my toes.

I didn't deserve him. I didn't deserve our relationship. I'd been such a coward.

No more.

I was taking a stand.

Brenda must have seen my conviction on my face because she tried again. "Whatever job you want. Whatever department. You choose your salary. Name it, and it's yours. All you have to do is go on the show and say five words: 'I slept with Evan Dawson.'"

Funnily enough, I wasn't even tempted. There was nothing she could have said to me to change my mind. I was going to do the right thing. No matter what it cost me.

"Ashton?"

No. No, no, no, no. This was not happening.

I turned in horror to see Evan standing behind me, wearing a mask of confusion, disbelief, and heartache.

"What are you doing here?" I asked, the words little more than a whisper.

CHAPTER TWENTY-FOUR

He'd heard me. There was no question of that. Little fissures formed on the surface of my heart, threatening to break. This was not how I'd wanted him to find out. I felt like I was going to throw up.

Brenda started directing the cameramen. "Turn the cameras this way. Get them both in the shot. Hurry."

"They asked me to come on *Sports Today* to talk about yesterday's game. But I guess that was all a ruse. Were you really going to go on air and say we'd had sex?" Evan asked.

This could not be happening. "What? No! I told Brenda no repeatedly. I would never do that to you."

"Then what is going on?"

I wanted to ask him to go someplace quieter, somewhere without an audience, but I didn't think he would leave if I asked him to. "A while back Brenda, who I'm sure you recognize, asked me to find out the truth about you. About whether or not you were actually a virgin. So I started talking to people you'd dated, like Whitley. Hanging out with you to uncover the truth. And then when you wanted to fake the engagement, Brenda thought—"

"She thought it would give you credibility," Evan finished, the disgust in his voice evident. "So you've been lying to me this entire time. While I was falling in love with you, it was all just . . . a job? A story?"

"No! It started out that way, and I wanted to tell you, but I couldn't figure out a way. My feelings for you are real. That was never a lie, even when I wanted it to be."

My words didn't seem to have any effect on him. "You couldn't figure out a way to tell me the truth? It's not hard. You just open your mouth and say the words. You didn't want to face the consequences of your actions, so you just lied and lied. I worked so hard to earn your trust, and the whole time you were lying and unworthy of mine."

What could I say to that? He was right. There had been a way to tell him; I just hadn't wanted to. I'd been a selfish chicken who was unworthy of his trust.

"I told her to have sex with you. To seduce you. Did she do it?" Brenda asked, the malicious glee in her voice evident.

The pain in Evan's eyes increased, which didn't seem possible. "The night of the reunion, was that what you were doing? Trying to seduce me for some story?"

How could he think that? "Evan, no. I would never do that. I was the one who stopped it."

"You heard what I said," Brenda kept interjecting, and I seriously considered punching her in the face just to get her to shut up. "I offered Ashton her dream job. Whatever she wants, as long as she tells the world all about you and your relationship. Do you really think she would turn that down? If you know anything about her, it's how ambitious she is."

"Don't listen to her," I said, even though I could see Brenda's words had found their mark.

"She wanted to pay you back. For what you and your friends did to her in high school."

"Shut up, Brenda!" She was going to ruin everything.

"Is that really what this is about?" Evan asked. "You've been waiting ten years to get me back? Like some kind of long con? To turn into my perfect woman and then destroy me?"

"No!" That had never been my intent. I could feel that I was losing him. That with every word he spoke and every protest I made, he was slipping farther away from me.

And I didn't know how to make it stop. My throat became so thick I could barely breathe. A crushing, shooting pain started in my stomach and then spread throughout my chest. I blinked away hot tears. I had to keep it together. I wouldn't break down and lose it. Not while I still had a chance of trying to convince him.

He looked down at the floor and then back up at me. "I would have given you everything. Every part of me. All of my future. And this was just a way to publicly humiliate me?"

"I'm sorry. That wasn't what happened."

"An apology is not a magical token you can turn in for instant forgiveness," he said.

But I was sorry. I had felt terrible about keeping a secret from him for such a long time. I didn't know how to make him understand that.

When I didn't respond, he said, "The worst part is you lied. Over and over again. You lied to me."

"I'm sorry," I repeated, and guilty, defensive anger sneaked its way in to mingle with my fear and sadness. "But I'm not the only one who lied."

"What?" He looked taken aback. "When did I lie?"

"You lied for your career, too." Maybe I was grasping at straws, but I wasn't thinking clearly and was throwing anything I could at him. "You lied about our engagement to get your contract renewed."

"That's not the same thing!"

"It was exactly the same."

"No, it wasn't. Because I did it only to be close to you! I couldn't have cared less about my contract. I wanted to be with you. You lied to destroy me. They aren't the same."

"She wanted to hurt you," Brenda added. I knew that if I lunged for her, Security would escort me from the building, and I might never get another chance to fix things with Evan. Not that I was anywhere close to doing that now. I had just accused him of lying! How was that going to solve anything?

"Well, mission accomplished," Evan said sadly. There was such a note of finality in his voice that I realized there was nothing I could say or do to change his mind. He walked over to me and held out his hand.

For one hopeful moment I thought he was offering it to me, wanting us to go somewhere to work things out, despite his anger.

Instead, he said, "I need the ring. It was my mother's."

"Your mother's ring?" My throat tightened even more, and I felt several tears escaping. He'd given me his beloved mother's ring? He'd said he'd have his assistant pick one up, and the entire time it had been his mom's? The ache in my chest intensified a hundredfold. "I didn't know."

"What does it matter?"

"It does matter. That you would let me wear this." Somehow it made everything worse. I sniffed, wiping at my nose.

He lifted his hand. "Please give it back."

With my tears blinding me, I pulled the ring off and let it drop into his palm. I noticed he made sure not to touch me.

"Not many people can pull a perfect blindside on me. You can at least feel good about that," Evan said before he turned to walk out of the studio.

"I love you!" I called in a panicked voice and watched as he stopped. My heart lurched with hope. I hadn't told him yet; could that be enough?

It wasn't. He squared his shoulders, lifted his head, and walked out of sight. The fissures covering my heart began to break apart, drifting away one piece at a time until there was nothing left.

"That was perfect," Brenda gushed. "Now just sign this release, and tomorrow we can discuss your new position."

A heavy, hollow emptiness began in my chest, spreading out like a dark stain until it filled every part of me. I was numb to the pain—for now. I knew it would destroy me later. "Did you really think you could get me to go on air and lie?"

"I don't care if you do or not." She gestured toward the cameras. "Either way, I already have a story to air."

That would just be the icing on the cake. Having my personal heartache and trauma played out as entertainment across the country.

"I quit."

It might have been too little too late, but I was done with Brenda and this network.

"Ha," she said. "I predicted it weeks ago. That you'd be the girl who'd give up her career for some guy."

"You don't understand. Although I'm not surprised someone like you wouldn't. I'm not choosing a guy or a relationship over this job. I'm choosing my integrity. I'm choosing me." I'd been gambling with my integrity for months, letting Brenda and my anger chip away at it one piece at a time. It was time for that to stop.

I wouldn't be this person any longer.

I pulled the microphone off my shirt and placed it on a nearby table.

"You should probably get professional help," I said to her as I made my way out of the studio.

Part of me should have felt triumphant at finally standing up to my boss, but all I felt was an overwhelming, acute sense of loss.

No job, no prospects. Soon I'd be unable to afford to live on my own.

And no Evan.

That hurt worst of all.

I hid in my condo. I had nowhere else to go, nothing I had to do. I'd already paid my rent through the end of the year, so I had until January first before I had to move out. My bank account was getting close to empty, and it didn't help that I occasionally ordered takeout. I didn't want to go to the grocery store.

At some point I texted Aubrey to give her the full details of the breakup, thinking that if I could write down the words, maybe everything would stop hurting so much. It turned out not to be very helpful, as I cried for about three hours straight after I'd finished.

I'd had to call and ask my parents if I could move back home at the beginning of the new year. While I'd braced myself for scolding and gloating, they were beyond kind about it, and not a single "I told you so" left their lips.

Maybe it wouldn't be so bad. Lots of people my age moved home again.

The one kindness the universe had given me was that Brenda had been unable to air the footage of Evan and me arguing. To my surprise, Rand emailed me to tell me about it, informing me that Brenda had been beyond furious because although Evan had an old release on file, I hadn't signed the form, and I was in every shot. It rendered everything they had filmed unusable. He sent it to me as a jokey email, as if we were still work buddies who wanted to mock our boss together.

I didn't know what he'd hoped to get out of it—maybe my reaction? But I blocked his email and felt some small relief that at least I'd been spared that public humiliation.

A couple of weeks after our breakup, around dinnertime, I heard a knock at my door. I actually had a sunshine-y moment of hope that Evan had come to see me. Realistically, I knew it wasn't him, but I was desperate for things to be better.

When I answered the door, I saw that I'd been right. It was my mom, my sisters, and my niece.

"Ashton, seriously. You stink. When is the last time you showered?" Rory asked, averting her face when she walked in.

"I don't know." It had been a while. I couldn't bring myself to care. What was the point of showering when there was no one around to appreciate it?

As they came inside, I went back to my nest on the couch. I'd made it up with blankets and pillows, and the seat cushion essentially had a permanent imprint of my butt. Aubrey began collecting the empty takeout containers on the coffee table, taking them into the kitchen and putting them in the trash.

My mom sat down on the couch next to me, and I felt a family therapy moment coming on.

"I know I'm depressed, Mom. But I'm sad. I'm allowed to be sad. I loved him, and I messed it all up." My mom nodded knowingly, and I was sure that by this point Aubrey had broken our attorney-client privilege and shared the whole story with my family. In fact, I was sure of it, given the sympathetic looks they were all shooting in my direction.

It was also probably why my parents had been so low-key about letting me move back home.

"You did something he didn't know how to handle," my mother said. "Kids with dependable parents who are around feel taken care of and safe. To kids like Evan, who feel abandoned or abused or lose their parents in an accident, the world doesn't feel safe at all. And in order to be safe, they have to be in control of everything.

"He thought he understood what the situation was between you, and you threw him a horrible curveball. I'm hoping that while he processes it, there's someone in his life who will show him that forgiveness is what will heal him, not anger."

That made some sense. And I knew all about how anger couldn't heal you and just left behind festering, gaping sores. I had wanted to destroy him for something I thought he'd done to me. I'd spent ten years hating him. But the best thing for me had been forgiving him. Even though I hadn't realized it at the time, forgiving him, beginning to trust in him, was what had made it so I could move on.

It had helped me become a better, stronger person.

"I don't think it will matter, Mom." I didn't have any hope that things would work out between Evan and me. "He hasn't called or texted. I've tried composing the perfect text to him a million times. The one that will make him accept my apology and beg me to get back together with him. But I just can't find the right words."

"So you're just giving up?"

"I'm not giving up," I retorted. "I'm accepting reality."

"Ashton, my daughter, I love you. But this is what you do. You're not 'accepting reality.' You are definitely giving up. You always take the easy way out. Instead of telling Evan the truth about your work situation, you pretended like it didn't exist. You literally did nothing and hoped it would all work out and that there wouldn't be any consequences for your inaction."

I gasped, unable to believe my own mother was talking this way to me.

She went on, still in full therapist mode. "And ever since high school, you make protecting yourself your number-one priority. You're never vulnerable. You don't take risks."

"I take risks!" I protested.

My mom smiled sadly at me. "I don't mean professionally. I mean personally. You keep everyone at arm's length, including Evan. He didn't deserve that."

I was in complete and total shock. Was she right? Was I just giving up?

"Maybe you need to make the first move. Show him how you feel instead of waiting for him to come to you. I think you're the one who needs to apologize and own your behavior."

Anger and denial roared up inside me, and I was about to tell my mom she had no idea what she was talking about when Aubrey asked, "Ashton, when was the last time you ate?"

Her question diffused my anger, which was probably the point. She'd always been good at running interference for me and my mother. "I'm not sure." My appetite had been completely killed, and I couldn't find the energy to eat on a regular basis. But I didn't want to tell her in front of Charlotte that I'd been too sad to eat.

"Your fridge has nothing but soy sauce packets and milk that has turned into cottage cheese. Mom, would you mind going to the store? I'm going to clear out whatever science experiments are happening in the refrigerator."

"Any special requests?" my mom asked, but I just shook my head. She promised she'd be back soon, and I tried not to think about what she'd just said to me. As she pulled her keys from her purse, I had to force myself to not think about when Evan went shopping for me after my surgery. The way he'd taken care of me, looked at me like he'd loved me.

And I'd ruined all of it.

My mom was right. I had screwed up even worse than I'd originally thought. I sucked in several deep breaths, trying to ignore the sharp shooting pains against my chest.

"Come on," Rory said, standing in front of me and offering me her hands. "Aubrey and I will clean your kitchen, but you have to clean yourself. We won't be able to tell if we cleaned away that funky smell until we know for sure it's not you."

She walked me to my bathroom, turning on the hot water and staying while I took off my clothes.

"Use soap. And shampoo," she said before turning on the ventilation fan and leaving me in my shower.

The water actually felt amazing. I'd forgotten how nice it was to be clean. I washed my hair two times and scrubbed myself all over.

I took the longest shower of my life, until the heat began to disappear. The water beating down on me felt so cleansing. Not just physically but emotionally as well.

I got out and changed, leaving my hair wet. I brushed through it, getting a couple of tangles clear.

My sisters were loudly discussing the state of my kitchen when I came back out to join them. "Good. You're no longer sporting a cloud of stench behind you," Rory said.

Aubrey stopped scrubbing my peninsula counter and said, "Do you remember when you last left your condo?"

I realized I hadn't since Evan and I broke up. The days all blended together. I could have used my daily sports shows to keep track, but I couldn't watch *SportsCenter* or *Sports Today* without breaking down in hysterical sobs.

Rory, who had never been a big fan of cleaning, came to sit next to me on the couch. She moved the yarn I'd halfheartedly attempted to keep working on out of her way. "What's this?"

"It was a sweater. For Evan for Christmas." There didn't seem much point in making it now, but it did occasionally help keep my hands busy.

She held up the partially constructed sweater. "You must have really loved him, given how bad you are at knitting. Did he know you're terrible? There wouldn't have been a better way to show him how much you truly loved him."

Rory was gently teasing me, trying to get me to smile. It didn't work, and so she changed tactics. "So things got pretty messed up?"

"Yeah. I made some really dumb decisions. I regret them." Which was probably the understatement of the year. There were no words for how bad I felt about the choices I'd made. Or, like my mom said, the choices I had just refused to make.

My sister moved my knitting to the floor at the side of the couch. "You know, Mom was telling me the other day that the decision-making parts of our brains aren't totally developed until we're twenty-five."

"You're saying I have an excuse."

"Yep. Factory installation error." She rubbed her hands together, playing with one of her rings. I recognized her telltale signs that she wanted to say something but wasn't sure that she should.

"Spit it out, Rory."

"Look, I'm not the person to tell other people how to live their lives. I'm barely keeping mine together. But at some point, you have to accept that this is your life now. Evan's not a part of it, and he's probably not coming back. You can't stop living just because he's gone. You need to eat and shower and go outside once in a while."

I nodded. Maybe Rory was right. I had to make some effort to be normal again. To try and live my life the way I had before Evan had become such an important part of it. I needed to fix the parts of me that felt too sad to do anything. Even if that meant faking until I made it.

I couldn't keep sitting around my condo feeling sorry for myself.

Or was that more of me taking the easy way out?

Maybe my mom was right, and I needed to put myself out there. Be vulnerable with Evan. Take a risk.

"Rory! Stop trying to counsel Ashton to get out of work," Aubrey said. Rory rolled her eyes with a smile and went back into the kitchen.

Charlotte was coloring in an *Alice in Wonderland* coloring book on the coffee table. I was a little envious of her and how easy her life was, to be able to get caught up in an art project and tune out the rest of the world.

She caught me looking at her and offered me a crayon. "Want to color?"

I took the blue crayon and sat down next to her on the floor. I colored on the left page, while she colored on the right. It was soothing and relaxing to focus all of my efforts on what I was doing, making something beautiful with my niece.

I put down the blue crayon and reached for the green, intending to color in some grass in my picture. I must have been gripping the crayon too hard when I started shading, because I managed to both break the sharpened tip and snap the crayon in half.

The wax paper made it so that the pieces still dangled together, but it was broken and useless.

Like me.

"What's wrong?" Charlotte asked.

I held up the crayon. "I broke it. I need to toss it out."

She took it from me and peeled back the paper. "It's fine, Aunt Ashton. Broken crayons can still color. See?"

At that I sobbed, like a dam had burst inside me, unleashing tears I didn't even know I had.

Charlotte came over and put her arms around my neck, hugging me tightly. "It's okay. Everything will be okay."

I hoped she was right.

CHAPTER TWENTY-FIVE

Turned out that Charlotte was right. So was Rory.

And even my mom.

I started to exercise and went back to my intramural basketball league, and everyone there was thrilled to see me. I kept my eyes away from the bleachers during the games, not wanting to remember what it was like to have Evan there cheering me on. I even went with my teammates to sing karaoke. My heart wasn't really in it.

I hoped someday it would be.

Christmas came and went, and I moved into my old room at my parents' house. Which still looked just as it had when I'd left for college. I decided that if I was living here, I was going to have a grown-up room. After I'd unpacked all my clothes, I pulled down the bulletin board where I'd thumbtacked ticket stubs and pictures from high school. As I peeled off the layers of photos, I found some candid pictures of Evan in our basement that I had forgotten about.

The pain was swift and fierce, and I had to sit down for a second until it passed.

It was like the moment that I heard about his renegotiated contract. Evan Dawson was currently the highest-paid athlete in the NFL. The numbers, nine figures, were mind-boggling. I was really, truly happy for him. He deserved it. And even though I was quietly cheering him on,

I'd had to fight off the urge to curl up in the fetal position and stay in bed for three days, until everyone stopped reporting about it.

I missed him so much.

Besides aching for Evan and going through the motions of my life, I had plenty of time to think. Turned out my mom was actually a pretty good therapist, and her insights turned out to be, well, insightful.

I did ignore my problems. I did always try to take the easy way out.

I had justified the bad decisions I'd made, even trying to share the blame. Like when I'd accused Evan of lying, too. He had been right. The two things weren't even remotely similar. I'd just wanted an excuse for my terrible behavior. I'd been deflecting and ignoring just how badly I'd betrayed him.

I'd betrayed him beyond belief, and it caused me pain on a daily basis. I'd taken his trust, something he didn't give lightly, and I'd smashed it all to pieces.

For what? Nothing. Nothing excused or rationalized the choices I'd made.

I was weak; I was wrong; I was selfish.

And I needed to confess that all to him.

So I did one of the scariest things I'd ever done. I didn't call or text, thinking that would again be me taking the easy way out. I couldn't go to his house, not knowing if he'd let me into his sanctuary.

Instead, I went to the stadium. I called in yet another favor with Nia, who had Malik contact one of the security guards to let me in. I waited outside the locker room after practice, wearing sunglasses and a hat, hoping that the few reporters there wouldn't recognize me.

I watched as players filed out of the locker room at different times— I knew the quarterbacks and offensive linemen would be among the last to leave.

Then . . . there he was. My heart leaped at the sight of him, crashing hard into my chest. Hope and fear warred inside me. I opened my mouth, and no words came out. But as if I'd spoken his name, Evan turned and saw me.

His hand tightened on his duffel bag as his mouth stretched into a thin line.

My first instinct was to think that this was a mistake. That I should leave and not bother him ever again.

"Easy way out," I muttered, making my way over to him. Time to be strong and to act.

He watched me approach, and just like during a game, his face didn't give away anything of what he was feeling.

"Hi. Can we talk? Please?" My voice shook, my words running all together.

Evan nodded curtly and then said, "This way."

I followed him to the players' parking lot, ignoring the curious looks from his teammates as we climbed into his SUV. He threw his bag in the back seat and then faced front, his hands on the steering wheel. I wanted to reach out. Hug him. Find a way to make this better.

I'd lost that right.

Folding my arms, I told myself I could do this. "Just because I can't say it enough, I'm sorry. I screwed up. Royally."

He didn't respond.

"And I know saying those words isn't a magical forgiveness token. I wanted to explain and to own my actions. When we . . ." I took in a deep breath. "When we talked at the ISEN station, I was freaking out. I wanted to excuse what I had done. And there's no excuse."

I gulped, trying to keep my voice steady. "When Brenda told us she wanted to prove you weren't a virgin, it was like I couldn't volunteer fast enough. It was a chance to get back at you. To try and hurt you the way you'd hurt me. I thought I hated you. It's been a decade, but I was still so angry at you. And then you told me the truth. I believed you. I didn't want to, but I did. You were just so wonderful and amazing. My feelings changed."

Evan shook his head, as if denying what I was saying.

"I've always been overly competitive. And I wanted this announcing job more than anything. I thought I had to be ruthless. Ambitious. Cut down everything in my path to get what I wanted. Especially when no one in my life believed I could do it. Except for you." My voice caught, and I took a second to collect myself. "You were open and vulnerable and so generous with me. And I betrayed all of that. I repaid it by being deceitful and selfish. I tried to equalize the playing field by accusing you of lying, but you were right. They weren't even remotely the same. I was being defensive and lashing out because I was so panicked by the idea of losing you. I was so focused on my pain and my loss that I didn't stop to really consider how deeply I must have hurt you."

This time he nodded and shifted in his seat.

"I think about that all the time now, how I must have hurt you, and it destroys me."

He rubbed the back of his neck.

I rushed on, wanting to get all the words out. "When it comes to my job, I'm all about risky moves. But in my personal life? Not really. My mom thinks it goes back to that high school stuff. That I'm afraid to be unguarded and trust people." I looked down at my hands. "And I should have trusted in us. In what we had. I knew for a long time that things were ruined at work because I chose you over them. I should have quit weeks before I did."

"You quit?" he asked, and the sound of his voice pierced me like an arrow.

"Yes. I know, too little too late. And Brenda offered me the world if I would sign the release form. I walked out instead."

His body shifted toward me, his gaze trained on my face, and I tried not to read too much into it. "I wish you'd told me in the beginning."

"If I'd told you, then what? We would have had a good laugh and moved on?" I let out a sigh. There I was, doing it again. Rationalizing my stupidity. "Sorry. You're right. I should have been honest with you. I shouldn't have taken that choice from you. I should have been up-front and let you decide for yourself whether or not you wanted to be with me. I was just scared of the consequences. I'm sorry."

"Ashton . . ."

I heard the regret in his voice. Not that I had expected anything from him, but there was a tone of finality that made me want to start crying.

"I know there's no excuse for what happened. No apology that I can offer that makes things better. Only that I promise to never do it again. I don't mean to be presumptuous. If you never want to see me again, I understand. It will kill me, but I get it."

I cleared my throat, blinking hard before continuing. "My feelings for you haven't changed. I love you. Always have, and I always will. So if you ever think you'd be able to trust me again, I'll be here."

I was moments away from bursting into sobs. And that wasn't what this was about. I wasn't going to cry on his shoulder and feel sorry for myself. I had to go. I opened the car door and got out, taking him in one last time, not knowing if this would be the last time I'd see him in person. "And I'll be waiting."

Walking away from his car was one of the hardest things I'd ever had to do. But since I hadn't let him make a choice about us in the first place, I was going to give that to him now.

He didn't contact me. Which seemed to be his answer to my offer. I held out hope since he didn't say anything to the media about our relationship ending, but I had to admit it was over. I needed to move on as best as I could with my life. I reached out to all the people in my social media network, telling them I was looking for a job with a sports station. I had accepted the fact that I'd probably have to move away from my family, but I was okay with it. Obviously I would miss them, but maybe it would be better for me to start over in a new city, where I wouldn't be plagued by memories of Evan.

My online plea for help seemed to have worked, as a couple of weeks after talking to Evan in his car, I got a phone call. "Hello?"

"Hi. I'm looking for Ashton Bailey."

"This is her." I expected it to be a collections agent. I'd had a bit of an issue staying current with things like my credit card bills. I probably could have gone to my parents for financial help, but I needed to retain some dignity.

"Hi, my name is Marian Monson. I'm the human resources director for KPRD."

"Excuse me?"

"I'm calling because your name was recommended to me. Our news and sports director is looking for an assistant, and I think you'd be excellent." She mentioned the salary, which was more than I'd ever hoped to make with my first real paying job and even included benefits. She didn't have to sell me, though; I was in. "Would you mind coming in for an interview tomorrow?"

"Yes, I'd love to! Yes!"

"Great." She laughed. "How's eleven o'clock?"

"Perfect!"

She promised to send me an email with the address and parking information for their building.

An actual job interview! I couldn't believe it.

"I'm looking forward to it, Ashton."

"Me too. And wait, before you go, can I ask you a question?"

"Absolutely. That's what I'm here for."

"Who recommended me for the job?" I wanted to know who to thank. There were a lot of possibilities. Maybe it had been Nia. Or Scooter Buxton.

"It was Evan Dawson."

For a second I couldn't breathe. Evan had recommended me? I thanked her, and we hung up, allowing me to have a full freak-out.

Why had Evan recommended me? And why now? Did this mean something? Had he started to forgive me? Or was he just being nice?

But why would he be nice?

Hope bloomed in my chest. Did he still love me? Was there a chance for us to get back together?

Before I could consider the repercussions too closely, I took out my phone and texted him.

> Thank you for getting me the job interview. It means a lot.

A lot? It meant everything. That he was thinking about me. Still cared. Had worried about me. But that was too much to put into a supposedly casual text.

I saw the three scrolling dots, and my breath kept catching, waiting to see if he would actually reply or if he would just ignore me.

> You're welcome. Come to the game this Sunday.

He hadn't asked me. It was almost more like a command. Maybe he was afraid to ask. Fearful that I might say no.

He couldn't possibly have known there was no way I could have denied him anything right then. And of course I was going to the game. Even if I'd been skipping games lately, it was the last playoff round before the Super Bowl, and there was no way I was going to miss it. I needed my Jacks to make a repeat appearance.

I needed Evan to have all the success in the world because he deserved it. My hands were shaking so hard that I had to retype my reply, like, fourteen times because I kept hitting the wrong buttons.

I'll be there.

He didn't respond right away, but I didn't need him to. I mean, I would have liked it, but it was enough that he was actually communicating with me. I didn't need for everything to be resolved today.

But my conviction to stay strong wasn't helped when he texted:

I miss you.

I miss you, too.

Knowing that Evan missed me gave me an inner strength I hadn't felt in a long time.

The next day went amazingly well. The interview was a slam dunk—it was like the job had been tailor-made for me. Marian told me there was a lot of room for advancement after I told her my hope was to be a commentator for KPRD someday. She mentioned that Keith Collinsworth planned on retiring in a few years, and they would find his replacement in-house. And they would support me along that career path. Marian and I were completely in sync in every question and answer, so much so that I felt like I'd known her for forever. At the end she told me to "expect to hear from us very, very soon."

Thankfully, she didn't ask me for any references from my old position.

And sure enough, as promised, she called the next day to offer me the job. I eagerly accepted and went out with my family to celebrate. I was tempted to call Evan and invite him along but worried it might be too much too soon. I didn't want to rush him if he was getting to a point where he felt like he could forgive me. Maybe we wouldn't get back together right away, and that had to be okay. Just having the chance to make this better was enough for now.

The morning of the game I tailgated with my parents, wanting to be close to where Evan was going to be. He was most likely already inside, and it took everything I had to not go searching for him.

Rory told me that, out of solidarity with me, my family had stopped using Evan's luxury box when we broke up. I didn't even know if it was still available to us, and I didn't ask because I didn't want to hear that the answer was no. We sat in our old season ticket seats. Aubrey and Justin had left the kids at home as it was a ridiculously cold day. The sun was shining, the sky a bright blue that reminded me of Evan's eyes, but super cold.

When the team came out on the field, I got to my feet, trying to find his jersey. I spotted him, and my heart skipped about thirty beats in a row. It's a wonder I didn't pass out cold on the concrete.

The pregame formalities were over, and the kickoff commenced. Everyone yelled, "Timber!" but I was totally focused on Evan standing on the sidelines.

And how nicely he filled out his football pants.

Now whenever the Jacks offense went in to play, I was more worried than ever about him getting sacked. One, because I didn't want him to get seriously hurt or maimed or concussed in any way; two, because he needed to keep playing so that the Jacks would win the game and go to the Super Bowl; and three, because I really wanted him to be conscious so we could talk after the game.

Because that had to be the whole point of this, right? That's why he wanted me at the game? So we could sort things out?

Evan took a few hits that had me back up on my feet and yelling at the refs, but nothing he didn't stand up and walk away from.

At the end of the first half, the Jacks were up by a touchdown. I would have preferred a much bigger lead. I turned to Rory. "Do you want to get some snacks? Stop by the bathroom?"

Weirdly, she wouldn't meet my eyes. "Nope. I want to stay right here. And so do you."

"Why?"

"No reason."

I was about to ask her what she was up to when a cameraman turned his camera on us. My whole family was up on the Jumbotron for the kiss camera. So my parents kissed, and Aubrey and Justin kissed. It was sweet, if a tad bit nauseating.

When they were done, the cameraman continued to stand there, his camera pointed at me. I turned toward Rory. "Just so you know, I don't care what he wants. I'm not kissing you."

"Good. I don't want you to kiss me."

"Why is he just standing there?"

Music rose up from the field, and there was what looked like a high school marching band moving in formation. The Jumbotron began to flash colors, and then I saw my name.

ASHTON BAILEY.

What . . . what was happening right now? I stood up, ignoring everyone and everything around me. I stared at the giant screen.

I LOVE YOU.
PLEASE BE MY WIFE.

There was a giant animated arrow pointing down, and I looked at the field. There, on the fifty-yard line, was Evan, still in his football pads, waving at me.

Hope, relief, and love exploded inside me.

"What are you waiting for?" Rory asked. "Do you not recognize a grand gesture when you see one? Get down there!"

I started climbing over my family. I had to get to him. I ran down the stairs and heard people talking all around me about what was happening.

"Aren't they already engaged?"

"What kind of froufrou garbage is this?"

"Man, she is going to own him their entire marriage. Look how whipped he is."

"How many proposals does one woman need?"

I only needed the one. This one. The real, actual one.

As I headed down the steps, Evan made his way over to the wall. When I got to the railing, he yelled, "Jump! I'll catch you."

It was a pretty big drop onto the field, but I didn't even hesitate. I knew he wouldn't let me get hurt. I swung my legs over the side and let myself go.

And he caught me. My breath left me for a moment when his arms connected with my body. He held on to me tightly for a moment against his smelly, sweaty, padded jersey, and I didn't even care. Because that look was back in his bright-blue eyes. A look that said he loved me.

Evan put me down on the ground, but I stayed close to him.

"Hi," he said flippantly. "So how've you been?"

It made me laugh, and I felt light and airy, like I might float away. "What are you doing?" I asked. "What is all this?"

"This was me realizing that my feelings for you haven't changed, either. That I love you." His hands rested on my waist, holding me close so it was easier for us to talk.

"I love you," I told him.

He kissed me on the tip of my nose. "I know you do. And since our conversation in my car, I've been doing nothing but thinking about you. About us. About what it would take for me to trust you again. It helped that you apologized and owned what you did. But I also realized that a long time ago, you thought I had betrayed you. And you were able to give me another chance. To trust me again. And that was the very least I could do for the woman I love. I decided that it didn't matter how we got here, that if you were willing to move forward, so was I. I'm sorry it took me so long to figure out. But what I do know is that I want you in my life. Forever."

"You could have just stopped by," I told him with a teasing grin, my heart fluttering over his words. "You didn't have to do all this."

"Rory convinced me otherwise."

"Rory?" I echoed, looking up at my family in the stands.

Although I couldn't be sure, I thought I heard her yell, "Grand gesture for the win!"

"I realized I want you to be my wife. The mother of our kids. And I went to your family to ask for their blessing."

My family? Oh, they had held out on me.

Evan kissed me gently, which elicited a lot of cheering and yells from the crowd. "Your parents took some convincing, but eventually everyone said yes. Even Joey gave me a 'good job, football man,' and during a tea party Charlotte haughtily said Uncle Satan could marry her aunt Ashton."

And I swear, right in that moment, I heard my mother yell, "I'm going to have more grandbabies!"

That made me throw my head back and laugh. I felt unbelievably happy and free. Like I'd found the other half of me and could finally feel complete.

"Your mother did make me promise to stay and fight when things got hard, because love is worth it. And I said I would."

"I promise to never lie to you again. Ever. About anything. Like that terrible pass to Sanchez in the first quarter. Ugh. Just awful."

He laughed and pulled me into a hug, squeezing me tightly. I closed my eyes. I had missed this.

"With that in mind," Evan said, pointing over his shoulder at the Jumbotron, "I have something to ask you." He walked over to his bag and pulled out a box. A ring box. For a second I was worried. I hoped he hadn't bought me a new ring. He came back and got down on one knee, sending the crowd into a frenzy. "I told you I'd never propose in a restaurant."

Being proposed to in one of my favorite places by my favorite person was infinitely better. Both of my hands went over my heart, trying to contain the joy I felt. "It's a good thing I showed up today! Or else this would have been really embarrassing."

He grinned at me. "I'm glad you're here."

"Me too." He'd probably never know exactly how much.

Evan opened the ring box, and tears blinded my vision when I saw it was his mother's ring.

My ring.

The crowd went insane. Someone started chanting the word *yes*, and soon the entire stadium was chanting along. "Yes, yes, yes, yes."

"I can get you a different one," he yelled.

"Don't you dare. This one is perfect. I love it," I yelled back as he slipped it onto my left ring finger. "And I love you."

The chanting became deafening, and it turned from "yes" to my name. "Ashton, Ashton, Ashton."

Evan had to shout, "Ashton! Will you marry me?"

"Do you hear that?" I asked him.

"The sound of seventy thousand people screaming your name? Kind of hard not to!"

"No. The sound of me saying yes!"

Evan got back to his feet and pulled me into a kiss, dipping me backward. The entire stadium went berserk, hollering and cheering.

He pulled back, grinning at me, and I'd never realized this kind of happiness could exist. He kept an arm around me while he waved to everyone in the stadium, and now they were chanting his nickname. "Awesome, Awesome, Awesome!"

I couldn't wait to become his wife. "I don't want a long engagement!"

"Me neither! We'd never make it!"

We kept waving and smiling until I felt like my face was going to freeze in a permanent grin. As soon as we left the field, cameras would be shoved in our faces, questions yelled at us, interviews given. But it would all be worth it.

Evan was worth it.

And I wouldn't have traded him and what we had for anything.

We started to walk off the field toward the Jacks' tunnel, where a horde of reporters and photographers waited for us.

"In case you were keeping track," Evan said just before we reached them, "that was Marriage Proposal Number One. And it's the only one I plan on making in my entire life."

"Then it's a good thing I plan on being your wife for the rest of my life." I paused. "But only if you win this playoff game and then get me one of those Super Bowl rings."

He laughed. "I will."

And he did.

AUTHOR'S NOTE

Thank you for coming along on this journey with me! I hope you enjoyed getting to know Evan and Ashton and reading their love story. If you'd like to find out when I've written something new, make sure you sign up for my newsletter at www.sariahwilson.com, where I most definitely will not spam you. (I'm happy when I send a newsletter once a month!)

And if you feel so inclined, I'd love for you to leave a review on Amazon, Goodreads, the bathroom wall at your local watering hole, the back of your electric bill, anyplace you want. I would be so grateful. Thanks!

ACKNOWLEDGMENTS

For everyone who is reading this—thank you. Thank you for your support, for your kind words, and for loving my characters and my stories as much as I do!

Thank you to Megan Mulder, editrix extraordinaire. I tell you all the time how much I appreciate you, how grateful I am for you, and how thankful I am for our relationship, and this is just more of the same. You are an amazing rock star. Thank you to Alison Dasho for stepping in and stepping up to help bring this book to the world. Thank you to the Montlake Romance team for everything you do that gets my books in the hands of readers. (I want to especially thank Angela, Kris, Kelsey, Adria, and Gabby.) And thank you for helping me celebrate my birthday last April—it was so much fun hanging out with all of you! Thanks as well to Charlotte Herscher. Please don't ever quit, because I've discovered that you make my books infinitely better. And thank you for your long-suffering patience with me and my inability to remember deadlines correctly.

Thank you to Sally, Leslie, and Angela for their copyediting. A special thanks to Erin Dameron Hill for my beautiful cover and to Wander Aguiar for his photos, which have made my recent covers possible.

For my children—I love you so much! We miss you, Kaleb—can't wait until you get back home to us! When this book comes out, we will have only eleven more months to go!

And for Kevin, my favorite person in the entire world. Love you more every day.

ABOUT THE AUTHOR

Bestselling author Sariah Wilson has never jumped out of an airplane or climbed Mount Everest, and she is not a former CIA operative. She is, however, madly, passionately in love with her soul mate and is a fervent believer in happily ever afters—which is why she writes romances like the Royals of Monterra series. After growing up in Southern California as the oldest of nine (yes, nine) children, she graduated from Brigham Young University with a semiuseless degree in history. The author of *#Starstruck*, she currently lives with the aforementioned soul mate and their four children in Utah, along with three tiger barb fish, a cat named Tiger, and a recently departed hamster who is buried in the backyard (and has nothing at all to do with tigers). For more information, visit her at www.SariahWilson.com.